RISE FROM RUIN

RUIN OR REDEMPTION

MARTI M MCNAIR

Hope You Enjoy
Marti M. McNair
x

REBSAM PUBLISHING

martimmcnair.com

Paperback ISBN 978-1-916721-06-7

eBook ISBN 978-1-916721-07-4

In loving memory of my Dad, John Hannay. You gave me a strong sense of right and wrong. You were always there when I needed you. You made me laugh, and taught me how to be thankful for all life's blessings. Forever in my heart.

CONTENTS

1

With bloodied hands and shattered hope we clawed our way through the rubble left by the explosion in the mines. We'd dragged Saxon's broken body - alongside the ghosts of those we couldn't save.

It was Robinia who orchestrated my rescue, with Spindle acting under her command. I should've disappeared then, slipped into the shadows while I still could. But I stayed. Stood my ground. Chose defiance over fear. Became a leader. The cave-dwellers and the Resistance stood side by side, bound by a fragile but burning hope.

We'd struck a blow Malus couldn't ignore. Omen's Keep had fallen. We stormed it, dragged out the scientists who'd twisted innocence into experiments, and freed the children hidden in their cages. Our momentum carried us further, infiltrating one of their settlements. We took what they held dear. Their wives. Their children. Now, the hostages were ours – and there were many. Our unity - and the victories we claimed together - drew the full, unrelenting wrath of Malus.

He hacked into our systems at the outpost with ease, his voice cold and triumphant as he summoned me to witness the full weight of his fury. The screen flickered to life. We watched, helpless, as our mountains crumbled under the force of his assault. Stone split like glass. Ridge-lines folded in on themselves. The place we had once called home - our sanctuary, was reduced to dust before our very eyes.

As we approached the toppled mountains, no one spoke. The silence wasn't chosen – it was stolen, ripped from our throats by the sight. Charred slopes slumped where proud cliffs once stood, their remains blanketed in ash. It looked less like a landscape and more like a battlefield where the earth had lost.

Smoke hung low, a ghostly shroud that blurred the edges of the devastation. It clung to our clothes, our skin, slipping down our throats with a dry burning bite. Every gasp felt like an intrusion, as though the air mourned the annihilation we'd stumbled into.

The river of molten lava had finally cooled, its once-glowing currents stilled into blackened stone. It had been more than a marvel - it was part of our ecosystem, the lifeblood that had warmed the water pools we had relied on each day. It was all gone. Swallowed by fire and fury, leaving an acrid tang of scorched earth and a sharp, metallic sting in the air. The scent alone was a warning, a bitter reminder that there was no mercy here – not for those already lost, nor for the lives it had yet to take.

Orion collapsed to his knees, his fingers tearing through the ash with desperate rage, as if he could claw Freya and Nova back from the ruin. Each scrape of his hands sent up grey plumes. His head bowed low, his shoulders heaving with the weight of his grief. Tears ran down his dirt-streaked face, vanishing into the dust beneath him.

Cooper stood a few paces away, pain written in every taut line of his face. His hands twitched at his sides, torn between reaching out to comfort Orion, but holding back, as if afraid his touch might break him further.

I couldn't bear the sight of it - the hollow ache in my chest threatened to spill over. I reached for Cooper's elbow, gripping it tightly. 'I thought we were doing the right thing,' I murmured, my voice thick with regret. 'But look what it's cost us.' I faltered, trembling with the realisation. 'Orion would still have his wife and daughter. You'd still have a sister and niece.'

His eyes met mine, wide and glassy, mirroring my own anguish as he spoke through gritted teeth. 'This is the price of war. Tragedy was inevitable, with or without you.'

Orion's forehead pressed against the dirt, his body quaking with gut-wrenching sobs.

I swallowed hard, my throat tight. 'I should've seen it coming, Cooper,' I murmured, my voice barely above a whisper. 'I should've known what they were capable of. How can I ever put this right?'

Before Cooper could answer, Astrid appeared at our side, her steps slowing as her gaze swept over the devastation. Her face pale, her lips trembled as though caught between words. Her eyes fixed on Orion - broken and sobbing in the ash. She knelt briefly, pressing her fingers into the dirt, then straightened with a sharp intake of breath. Her grief shifted, hardening into resolve. 'We need to move quickly,' she said, urgency threading through her voice. 'We have to get into the underground chambers. Remember, we lived deep in those caves - some of the caverns lie far below ground level. The mountains may have fallen, but not everything is lost.'

Zander's voice rang out. 'Jasmine.' He stood by the vehicle, waving me over. 'Spruce is on the radio - he's worried Malus might trace the signal if he stays on too long. You need to come quick.'

The parched earth crunched beneath my boots as I hurried across the dusty ground, the dry heat pressing down on me like a weight. Inside the vehicle at the back, a table had been pulled out, maps spread across its surface. Minx, Felix, and Larch leaned over them, their faces grim but focused, fingers tracing paths that could lead to salvation - or deeper into ruin.

I grabbed the radio. 'Spruce,' I said, my greeting strained. 'It's worse here than we ever imagined. A hundred times worse than what Malus showed us on the screen. '

Silence hung for a beat before the radio crackled. 'I don't have long. If Malus picks up on this signal, it's over for all of us,' he said, his words rushed. 'The convoy's on its way, medics included. They'll do what they can for your injured. But, Jasmine.' He paused, a hint of desperation creeping into his tone. 'Get them, and any survivors, back here. Fast.'

Larch looked up from the table, his eyes locking with mine. In them, I saw the worry etched deep, carved there by his fear for Ash. 'Has there been any word from our operatives embedded in the government?'

A pause. Too long. 'Nothing from Ash,' Spruce said. 'It's too risky. Only Taxus got through. He said they're jamming Malus's signals to keep the drones off your back.' He hesitated. 'Still, you know Malus. He'll assume we're planning a rescue. It's only a matter of time before he acts.'

My gaze flicked to the wing mirror, scanning the barren wasteland that stretched endlessly behind us. Nothing moved, but the emptiness itself felt like a threat. 'We're exposed here,' I said, forcing the words past the dryness in my mouth. I gripped the radio tighter to stop my hands trembling. 'There's nowhere to take a stand.'

'You'll need to move fast,' Spruce replied. 'It's only a matter of time before they come.'

Panic pushed my thoughts forward. 'What about our drones over Ruin? Has there been any sign of Coral or Spindle?' The thought of them burning in the Cleansing Chamber made my heart race. 'Have we heard from anyone on the Island?'

Spruce's voice came in a low rasp. 'Nothing yet. Everyone's

probably lying low to avoid suspicion. But the second we see or hear anything, I'll contact you.'

The radio crackled into static once more. Around me, unspoken fears settled – heavy, suffocating, filled with a thousand questions no one dared to voice.

I drew a deep breath, forcing down the swell of anxiety growing in my chest. 'Keep me updated on the prisoner interrogations, and don't stop combing through the documents from Omen's Keep. We've lost our edge, and we need to find a strategy that puts us ahead of Malus - now more than ever.'

'Robinia's already on it,' Spruce replied. 'She's working through the files while tending to the children's welfare. Aspen's analysing the blood samples he took from the scientists. He'll monitor their progress while they're off Control. He sent medication for you with Linden - in the event your condition worsens under stress.'

A low rumble came from the distance. I whipped my head toward the wing mirror. Five massive vehicles, identical to ours, tore across the landscape, kicking up dense clouds of orange dust as they raced towards us. 'They're here,' I said, as every muscle in my body tensed. 'Unless Malus's soldiers have commandeered your vehicles.'

'We'd have been alerted if that had happened.' Spruce assured me. 'We've sent plenty of water and supplies. I'll sign off for now but will check in later.'

The line went dead, and I set the radio aside, my thoughts churning. As I moved to the back of the vehicle, my eyes met Larch's. His stare pinned me in place, fear carved deep on his face, but it looked a lot like blame.

A sharp pain twisted in my gut as I said, my voice tight, 'The last thing I wanted was for him to go back. You know that. But it was Ash's decision.'

'You could've stopped him,' Larch replied, his voice filled with anger. 'You knew the risks, and you still let him go. If

Ash doesn't make it.' He stopped, looked away, his jaw clenched.

A heavy stillness settled over the vehicle, the kind that made your skin crawl. It was Minx who broke it, her words cutting through the uneasy quiet. 'The damage - it's most likely around the hot pools, going by the amount of lava that's seeped out.' She paused. 'If that's true, maybe - just maybe - some of our people are still alive.'

Felix's brow furrowed. 'Won't there be danger from toxic fumes?'

'There's a good chance,' I admitted, the stench of smoke and decay already burning my nostrils. 'Gas from the lava pools could be trapped down there. Sulphur, maybe worse.' I exhaled, the breath tight in my chest. 'But what choice do we have?'

Larch leaned over the map. 'We could enter through the tunnels here,' he said, his fingers tracing a route along the faded lines. 'And work our way toward the crags that are still standing.'

A sudden tap on the window startled me. Linden's face loomed, distorted behind the dirt-caked glass. His eyes narrowed as he squinted through the grime. 'Jasmine,' he said, his voice dulled by the pane. 'Can I have a word? I won't keep you long.'

I nodded before turning back to Larch and glancing at the map. 'See if you can find a secondary route as well. Just in case the one you're looking at is blocked.'

Larch gave a curt nod. I pushed open the vehicle door and stepped out into the heat, bracing myself for whatever information Linden was about to impart.

'Any news on Spindle?' My voice wavered. 'I can't help but feel Spruce is holding something back.'

Linden stepped closer, his hands resting on my shoulders. 'He's not hiding anything,' he said, softly. 'Spruce knows how much Spindle means to all of us. He'll do everything he can to bring him back. So will I.'

I bit my bottom lip, but the words tumbled out before I could stop them. 'Can we trust him to do everything in his power to save them?'

His reply came without hesitation. 'Absolutely. As soon as we re-establish contact with our operatives on Ruin, we'll have a clearer picture of what's happening and how to proceed.'

Something in his tone steadied me. But not enough. 'What chance do we have against Malus?' I asked. 'With weapons like this?' My shoulders slumped. 'He brought down mountains.'

Linden's lips thinned. 'The world has known weapons like this before - long before the End of Days. Back then, people believed they could control everything. Even the weather.' He shook his head, eyes dark. 'It's terrifying, the kind of firepower Malus has at his fingertips.'

Whatever he saw in my face made him hesitate, if only for a moment. When he spoke again, his tone softened. 'In some ways, we're fortunate that weather manipulation died out when the sun was harnessed. But they still have weapons - earthquakes, tremors . . . enough to shatter cities.'

The task ahead loomed, impossible. I wiped a trembling hand across my face. 'How are we supposed to fight this? How do you plan against someone with that kind of power?' My voice cracked. 'Do we even have any scientists in the Resistance?'

A flicker of unease crossed his face. 'We have a few, but I doubt any with this kind of knowledge. Perhaps they, along with some of our engineers, might offer some insight. We'll need to look into it when we're back at the outpost.' He looked unsure of himself. 'But honestly, we've never had to think this far ahead. It's the first time in generations that warfare like this has been attempted.'

My head swam as he shifted the conversation. 'Aspen asked

me to scan your brain and send him the results,' he said, keeping his tone light. 'He wants to check for any changes since your last X-ray. You took off before he had the chance, so he made sure I came prepared.' He gestured toward his vehicle. 'Let's get it done now. Then you can get back to planning the cave rescue.'

As we walked arm in arm, the dense, smoky clouds shifted, parting just enough to reveal a glimpse of the Sun. Its edges blurred in the haze, as it sank lower in the horizon. A chill ran through me, as the dying light cast a gloom over the rugged peaks left standing.

'Coral's words won't leave me,' I murmured, my gaze fixed on the hazy sky. 'Back on Ruin, when we thought it was the end, she asked if the Sun could be unharnessed.'

Linden squeezed my arm. 'Let's not go there yet. We've got enough to fight without chasing shadows of the past.'

Thunder rolled in the distance, echoing through the stillness. This wasn't just a storm - it was an ugly reminder of Malus's power to shroud our world in fear, using nature itself as a weapon of mass destruction.

2

The first light of dawn clawed feebly at the edges of darkness. It spilled a pale, tentative glow over the work-site. Spruce hadn't just delivered the desperately needed medical supplies - he'd brought pulleys, ropes, and heavy excavation tools that looked like relics from another era. I was amazed his people knew how to use them.

'Did you manage any sleep?' I asked Linden as he emerged from his vehicle, his face drawn.

'Not much,' he admitted. 'I faxed your X-ray over to Aspen. I'm sure he'll want a word with you before long.'

The ignorance I felt pressed down on me. 'I need to understand all of it – our technology, how the radio waves work, and what we can do to improve communications. I can't afford to stay in the dark any longer.'

Linden's hand rested lightly on my elbow. 'Jasmine, you're already juggling so much with barely enough hours in the day. Don't be too hard on yourself.'

I raised a hand to shield my eyes, scanning the horizon where streaks of dawn melted into the landscape. 'How long do you think we have before Malus's army reaches us?'

His expression darkened. 'Our operatives haven't sent word so we can only guess. It's a narrow window - maybe a couple of days, if that.' He hesitated, then met my gaze, his tone firm. 'You can't be here when that happens. The moment we spot drones overhead, that's our signal to leave.'

The camp stirred to life as shadowy figures emerged from their tents. Zander and Cooper approached, their footsteps echoing on crust-hardened earth. Zander carried a map, its edges frayed and stained from use. He snapped it open, revealing a scribbled sprawl of lines, dots, and arrows he'd marked on it.

He crouched, spreading the map across the ground, and jabbed a finger at two key positions. 'These are our best entry points. If we dig in these locations, we should be able to access the tunnels that run beneath the remaining mountains.' He looked up. 'Are you good with me assigning men and machinery to these spots? It's going to be tight, but it's our best options.'

'The sooner, the better,' I said, nodding. 'See to it that everyone's fed before we move out. Once we start, there'll be no stopping.'

Linden's eyes swept over the devastation. 'Do you really believe anyone could've survived it?'

A lump rose in my throat. 'We have to believe,' I murmured, the image of Freya and Nova flashing through my mind - trapped, screaming for help.

The sharp clang of metal sliced through our dread, drawing our attention to one of the hulking armoured vehicles. Machinery groaned as it was hoisted off, the gathered men bracing themselves to help unload the tools. The mood shifted - despair giving way to determination.

At one of the designated sites, I watched a massive machine hammer away, each strike shaking the ground beneath my feet. The deafening roar of grinding metal against stone echoed in the air. The atmosphere thickened with the sharp scent of disturbed earth, the dust swirling around us.

We worked without pause, straining as we hauled load after load of soil and stone from the expanding hole. Each barrowful added to the mountain of debris piling up nearby. Then, the pounding stopped, and the abrupt silence struck harder than the noise had. The machine operator wiped a sleeve across his grimy forehead and waved urgently. 'Jasmine, we've got an entrance.'

As the dust settled, the opening gaped beneath us from the hole we'd cut in the earth. Shafts of light pierced through the orange haze, illuminating the newly unearthed passage.

Zander stepped forward. 'Lower me down on a rope. I'll see how far the passage goes. Get word to Cooper's team - they need to know we've broken through.'

'You go,' I said, turning to Minx, 'Let Cooper know I'm going in with Zander.'

Minx's expression hardened. 'No way,' she said, her tone flat. 'We've no idea how stable it is down there. I'll go instead. You're needed here to coordinate.'

Zander tightened the rope over his shoulder and around his middle. 'What if Spruce makes contact. Minx is right, you need to be here.'

Their logic gnawed at my conscience. 'Okay. But be careful. At the first sign of trouble, you both get back here. No heroics.'

They descended into the chasm, their silhouettes swallowed by the encroaching darkness. The faint scrape of the rope against the jagged edges was the last sound before the shadows claimed them.

I turned to Felix. 'Send word to Cooper that Zander and Minx are underground. Any further digging could risk the tunnel collapsing. If they can't reach the settlements from this entry point, we'll have him continue digging at his location.'

As he sprinted off, I turned towards the camp, my thoughts

racing and my gut churning, bracing for the next update from the outpost.

* * *

Linden and Larch were tucked inside Linden's vehicle, surrounded by a heap of medical supplies. Larch sorted through bandages, arranging them by shape and size, while Linden carefully labelled vials of painkillers. On a cluttered table nearby, a hand-held monitor flickered with the scanned image of my brain, its complex grey contours holding secrets only Aspen might uncover.

'Have you heard from anyone at the outpost?' I asked, glancing again at the monitor, debating whether to contact them about the tunnel access.

'Not yet,' Linden replied, catching the direction of my gaze. 'Are you worried about what Aspen might find?'

'I'm more worried about those trapped in the caves - and about Coral and Spindle,' I said, with a sigh. 'But yes, it would be good to know if my condition's worsened. Honestly, I don't feel any different than before, so let's not dwell on it.'

Larch remained tense around me, even though we shared the same fears for Ash's safety. I knew the enormous risks he took by going back to the capital. 'Ash has always been fiercely competitive,' I began, hoping to alleviate Larch's fears. 'Back on Ruin, he was a remarkable athlete, pushing all of us to be better. Salix was his best friend - someone who always had his back. I'm sure, wherever Salix is now, he's watching over Ash, giving him the strength he needs.' I paused, memories of simpler times cluttering my mind. 'And according to Robinia, the intel Ash has provided in the short time he's held his position inside the government has been game-changing. He's not just a soldier in this fight - he's going to hold high office in the new government once we take Malus and his masters down.'

Though each of us had our roles and sacrifices to shoulder, I hoped my words offered Larch some measure of comfort in the midst of uncertainty. Yet, the tension between us clung like a shadow. He returned to stacking bandages, without uttering a word. I silently prayed we'd hear from Ash soon and ease both our troubled minds.

The sudden crackle of the radio jolted me from my thoughts. I rushed over, snatching the handset just as Spruce's voice cut through the static.

'I need to speak with Jasmine right away.'

I brought the handset close to my lips, 'It's me. What is it?'

His voice quivered. 'It's Malus . . . he's been in touch. I don't know how he's hacking into our system, but he specifically wanted to speak with you.'

My heart thudded against my chest, my grip tightening around the radio until my knuckles turned white. 'Why would he reach out to the outpost for me? He must know I'm here, rescuing the survivors from the caves.'

'Who knows how Malus's mind works?' Spruce said, his voice tinged with frustration. 'He might think you'd see a rescue mission as a lost cause, or that you'd take the safer route - hide away and let others risk their lives for their loved ones.'

'No, he knows I would come here.' My mind raced for answers as the possibility hit me. 'Could he find the outpost location by tapping into our systems? By tracing our calls?'

'Anything's possible,' Spruce replied. 'Any communication involving him - or even between you and me - puts us at risk. But one thing's clear now - he's not as powerful as we believed. If he were, his retaliation would've caused far more damage and he'd have struck again by now.'

'They're probably still scrambling to figure out how we pulled off the attacks on Omen's Keep and the settlement,' I replied, steadying my racing thoughts. 'What else was said?'

Spruce hesitated, choosing his words with care. 'To buy us

some time, I told him you were injured and in surgery.' He let out a long low breath. 'He asked me to pass on a proposal.'

'What kind of proposal?'

Spruce paused. When he spoke again, the words came slowly. 'He wants to arrange a hostage swap.'

'Coral and Spindle,' I said, my voice trembling. A spark of hope flitted through me as well as the cold grip of fear.

'Yes,' Spruce said, his tone heavy. 'He wants them in exchange for everyone captured from Omen's Keep, as well as the children who were experimented on. He also wants the families you took from the settlement - but there's more.'

A chill crawled down my spine. It had to be me - Malus was desperate to drag me back into his clutches. 'I'll do it,' I whispered, my voice barely a breath. 'I'll hand myself over to save them.'

'Even if that was what he wanted, we can't let him take you.' There was no room for argument in his tone. 'Our success depends on your medical history with Aspen - on figuring out why Control doesn't affect you. It's Robinia and Rowan. He warned that if we don't surrender them both, he'll bring down the remaining mountains.'

'What he's asking is impossible. Rowan is dead,' I said, struggling to make sense of Malus's demand. 'I thought when Zander disabled her chip, Malus would believe she was dead too. Why does he want them back?'

His voice took on a weight of foreboding. 'It could be a warning - a chilling message to anyone pretending to be under Control. If you deceive the government - this will be your fate. What he intends for Robinia, in full public view, will be far worse than any cleansing and worse than death itself.' As for Rowan, I'm not sure. Maybe he wants to parade her as a heroine - if he thinks she's still our prisoner. Or maybe, he's just calling our bluff.'

3

Bodies, caked in blood and grime, were hauled up from what could only be called an abyss of despair. The dead lay in solemn rows, their forms draped in tattered shrouds that failed to conceal the horrors they had endured. Linden tended to the living, moving between them. Each life saved was a fragile flicker of light against the crushing darkness.

Zander slumped onto a sun-baked rock, his hands trembling as he wiped sweat from his face, fresh tears welling in his eyes. He raised his flask to his lips, gulping back tepid water.

'Are there any signs of Freya or Nova yet?' I asked.

His gaze shifted to Orion, crouched at the edge of the chasm, breath ragged, anguish carved into every line of his face. 'We had to drag him out,' Zander said, shaking his head. 'He was clawing at the rubble, desperate to get through - like he thought sheer willpower could move it. Honestly, it's a miracle he's still got any nails or fingers left.'

I scanned the harrowing scene, my eyes settling on Minx as she guided dazed survivors toward a waiting vehicle. The dust-covered bus stood ready, its vulnerable cargo bound for the outpost. A pang of familiarity gripped me as I watched her, recognising the way she resembled Rowan. I pushed the thought aside.

'Do you think we should send Orion back with the survivors?' I asked. 'Being here . . . it must be too painful for him.'

'Sending him back will only throw fuel on the fire of his grief. He needs to be here,' Zander said, empathy flitting across his face.

'You're right,' I said, feeling the strain coil in my chest. 'But I'm terrified of how he'll react if we fail to find them.'

Zander met my gaze. 'We've got this. Cooper, Minx, Astrid, and I will handle the rescue. Larch and Linden can tend to the injured until backup arrives. You should return to the outpost. It's the best place right now for you to be.'

I felt sick as I wrestled with the decision, my heart torn between duty and instinct. The pull to stay was strong, but deep down, I knew what had to be done. Leadership wasn't just about being in the thick of it - it was about making the call, even when it ripped you apart. Steeling myself, I nodded. 'I'll leave with the next group of survivors,' I said, forcing the words. 'But we have to start evacuating the rest from the mountains. Malus won't bide his time - he'll strike again, and soon.'

A shadow of doubt flashed in Zander's eyes. 'Many are refusing to leave,' he said, his jaw tightening. 'Cooper's doing his best to persuade them the outpost is safe, but the mistrust runs deep. After everything that's happened between our people and the Resistance, some would rather perish in their homes than take the risk.'

'Then I'll go into the caves and speak to them myself. I won't stand by and let them die.'

Zander's lips tightened, he knew better than to argue with me. 'I'll take you to where the tribal leaders are assisting with the rescue,' he said, already preparing to return to the tunnels.

I followed him into the hole, the rope around my waist

pulled tight. As we neared the chambers, the devastation slammed in to me. A once bustling stronghold of life and energy had become a tomb. The main cavern, our sanctuary, lay in ruins, its vastness reduced to ragged rubble.

Narrow cracks split the ceiling, letting in faint shafts of sunlight - pale, ghostly reminders of the world above. The space hung thick with choking dust. My throat tightened as I took it all in - the wreckage, the silence, the broken remains of what had once been home. Obliterated. Gone.

The anguished cries of the injured echoed faintly through the devastation. A stark reminder of what we'd lost. We followed the sound, weaving through uneven gaps in the piles of collapsed stone.

Crawling through the narrow passage, the air thickened with every inch. Dirt clung to our skin, turning sweat to grit. At the end, Zander didn't pause. He vanished into a jagged hole above. I hauled myself upright, heart hammering, and reached for the ledge. Dirt and small stones broke loose beneath his boots, peppering my face as I climbed.

At last, we emerged into the small clearing Zander had described. The air felt heavier here, thick with grief and the harsh tang of destruction. All around us, figures moved in the dim light, pulling survivors from the ruins.

I wondered how the tribal leaders would receive me, knowing it was my rallying cry that had sent their fighters to war. Now innocents were paying the price. Their frantic digging stopped as they noticed our arrival, and I prepared myself for what was to come. To my relief, their hardened expressions softened, and even in the midst of exhaustion, a few managed faint, weary smiles.

Falconer, the first to step forward, caught my eye. I remembered the first time I met him, when looking for Larch in his settlement. Now, his presence calmed me.

'Jasmine, it's good to see you,' he said, his voice rough but warm.

I clasped Falconer's hand, and he pulled me into a firm embrace. 'I'm so sorry,' I whispered, my voice cracking.

'This is what war brings,' he replied, his breath warm against my ear. 'We'll only know peace when the government is destroyed and the chains of tyranny broken. You must keep your word, Jasmine, and free the world from our oppressors. That's how you honour those who've fallen.'

His words settled deep in my heart, but the conviction in his tone lit a spark within me. One by one, the other leaders stepped forward, their eyes filled with sorrow. They all nodded in agreement, patting me on the back and murmuring words of encouragement.

Falconer placed a hand on my shoulder, meeting my gaze. 'We're still with you,' he said, his voice carrying the strength of everyone standing there.

I blew out a shaky breath. 'Thank you,' I whispered. 'You don't know how much that means to me. But please - you must convince everyone to evacuate. The transport is ready to take them to the outpost. Malus will attack again, and I can't bear to see more innocents slaughtered.'

Falconer's features tightened. 'Some are too old, and too frail,' he said quietly. 'They've lived their entire lives in these mountains, and no matter what's coming, they've made their choice to stay. We can warn them, but we can't force them. They have free will, Jasmine. We have to respect that, even if it breaks us.'

Cooper's voice echoed faintly up the tunnel. 'Jasmine, you need to come. We've found Jaz. She's in a bad way, but she's awake and asking for you.'

The name froze me in place. Jaz - once my nemesis, the one I had been so sure had conspired against me. For months, I had believed her whispers had fuelled Klin's treachery. But it hadn't been her. It was Klin who had betrayed me, Klin who had led the ambush. Klin who had killed Rowan.

Rowan - fierce, unyielding Rowan - had thrown herself in front of me as Klin's spear hurtled forward. She hadn't hesitated. She hadn't faltered. She gave her life so I could live. Klin and his gang had been dragged away, shoved into the pit like the traitors they were.

When Malus unleashed his fury, the collapse swallowed them whole. Rocks would have silenced their screams. Bones, if they remained, were now scattered and buried deep, lost to time and memory.

I felt nothing for them - no pity, no sorrow, no hatred. They'd sealed their fate the moment they turned against me. Their end was inevitable, a reckoning they'd brought upon themselves.

'Convince as many as you can to join us. That's all I ask,' I said, despite the turmoil I felt. I turned to leave, clutching onto the fragile hope that we'd all reunite at the outpost soon. We descended the narrow shaft, the walls pressing in around us.

Cooper waited at the base. 'This way,' he said, leading us to another narrow tunnel.

It was dark, claustrophobic, and unrelenting. Finally, we emerged into a newly cleared space. The air here was cooler, but it carried the metallic scent of blood. Shadows moved against the stone walls as rescuers worked tirelessly, their murmurs often obliterated by groans of the injured.

Jaz lay on a makeshift stretcher - utterly still, her face a mask of grey dust. Her lips were a faint, unnatural blue, and grime with dried blood caked her multi-coloured hair. I stood frozen for a moment, the weight of seeing her like this crushing me. Without further thought, I reached out and took her trembling hand. Despite the coldness of her skin I could feel life.

Her voice barely scraped through in a fragile whisper. 'Freya and Nova were with me when the caves collapsed. They must be close to where I was found. You . . . you have to save them.'

I opened my mouth to speak, but Cooper's voice cut through before I could respond. 'We're already on it. We're shifting the rubble, but the ground's unstable. Another rock-slide could bury us all. We're doing everything we can to find them.'

'Jasmine, I was coming to warn you.' A weak tremor ran through her words. 'But Klin got to me first.'

'Let's not focus on that now,' I said, squeezing her hand gently. 'We'll get you to the surface, and Linden will check you over. What about Ella, or any of the others? Can you remember where they were before the collapse?'

Jaz took a shallow breath. 'Freya took over nursing me to give Ella a break. Ella could be anywhere.'

I gestured towards the two men lifting the stretcher. 'Get her out of here,' I said. 'I'll follow on soon.'

As they moved her, I remembered Saxon - his limp form, slumped on a makeshift stretcher we'd pieced together from wooden planks. We'd bound him to it from the torn leather leashes ripped from the mine warden's whips. Another catastrophe deep in the earth's gut, another frantic race against time to pull someone back from the brink. How many more lives would be consumed by this endless cycle of violence and death before it finally stopped?

'Are you okay?' Zander asked, concern crossing his face.

I couldn't tell him the truth - that his father's ghost was weighing on me. The memory of us fighting with everything we had to keep him alive, only to watch him slip away. It still cut deeply.

Instead, I squeezed Zander's fingers, trying to offer him the reassurance I couldn't find for myself. 'Come on,' I said, forcing strength into my voice. Then I turned to Cooper, 'Take me to where they're digging for Freya and Nova.'

Once again, we pushed through the cramped crawl space, stirring the dust and grit. Stones were lifted, then shoved aside, revealing gaps in the rubble that seemed to reach deeper into the earth. As we worked, fragments of our past emerged - chipped pottery, shredded fabric, carved trinkets half-buried in the ruins.

It hit me. It wasn't just the destruction of communities we'd witnessed - it was the collapse of an entire ecosystem. The caves had cradled a hidden world, teeming with life and secrets; a delicate balance. If only we'd known its rhythm, had understood it, we might have saved the barren lands and the fractured islands.

A voice rang out from one of the helpers. 'Cooper, we've found someone.'

Cooper darted forward, and I followed close behind. We reached the spot where the stones had been cleared, and there they were. Freya lay curled around Nova, her arms locked in a protective embrace, a mother's instinctive shield. Cooper released a raw, feral wail - the sound of a heart shattering beyond repair.

I looked at the bodies. Their eyes were closed, not in rest, but in the final grip of death. A suffocating silence cloaked us, broken only by the agonising sound of Cooper's sobs, each one a raw scream of agony. Zander held him tight until his cries slowly petered out.

I balled my fists, battling the flood of emotions threatening to break through. My heart throbbed with a pain so intense, I feared it might explode inside me. I fought to hold it together. Every fibre of my being screamed to crumble, but I couldn't. Not now. I forced my focus onto Cooper and Zander, clinging to the thought that I had to be strong.

Swallowing the lump in my throat, I nodded to the men

working to free them. 'Treat them with the utmost respect,' I said, as I fought back tears. 'Have Linden make them look at peace. And when that's done, let Orion say goodbye.'

4

Orion dropped to his knees beside the stretcher, his body shaking violently as he held the lifeless bodies of his wife and child. Soul-shattering howls ripped from his chest. Grief shattered him. His face, a ruin - eyes inflamed and glassy, lips cracked, tears cutting rivers through the dirt on his face. He called their names, as if saying them over and over might bring them back.

Later, he moved to Cooper's side. Cooper sat with his legs drawn up, hands tangled in his hair, the weight of grief pressing down on him. Silent tears slipped through his fingers. Beside him, Orion wept, and together they formed a portrait of torment - two souls locked in shared suffering.

My lips quivered as the words slipped out. 'What have I done? I should've known there would be consequences.'

Felix met my gaze, his sorrow plain to see. 'We had no choice. We acted when the moment demanded it, and you dealt a crippling blow to Malus. The blame doesn't rest on you. It belongs to our oppressors.'

'You should go back with this convoy,' Zander said, his voice heavy with exhaustion. 'Time's running out, and if Malus tries to contact you again and you're still unavailable, he'll grow suspicious. I'll stay here and help bury the dead.'

A sharp, throbbing pain struck my temple - a cruel reminder of how much my body was beginning to betray me. 'Yes, I'll go back.' I kneaded away a strange tingling in my fingers. My eyes fixed on Zander. 'Take care of them,' I said, nodding toward Cooper and Orion. 'And come find me when you return.'

* * *

The convoy of vehicles crept across the vast orange plain, a cloud of orange dust following in their wake. Each vehicle groaned under the weight of injured and traumatised survivors. Their faces drawn with fatigue and the hollow stare of those who had witnessed too much.

We stopped twice, the drivers dragging themselves from their seats to refuel, their movements sluggish from exertion. We rolled past the haunting remains of the bone cemetery, and as the air thinned, our breathing struggled. Linden handed out inhalers he'd prepared in advance. Each gasp from the devices was a lifeline, keeping the convoy moving forward through the suffocating wasteland.

My mind drifted to Orion. The weight of his loss crushed the breath from my chest, twisting something raw deep inside. Guilt gnawed at me relentlessly - for leaving before I could stand beside Freya and Nova's graves - for not being there to say a proper goodbye. But I pushed the thought aside, telling myself this separation was only temporary. Once the war ended, I'd give them the resting place they truly deserved. A place of honour, peace and remembrance.

Then Spindle and Coral filled my mind, and I sent up a silent prayer for any scrap of news about their fate. Clinging to hope, I believed we'd re-established contact with our operatives on Ruin - that even now, they were working to secure their escape or, if nothing else, to clear a path for a rescue mission.

Nothing would keep me from being there when the moment came. I ached to see Spindle again, to hold him close and dare to dream of a future together - a future free of this constant struggle. But that dream felt fragile, tainted by the reality of my condition. If only my body weren't failing me, I might stand a chance of making it real.

The convoy finally rumbled into the gloomy tunnel of the outpost, the dim light casting long, flickering shadows on the cold, stone walls. Medics surged forward pulling the injured from the vehicles and loading them onto stretchers. Orders were shouted, as they assessed wounds and stabilised the weakest. Able-bodied survivors were ushered toward a welcoming official seated at a makeshift desk, his pen scratching across a logbook as he recorded each new arrival.

I jumped down from the vehicle, and found myself face to face with Aspen. His eyes lit up, and before I could say a word, he pulled me close. His arms wrapped around me as if he could shield me from everything we had endured.

'It's good to see you,' he said, pressing a gentle kiss to the top of my head.

'It's good to see you too.' For a moment, the ice-cold pain gripping my heart thawed as he held me. 'It was awful, Aspen,' I said, the words trembling. 'If Malus discovers our location, we're all as good as dead. There's nowhere left for us to hide.'

Aspen offered a smile, one that didn't reach the worry lingering in his eyes. 'We'll figure it out before he finds us.' His tone was firm, as if his conviction alone could save us from Malus's capabilities. 'Robinia wants to speak with you. She's been working around the clock, deciphering codes and helping our operatives hack deeper into Malus's systems.'

He hesitated, his expression subdued as he shifted his focus to me. 'However, before you do anything, we need to talk about your condition. I need to give you a proper examination. Have you experienced any more side effects?'

I rubbed the side of my head, wincing as a sharp, stabbing pain flared behind my temple. 'Just here,' I muttered.

Aspen frowned, slipping his arm through mine. 'Come on.' He guided me toward the lift. 'We've set up a small suite for you. You can wash up, get some rest, and then head to the medical bay. And, for once, Jasmine, grab something to eat too. You look like you're running on empty fumes.'

I did need food, but my thoughts were elsewhere. 'How's Spruce holding up in Operations?' I asked, unable to hide the doubt creeping into my tone. 'I probably shouldn't say this, but I still don't trust him. Linden keeps telling me to let it go, but I just . . . can't.'

Aspen sighed, his grip on my arm tightening. 'He's committed to your leadership. Don't think too badly of him. He was part of the old Resistance for so long that his loyalty was tested. He was following orders from men he believed in, but realises his mistake.'

After days swallowed by ash and hollow grief, returning to the outpost felt like a myth made real. I was struck once more by the impossible comfort buried beneath the earth - a refuge that didn't belong to this shattered world. Perhaps that was its purpose - humanity's last stand, hidden underground just before the End of Days consumed everything.

I'd seen most of the outpost already - the medical bay, the canteen, the operations room, the tight, functional living quarters. Even down to the underground greenhouses and the labs where they grew synthetic meat. But nothing prepared me for what lay behind the door Aspen now opened.

The room beyond glowed with a soft, inviting light that spilled gently across the space. A plush bed, dressed in deep, rich fabrics, added a surprising touch of comfort to the otherwise no-nonsense surroundings. The muffled hum of a wall heater filled the quiet, its warmth spreading through the air. Beyond another archway, a long steel table stood at the centre of the adjoining room, its polished surface catching the light. Ten high-backed chairs circled it.

I took it all in. 'It's all too much. I don't need such elaborate quarters.'

Aspen saw it differently. 'Look on this room as a place for your war cabinet to meet - a private office where plans can be discussed away from prying eyes.'

Another door to the right swung open, revealing a tiny bathroom. A porcelain washbasin clung to the wall, its silver tap dull with age. A toilet stood in the corner, but the real marvel stood against the far wall - a relic of a forgotten time.

Aspen noticed me stare at it. 'It's called a bathtub,' he said, as his lips curled into a kind smile. 'We thought you deserved some comfort after everything you've gone through.'

He strode over, turned the shiny tap, and a rush of water thundered into the tub. Within seconds, steam coiled into the air. Heat licked at my skin, the scent of old pipes and something almost clean filling my lungs.

'They had these before the End of Days,' Aspen said, watching the water rise. 'People would soak in them, using scented bubbles to melt their worries away. Maybe the government's elite still do, in whatever secret homes they have away from the Midpoints. But people like us? We were never meant to know luxury.'

I fought back a sob. 'Thank you,' I whispered, my voice shaking. 'I don't deserve this.'

'Yes, you do,' he said, his voice soft and full of tenderness. He pressed a plastic key card into my palm. 'Come to the medical bay when you're ready.'

Just as he turned to go, I called after him. 'Aspen - have you heard anything from Ruin?'

His features hardened. 'No, nothing yet.'

* * *

Once Aspen left, loneliness settled - heavy as the ache in my heart. I stripped off my filthy clothes and dipped a hand into the bathwater - perfectly warm. Climbing in, I let the heat cover me, my scarred back pressing gratefully against the tub's curve. A sigh slipped from my lips. The water didn't have the crisp, mineral purity of the cave pools, but it offered its own kind of bliss. I surrendered to it. When I finally surfaced, the waster lay clouded.

I wrapped a towel around myself and stretched out on the bed - huge, firm, and layered with thick covers and plush pillows. A world apart from Ruin's rigid bunks with threadbare mattresses, and the makeshift beds in the caves.

No matter how much I twisted and turned, comfort eluded me. The bed felt too big, the covers stifling, the pillows unwilling to mould to my neck. I yanked a blanket and the flattest pillow I could find, then settled on the floor. The hard, cool surface brought relief. Curling into a tight ball, exhaustion took over, and I slipped into a deep, dreamless sleep.

I jolted awake, drenched in cold sweat, my heart hammering against my ribs. The lavish suite felt alien, its shadows stretching long and menacing across the floor. My gaze flickered to the open bathroom door, then to the table and chairs beyond the archway - yet none of it felt real. None of it felt like mine. Then it hit me - I didn't know who I was, let alone where I was.

With effort, I pushed myself upright, clutching the blanket as my mind fought to pierce the thick fog clinging to my brain. The steady ticking of a wall clock filled the silence while I willed my memories to surface. Slowly, the pieces slid into place. Jasmine. The outpost. Safe.

* * *

The cool, sterile medical bed offered no comfort as Aspen moved beside me, drawing blood from my arm. The needle's slight pinch barely registered - drowned by the tangle of thoughts swirling behind my eyes.

Aspen kept the mood light. 'So, what do you think of the clothes we left for you in the cupboard?' His brow arched, a playful spark in his eyes.

I sighed, shifting against the padded surface. 'I'm not used to having so much. I don't need all of it.'

A knowing smile tugged at Aspen's mouth. 'I told Spruce you'd say that. It's not like Ruin here. Don't get me wrong, we're not drowning in abundance, but we allow ourselves a few comforts. Still, with the new arrivals from the caves, we'll have to rethink how we manage things.' He placed the vial of blood into a rack on his desk.

Returning to my side, he flicked on a small torch, the beam flaring to life as he leaned in, tilting my chin. Light swept across my eyes. 'Any more dizzy spells?' he asked. 'Muscle cramps? Memory loss?'

I blinked against the sharp beam before focusing on his face. 'Just the headache I already mentioned,' I said, keeping quiet about the disorientation I'd felt upon waking. I blamed that on jolting awake from a deep sleep, so didn't feel the need to speak of it. 'Have you had a chance to look at the brain scan Linden sent over?'

Aspen cleared his throat. 'The scan he sent . . . it wasn't exactly clear,' he said, as if carefully choosing his words, only saying what he needed to. 'Now that you're here, we'll run another,' he added, his gaze shifting from mine. 'Then maybe afterwards, we can sit down and talk properly about your condition.'

His hesitation, coupled with the faint tremor in his voice,

betrayed an undercurrent of unease. It wasn't just what he said, but what he didn't - and how his speech stumbled. The silence that threaded between each carefully chosen word spoke louder than the sentiment itself. I had a feeling he either couldn't - or wouldn't - admit that my condition was worse than he wanted me to know.

5

I stepped into the Operations Room, where operatives were absorbed in their tasks. A quiet murmur of conversation drifted through the room, punctuated by the steady tap of fingers on keys and the occasional rustle of papers. The air hummed with silent focus and unspoken urgency.

Spruce stood unmoving at the centre, his posture rigid with command. His gaze fixed on the large plasma screen displaying a haunting image of our fallen mountains. As I approached, the hard lines of his face eased, his stern expression giving way to a welcoming smile.

'How are you feeling?' he asked, his voice warm. 'I'm glad you're back safe.' He led me towards his desk, nodding towards an empty chair nearby. 'Pull it over and sit down.'

'Thanks for your concern. I'm fine, really,' I said, my gaze shifting to the plasma screen. The broken remnants of our home sprawled across the land held my gaze. A chill crept up my spine. 'Why are you showing the devastation up there?' I asked, studying the disturbing image.

Spruce's brow knitted as his gaze flitted between the screen and me. 'We can't control that image,' he said. 'Malus put it there. No matter what we do, we can't take it down. It only disappears when he appears on the screen to speak to you.'

A knot tightened in my stomach. 'He's controlling it?'

Spruce exhaled; his features tightened. 'Our technicians think it's some kind of system corruption - his way of stalling us, maybe even hacking in to trace our location. We're doing everything we can to regain control.'

I clenched my fists. 'We're running out of time,' I said, a heavy dread settling over me. 'We need to find a way to put an end to Malus for good.'

His brow furrowed, his features tight with concern. 'I agree, Jasmine. Time isn't on our side.' A small smile tugged at his lips - just enough to let a glimmer of hope pierce the tension. 'But on the bright side, our hackers are still inside his system, thanks to Larch. We don't know if they've gone undetected. Malus's people could be watching, trying to uncover our objective, maybe even tracking the interference straight back to us. So, for now, we still have access to the schematics of Midpoints across all the islands - including government facilities and the private compounds where they've built homes for themselves and their families.'

I fell silent for a few moments, my thoughts spinning. Then, unexpectedly, a spark of optimism cut through my doubt. 'Do you think we could find where the pre-End of Days rulers kept the Sun-harnessing machinery?'

My mind sharpened, sifting through the stories Mary had shared with Coral and me. 'The project had the initials SIAJ. Mary didn't know what it meant, but the common folk called it *Star in a Jar.*'

Spruce's eyes narrowed. His fingers drummed a rhythm against the edge of his desk. 'Why do you think finding that location will help us against Malus?'

I hesitated, searching for a solid reason. It was just a hunch - it was an insistent whisper in the back of my mind that there was more. I was certain the buried within that ancient machinery lay something vital. Something that could change everything.

'It's where this whole tragic story began,' I said, turning the thought over in my head. 'Maybe it's where it will end.'

He leaned back in his chair, fingers laced together in his lap. 'Robinia is already combing through the documentation from Omen's Keep. If you truly believe this could be the key to ending the regime, I'll have someone look into it,' he said, his tone reluctant.

'It's not just about ending the regime,' I said, my confidence growing. 'It's about restoring the Earth to its rightful state. What good is victory if we're left with a planet that can't sustain us?'

Spruce nodded, resolve settling in his expression. 'You have my full support, Jasmine. We'll see what we can find.'

'Thank you,' I said, relief flooding through me. At least he was on board. 'Next, we need to address Malus's demand for a hostage swap. Even if Robinia were willing to sacrifice herself, we don't have Rowan.'

Spruce's jaw tightened. 'I'd let the world burn before handing Robinia over to Malus. Right now, we need to think carefully about what we say to him - to buy ourselves some time. And we need a solid plan to extract Coral and Spindle. Once we make contact with our operatives on Ruin, we'll have a clearer picture of what we're dealing with.'

I drew in a deep breath. 'I might have an idea,' I said, my voice dipping as I leaned closer. 'Minx looks like Rowan. If we shaved her head, she could pass for her - at least from a distance.' I locked eyes with Spruce, letting the gravity of my proposal sink in. 'We could stage a swap? Use Minx as a decoy to lure Malus into a trap?'

Spruce inhaled sharply, his eyes widening. 'I never imagined you'd suggest offering anyone other than yourself as a sacrifice.'

I cut in before he could go any further. 'No, I'd never do that. I'm trying to find a way to use her to our advantage - without actually handing her over or putting her in danger.'

His features tightened, tension radiating through his expression.'They've got advanced facial recognition. I'm fairly sure they'd see through the deception.' Despite his scepticism, he paused - a glint of intrigue breaking through. 'Still, it's an interesting idea. Let me give it some more thought. There might be another way to make it work.'

Robinia stormed in, a stack of folders clutched tightly in her arms. She rushed over, dropping the files on Spruce's desk before wrapping me in a fierce hug. 'Welcome back,' she said, relief shining in her eyes. 'I would've come sooner, but I assumed you'd be resting after the examination.'

Grinning, I hugged her back just as tightly. 'I'll have plenty of time to rest once the war is won.'

My gaze drifted to the files now sprawled across the desk. 'I can see you've been busy. I don't think I've ever seen this much paper. On Ruin, we grew up believing it was a scarce resource.'

She ran a finger over the stack of files. 'It is scarce,' she said, her eyes lingering on the pile. 'They've been carefully preserved, not recycled.'

I pulled one of the files toward me, flipped it open, and skimmed the first few pages. 'Have you found anything useful?' I asked, curious where she'd begun.

'I'm sorting through them in batches,' she said, with a sigh. 'Starting with the most recent dates and working my way back. Most of what I've read are reports on the children they took - why they took them, and the horrifying reasons behind their experiments. We know they used the children's skin for grafts.'

My mind flashed back to when Zander and I first captured

Rowan. 'Rowan promised Zander a skin transplant to heal his burns if he agreed to help set her free.'

Robinia shuddered. 'If only it were that simple,' she murmured, drawing a shaky breath. 'We've since uncovered something far darker. The skin was taken from children - for the collagen.' Her voice was thick with revulsion, and each word laden with horror. 'They processed it into a paste, a sticky gel to smear across their faces, clinging to the illusion of youth.'

My blood simmered at their twisted vanity and ruthless ambition. 'We need to expose the real masterminds behind this world order,' I said. 'Malus is just a pawn. The true masters pull the strings from the shadows.'

I sat frozen in suffocating stillness, the weight of their crimes pressing down on me. Despite the pulse thudding in my ears, my thoughts remained clear and sharp. I didn't need to speak the words - they were already burned into my soul, branding me with purpose. They would pay. Every last one of them. For the sins they cloaked in veils of power and corruption. No matter what it took, I would see them fall.

6

I decided to join Robinina to speak with one of the scientists from Omen's Keep, a man named Hemlock. It took effort not to recoil as I stepped into his holding cell. He was seated on a narrow bench, spine hunched, wrists shackled. His face was a ruin of exhaustion. Sunken cheeks, skin sallow and stretched thin. Eyes so bloodshot, it looked as though the vessels had burst from weeks of sleepless guilt.

I tried to meet his gaze. Failed. A shiver slipped beneath my skin and settled in my bones. 'Are you thirsty?' I asked, the words tasting bitter on my tongue. I had no real intention of giving him anything - not yet. This was a ploy, a test to see how deeply he was still entangled in Control's grip.

Zander had shown kindness to Rowan; it had worked in our favour, winning her loyalty completely. There was little to lose by testing his theory again - perhaps even more to gain.

He didn't answer. His gaze stayed locked on his fingers as if they were talismans, capable of whisking him far from our reach. I leaned toward Robinia, seated firmly beside me, and whispered in her ear. 'What's your take? You've weaned more people off Control than anyone.'

Her eyes stayed locked on him, reading the subtle fractures beneath his calm demeanour. 'I think you're worried, Professor Hemlock,' Robinia said, her gaze dropping to her notes before meeting his eyes again. She smiled. 'Do you prefer the formalities, or shall we just use your name? We wouldn't want to disrespect you, after all.'

He sat like an empty vessel, his eyes flitting between me and Robinia.

Clearing her throat, she continued. 'Hemlock, I believe you're starting to feel something - for the first time in a long while - outside of Control's grip. And it terrifies you. You're afraid because you're beginning to understand emotions. Emotions you haven't felt in years. Am I right?'

He said nothing, but a shadow flickered across his face. His posture shifted - restless, uneasy. As if her words had stirred something buried deep within him.

'Do you remember being a child on Ruin, before you came of age?' Robinia's voice softened. 'Or has that memory been pushed so far back that it's lost to you now?' She leaned forward a little, clasping her hands on the table. 'You once laughed, cried, felt anger - maybe even hatred. And perhaps, just once, you felt the joy of love. It was never encouraged, but those emotions were there, simmering beneath the surface before they were stolen from you.' Her voice dropped to a whisper, coaxing. 'Think hard . . . go on.'

Hemlock fidgeted in his chair, his fingers twitching in his lap. A deep, throaty gulp escaped his lips, as if he were swallowing back words that fought to surface. His eyes glistened, tears pooling, threatening to spill. He bit down hard on his lip, a last, desperate attempt to halt the fear brewing inside him.

A sudden knock on the door granted Hemlock a momentary reprieve. The door creaked open, and Felix's head appeared around the frame, his eyes bright with excitement. 'Jasmine, Spruce needs you in the Operations Room,' he said, barely containing his energy. 'Ash has made contact - he's safe and still in play.'

As Felix's words sank in, relief poured through me. Robinia met my gaze, the same park of hope shining back at me.

'We need to get word to Larch,' I said, rising to my feet. I gestured for Felix to take my seat beside Robinia. 'Stay here and have a friendly chat with Hemlock.' I said his name like a curse, unable to hide my contempt.

* * *

Spruce handed me the cryptic note Ash had sent through the fax. The paper crinkled under my fingers as I unfolded it, my pulse quickening. 'Can we be absolutely certain this is from Ash?' I asked, unease creeping in. 'What if it's a trap - a ploy from Malus to deceive us?'

'All the codes check out,' Spruce said. 'Our analyst has already scanned it into her software. She's working on the decryption now - we should have the full context within five minutes.'

The five minutes stretched into an eternity, each second dragging, tightening the anticipation coiling in my chest. Just as I was about to voice my impatience, the analyst marched over, and handed a tablet to Spruce.

'Gather around, everyone,' Spruce called, his attention fixed on the small screen. The room fell silent as we all leaned in, waiting for him to read the message from Ash. 'I'm back at my post. Although not yet suspected, it's only a matter of time. Malus is conducting a full sweep of interrogations. Some have chosen to take cyanide pills rather than risk capture. There's a rumour that government scientists are weeks away from decoding dreams and thought control. If this is the case, the Resistance needs to act now.'

The muscles in Spruce's jaw stiffened as he read Ash's

message aloud. 'I had to get this message through, even though it puts me and others at greater risk. But I had no choice. Shadows move in silence across the soiled land, weaving a storm to uproot the poisonous bloom and soothe the soil beneath.' Spruce paused, took in a deep breath. 'I can't say more in fear this message is intercepted, and our codes are deciphered.' Spruce fell silent, his brow furrowing as he processed the implications.

'What does he mean by all that talk of shadows on the spoiled land?' I asked, with a frown.

'It's a code,' Spruce said. 'Those in the Resistance on Ruin are preparing to overthrow Aconite and seize control of the island.'

'Does he say when or how?' I asked.

His eyes returned to the monitor. 'All is secure at the eastern crest. Will join the tree keeper and threads from the loom. Setting off to the spoiled land to spark the wind and will try to retrieve the weaver and the pearl.' He paused, glancing up at me. 'Ash has managed to get hold of a watercraft at the mainland pier. He's meeting Taxus and some of Spindle's crew. They're heading to Ruin to assist with the rebellion and rescue Spindle and Coral.'

The air tightened in my chest. 'When do they leave?'

'He doesn't say,' Spruce said. 'He finishes with this, which translates to, 'If this is my last means of communication, tell my father I'm honoured to be his son, and I'm sorry I didn't have much time with him. Tell Jasmine I'll do my best to bring Spindle and Coral back. I'll die before letting her down.'

An uncomfortable silence filled the Operations Room. The hum of machinery seemed distant, drowned beneath the weight of the message. Operatives exchanged grim, silent glances - the gravity of Ash's situation settling over us all.

'Back to your stations,' Spruce commanded, his voice cutting through our worry. He turned to me, his expression sombre. 'We can't have operatives taking matters into their own hands without orders. This kind of recklessness could cost us everything. Look at what's already happened.'

His words stung. I had been reckless, chasing opportunities that came with a heavy cost. But without that risk, we'd still be stuck, no closer to the freedom we so desperately craved. And now, we had the fear of government scientists soon being able to decode our thoughts and dreams. 'It's all or nothing now, Spruce,' I said, shaking my head. 'We need to strike again - hit them from every side. Target the last place they'd expect - break into the capital's Midpoint, cause havoc, cripple their communications, their weapons. At the same time, hit other key locations. It's our only shot. Ash doesn't have any other choice but to press forward.'

'We're stretched too thin already, Jasmine. We don't have the manpower to hit multiple targets at once.'

'Then we need to be smart. There's got to be a way.'

One of the operatives raised his hand. 'Movement at sector four.' His fingers flew over the keyboard, calling up the area on his monitor, and within moments, Spruce and I were beside him.

'It's our convoy,' Spruce said, as the vehicles appeared on the screen. 'They've come home.'

A deep breath of relief escaped me. 'I'll head over to the tunnel and meet them.'

Spruce turned to me, his brow creasing as his eyes met mine. 'Are you all right?' he asked.

I blinked, confused. 'Sure . . . why?'

He pointed to my face. 'Your nose is bleeding.'

I wiped it with the back of my hand, barely registering it, but when I glanced down, a streak of blood glistened against my skin. I froze, staring at the crimson smear for a moment before the pressure at the top of my head rose. 'I'll go clean this up,' I muttered, feeling the trickle quicken alongside the thud in my temples. 'Pass a key card to Zander and Cooper for my room and have them meet me there.'

* * *

I gazed into the mirror above the sink. The blood was gone now, but my nose still throbbed. It was tender, as though it had been struck. A wave of nausea twisted in my stomach, and I gripped the sink to steady myself. Just as the dizziness threatened to pull me under, a sharp knock echoed from the bedroom door, followed by the unmistakable swish as it opened.

Stepping out of the bathroom, I found two men seated on the high-backed chairs at my table. For a long moment, I stood watching them, confusion clouding my thoughts. Who the hell were they? And what were they doing in my room?

7

The fog in my mind lingered for a few minutes before recognition slowly sharpened the edges. Zander's square jaw, his skin marred with burn scars that told their own stories, his eyes sharp and vigilant. And Cooper - his broad shoulders hunched slightly as if the grief he still carried was too much to bear. The confusion melted away as it dawned on me that it was them.

'When did you get back?' I asked, a rush of relief flooding through me. 'If I'd known, I'd have come to meet you.'

They exchanged a brief glance - a silent conversation passing between them. A troubled look replaced Zander's usual calm, while Cooper's eyes narrowed. They didn't need to speak; the unease between them said enough. Something was off - and I didn't have a clue what.

'What's wrong,' I asked, walking over to them. 'Why are you both looking at me like that?'

It was Cooper who finally spoke. 'Jasmine, you knew we'd arrived. You had a nosebleed in the Operations Room and came back here to clean up. You sent word for us to meet you here. Spruce gave us a key . . . do you not remember?'

A pounding pain beat against my skull. I pressed my palm to my forehead. 'I have the beginnings of a migraine,' I murmured, forcing a weak smile. 'It'll pass soon.' I exhaled, willing my heart to stop hammering. 'But yes - of course - silly me. I forgot I'd sent for you.' The lie sat like a lump in my mouth, clumsy and unconvincing, as if I was trying to persuade myself as much as them.

I straightened, shoving aside the fog in my brain. 'Does Larch know we've heard from Ash?' My voice came out sharper than I intended, but I couldn't afford hesitation. Not now. Not when everything hinged on control. If they sensed a crack, even the smallest one, doubt would seep in at my ability to lead. And that was the last thing I could allow.

'Spruce briefed all of us.' Cooper said. 'Larch is relieved Ash is safe, but he's still on edge. Spruce too - he says it must be bad. Ash doesn't make decisions like this without consulting anyone.'

I lowered myself onto one of the chairs. 'I told Spruce already - Ash didn't have a choice. He's a sitting target where he is. He'd rather be out there, taking action, making a difference, than waiting around to get caught. I'd do the same in his position.' My fingers curled into a fist against the table. 'Which brings me to my next point - when do we set off for Ruin? He needs backup, and we can't leave him to face this alone.'

Cooper rubbed a thumb over his jaw before leaning forward. 'Hold on, Jasmine. Charging in won't help him - it might even make things worse. We need to be smart about this, use every resource we've got.' He placed his elbows on the table, steepled his fingers, thumbs pressing to his forehead. 'We can't just react. We need to think strategically. Look at this from all angles. Which means you have to be able to work with Spruce.' His shoulders squared, waiting for my argument. Hearing none, he continued. 'This isn't just about getting there fast. It's about getting there with the right moves - making sure we all make it out in one piece.'

Before I could respond, Zander pushed back in his chair, arms crossing tightly over his chest. 'And before you go anywhere,' he cut in. 'Aspen needs to check you over - make sure you're fit to go.' He jabbed a finger in my direction, eyebrows lifting in challenge, daring me to protest. 'We can't afford to stop and mop up your bloody nose in the middle of a fight. You need to be at full strength.' His tone softened. 'The last thing we need is you hitting the ground mid-battle because you were too damn stubborn to get checked.'

I sighed. 'Alright, you've both made your point.' Rising to my feet, I rolled the tension from my shoulders. 'I'll go see Aspen now. But after that, I want everyone in the Operations Room. We don't waste time - we plan.'

* * *

Aspen fastened the blood pressure cuff around my arm. His focus fixed on the readings. 'Your vitals are normal,' he muttered, though his tone carried a note of something unreadable. Caution? Doubt?

The cuff released with a soft hiss, but he didn't step back. Instead, he hesitated. 'I want to run some comparisons on your blood.' He met my gaze with a confident smile. 'I need to check it against the samples I took from the prisoners - both when they were still under Control and now that they've been off it. We need to see if anything's changed.'

I flexed my arm as Aspen removed the cuff. My gaze drifted to the row of vials lined up on his desk. 'How are the hostages?' I asked. 'I mean . . . now they're off Control - can you see them cracking?'

Aspen held up the syringe. 'They're confused. Disoriented. Like waking from a nightmare they can't quite remember.' He slid the needle into my arm. 'As for your blood . . . it's just a theory, but a promising one.' A spark of something - hope? It lit up his eyes. 'I believe I've identified a unique enzyme. If I can isolate it, it might be the key to undoing what Control has done.' His eyes held mine, stead and sure. 'It could be our antidote.'

'Aspen, that's incredible,' I said, the importance of his words sinking in. 'And all this time, I thought there was something wrong. When do you think it will be ready?'

'It's hard to say,' he said, his voice tight. 'That's why I didn't want to tell you until I was sure. We're making progress, but isolating the enzyme is just the first step.' He looked up, his uncertainty clouding his features. 'Distributing it? That's another beast entirely. We'll need to establish safe channels, mobilise every resource we've got, and ensure it reaches the right people - those who need it most. Government guards, soldiers, those who've been programmed to fight against us.' The stakes were clear in his voice. 'We also don't know how long it will take to work in each person's system. We might not even know if it's working until it's too late.'

'You need to give me a clean bill of health for the emergency meeting I'm calling,' I said, my tone sharp with determination. 'And I need that antidote ready in two days. I don't care what it takes -just have it ready.'

'I'll only falsify your health status if you let me go with you - whatever you're planning. Someone who understands your condition needs to be by your side, ready to step in if you start to struggle.'

'I appreciate your concern, but I can't let you come with me. Your time is better spent here. Even if you manage to find the antidote before I leave, we need to focus on mass production. We can't afford for you to be distracted by my condition. Too many lives depend on what you're creating right now.'

* * *

We decided to meet in my bedroom suite. It felt as though the weight of the entire world had settled into its quiet corners - a stark contrast to the relentless working of the Operations Room. There were no blinking screens, no frantic murmurs - just silence.

I stood at the head of the table, my gaze sweeping over each face in turn. Every set of eyes held the same look of understanding - the consequences of what lay ahead - and the knowledge that everything hinged on our next move.

Spruce perched on the edge of his seat, his hands clenched tightly. Robinia and Larch exchanged a silent glance. Cooper leaned forward, muscles taut and ready. Minx twisted a strand of auburn hair around her finger, slow and deliberate. Felix's fingers drummed an uneven beat against his knee. Astrid sat rigid, her gaze fixed on me - unblinking, unwavering. Zander sat with arms folded, his sharp eyes darting between us, calculating, as if he already knew how this would play out. And then there was Orion, his presence heavy with sorrow, the grief still lingering in him.

There was no time left for debate. That moment had passed, and my voice sliced through the charged silence. 'We can't wait any longer. I'm taking a crew to the island of Ruin immediately to aid the rebellion. With any luck, we'll reach Ash and the others before whatever's planned comes to a head.'

I locked eyes with Spruce. 'If any messages arrive from the island, inform them reinforcements are on their way. Also, find a way for me to cross the Pewter Sea undetected. Mary slipped aboard a trader's vessel - there must be others out there beyond Control's grasp.'

'Robinia,' I said, my tone resolute. 'I can't thank you enough for everything you've done - and continue to do. You've cared for the refugees from the mountains and the children from

Omen's Keep, all while sifting through documents filled with unspeakable horrors. You've shouldered so much, yet you keep going.'

There was no hesitation in her reply. 'Just tell me what you need, Jasmine.'

I nodded. 'I know operatives are already looking into this, but I need you to coordinate with them. There's a reactor that brought about the End of Days - it may be listed under a project called SIAJ. I need every shred of information on it. Does it still exist,? If so, where is it kept? What condition is it in? Most importantly, can it be used to reverse the damage to the Sun?' I leaned in, lowering my voice. 'The elite hoard luxuries at their settlements, recreating gardens and playgrounds while the rest of the world is left in ruins. There has to be a reason. See what you can find.'

The door parted and Aspen strode in. He nodded briefly. 'You'll be pleased to know, you've never been healthier, Jasmine.'

I smiled, relieved by how confident he sounded. 'Perfect timing. I was just about to give an update on your progress with the antidote.'

He pulled out a chair and slumped into it. 'I'm close to a breakthrough, but with a two-day deadline, we'll have to release it untested. I will have no time to refine it - we can only hope it works as intended.' He ran a hand over his head. 'I'll analyse your DNA samples, Jasmine - see if I can tailor the formula to your biology. If I'm lucky, I might even find a way to accelerate its effects using your genetic markers.'

A ripple of relief swept through the room. Shoulders eased, brows relaxed, and a few wary smiles flickered to life. Aspen's words - *on the verge of a breakthrough* - hung like a promise.

Just as the room began to hum with newfound hope, a sharp beep silenced the moment - Spruce's pager. We froze, every head turning as he drew the device from his pocket, his face unreadable. Then. Voice crackled through from the Operations Room.

'Malus is live on the plasma screen. We need you back here immediately.'

The words hit like a hammer, crushing the fragile optimism that had only just begun to take root.

8

We stood in the Operations Room, every eye fixed on the large screen as Malus's looming figure appeared. I knew each word from his mouth would land like a threat, ready to shatter the fragile hope we'd only just begun to grasp.

'Jasmine, I see you've recovered. Excellent. Breaking you will be all the more satisfying.'

'You've already done your worst - there's nothing left to break. Every wound you slashed across my soul, every twisted lie, every betrayal, has left me wrecked beyond repair. The hatred I feel for you burns hotter than any fire, yet it festers cold and hollow, rotting in my chest. So, when I come for you, pray you're already dead - because my fury will not stop, and it will not spare you.'

He laugh - loud and merciless. 'If you think you've suffered the worst, you're in for a rude awakening. Everything until now? Just the warm-up. And trust me - I'll savour every moment as I tear you apart, piece by piece.'

My fingers curled into fists, nails biting into my palms - but I held my ground. My voice held firm. 'Enough with the theatrics. Just tell me what you want.'

His gaze slid over me as if I were nothing, settling on Robinia with a predator's gleam. A slow, smug smile curled at his lips. 'I want a hostage swap,' he announced, arrogance lacing from every syllable. 'Coral and Spindle in exchange for Robinia, Rowan, and every woman and child from the settlement. I also want my medics and scientists returned from Omen's Keep - along with the children you so foolishly freed.'

He gave a careless shrug. 'As for the documents you stole - keep them. They're outdated. All they'll reveal is how far we've come - how thoroughly we've perfected our methods, thanks to human experimentation.'

I forced steel into my voice, locking down the chaos churning inside me. 'Rowan is my prisoner, Malus,' I said, every word deliberate, measured. 'You can have her back, but she's in bad shape. I had to take her arm - there was no other way to stop the microchip from tracking her.' I studied his face, searching for a sign of empathy, my pulse hammering in my throat. 'She never recovered fully. She's barely clinging to life. Move her now, and she won't survive. Is that what you want for her?'

His reply dripping with mock adoration. 'You took her arm. I have to say, I'm impressed. I never thought you had it in you, Jasmine.' He tilted his head, eyes gleaming with dark delight. 'She was one of your little friends, wasn't she? My, how you've changed. I want proof of life - that she's in the condition you claim.'

'I'll need time to set this up. A live feed isn't possible - not from where we're keeping her. It'll have to be a recording.'

As Malus and exchanged blows in words, dread pooled, seeping into every corner of the room. My comrades must have thought me reckless - mad, even - to offer something so far beyond our reach. How could I possibly prove life - where there was none?

'In return, I want to see footage of Coral and Spindle. You can have everything you've demanded - except Rowan.' I turned to Robinia, letting the ice in my voice slice through the air. 'We have no use for you anymore. When I was at my lowest, back on Ruin, you showed no compassion. You toyed with feelings I barely understood - played games that nearly shattered me. You thought I was your friend, Robinia. You were wrong.' I gave a curt nod to Zander. 'Take her. Lock her up with the others.'

Robinia's eyes flared in disbelief, her voice thin with panic. 'Jasmine, how can you do this?' She thrashed against Zander's grip, her cries rising to a frantic pitch. 'Everything I did was to protect you.'

Her words hit hard, cracking the cold barrier I'd begun to build. The pain in her voice was real - but not enough to stop me. I turned back to face Malus, the fire in my chest flaring hotter. 'Now, show me Coral and Spindle - then I'll send coordinates for your precious cargo.'

Spruce stepped forward, disbelief etched across his face. He raised a hand, palm open. 'Jasmine, this is madness,' he said, through gritted teeth. 'You can't.' Not with Rowan. You're letting rage cloud your judgement.' He stepped closer, desperation bleeding into every movement. 'You're not just giving up Robinia - you're throwing away everything we've built. This could destroy us.' The urgency in his tone was unmistakable - but so was the fear in his eyes. Fear that I was slipping into something darker than even Malus.

In a single stride, Cooper was at Spruce's side, laying a firm hand on his shoulder. 'Back off,' he said, his eyes cold, his voice like steel.'Let Jasmine do her job.'

The plasma screen flickered then blacked as if the feed had been cut. It slowly returned, revealing a cramped, dimly lit room. Shadows clung to the cold concrete walls, stretching and shifting as if alive in the silence. At the far end, two glass cages stood like grim monuments, each punctured with small air holes near the top.

In one cage, Spindle sat slumped, his body hunched over the metal bench, his head buried in his hands as though he could block out the world. In the other, Coral leaned heavily against the glass, her eyes fixed on Spindle, concern etched on her face.

'Coral . . . Spindle,' I called, my voice cracking as I fought to force the lump in my throat down. 'Can you hear me?'

The only answer was the faint, rasping sound of their shallow breaths. Then, slowly, Spindle raised his head, his face bruised and misshapen. Something caught his attention - perhaps the blinking red light of the wall camera - pulling his weary gaze towards us.

He tapped the glass, urging Coral to notice, to look. But there was no frantic pleading, no desperate cry for help. They simply sat there, still and broken, each trapped in their own stifling agony.

Blankets were draped around their shoulders, and a solitary bucket sat in the corner of each cage. There was nothing else - no comforts, just the bare minimum required to keep them alive in a place that had stripped them of everything else.

'They can't see or hear us,' Spruce murmured. 'But they know someone's watching. They probably think it's Malus.'

As if the mere mention of his name had summoned him, the scene shifted abruptly. Malus's face appeared, his twisted smile spreading across his snake-like lips. His eyes gleamed with satisfaction, the look of a man who thrived on human suffering. 'Now,' he purred, his tone demanding. 'You said you would give me co-ordinates of where to collect my people.'

'Do you think I'm a fool?' I said, my voice filled with fury. 'You'll get them, but not straight away. We'll take them to the location first and leave them in the vehicle for you. But I'll send you a live feed of their journey, so you can watch as they're loaded and delivered, every step of the way. And I want Coral and Spindle in return. As an act of trust, I'll allow you to choose the location for their exchange. Just let us know and we'll collect them. I only ask for fourteen days grace to be able to organise the live feeds and the recording of Rowan. We don't have the advanced tech you do. Our people are scattered across the mainland. This will take time.'

'I'll give you ten days,' he said, his words dripping with evil. 'At that point, I will call back in and require the co-ordinates for the swap, a live feed of the hostages being loaded, and a film of poor Rowan on her deathbed. Remember, I have more mountains to collapse should you renege on our agreement.'

With that, the screen cut to black, plunging us into a suffocating void. Seconds later, the image flickered back to life, and once again, we were confronted with the image of the toppled mountain range. A reminder of the devastation he could unleash.

'What the hell are you playing at?' Spruce snapped, his voice thick with frustration as he cursed under his breath. 'Not once did you stop to think. Not once did you ask for our opinion on any of this.'

'Listen up,' I shouted, silencing his anger. 'We're not giving Robinia - or anyone - back to that monster. We're buying time, and Malus just handed us the perfect opening.' I let out a long, slow breath. 'We now know where Coral and Spindle are being held. It's the same holding pen where Coral and I were kept before our trial.' My heart raced as the memories came flooding back. 'We won't need to waste time looking for them or waiting for our people on the ground to tell us. We've saved precious time with this knowledge.'

I glanced at Cooper. 'Fetch Robinia and Zander, and take

them to my suite.' My eyes met Spruce's. 'Ruin has a network of underground tunnels - used for holding their cloned livestock. I need a full map of them, every entrance and exit. Coral and I only saw a fraction of what's down there, but I'm certain there's more. And that might be the key to turning our attack on Ruin to our favour.'

9

As we gathered around the table in my suite, the tension was almost tangible. All faces were lined with exhaustion, suspicion, and something deeper - wounded trust. I curled my fingers around the edge of the table as I met each of their gazes in turn. Robinia, who met my stare head-on, was defiant and clearly waiting for an explanation - hurt, obviously, by the way I had treated her.

'I owe you all an apology,' I said, my voice sincere. 'I should've given you a heads-up before making the deal with Malus. It was done on the spur of the moment, thinking I could buy us time. But I see now that all I did was betray your trust.' I reached across the table, hoping Robinia would take my hand. 'And you, more than anyone, deserved better.'

Robinia's brow furrowed, her lips parting slightly, but she said nothing.

'I had to make it real. Malus isn't easily fooled. If I'd treated you with warmth, with the respect you deserve - he would have seen right through it. He had to believe you were nothing to me - just a piece to be traded, another pawn in the game. It was the only way to sell the deception, to make him think he had the upper hand.' My fingers tightened into a fist as I waited for Robinia to take it. 'But that doesn't excuse how I treated you. I crossed a line, and for that, I'm sorry.'

For a moment, the silence stretched between us. Then Robinia leaned forward, resting her palm on my balled hand. 'You made me doubt you,' she said. 'And worse - you made me doubt myself.'

My chest ached, but I nodded. 'I know. And I can't undo that. All I can ask you to believe is that I never once regretted or faked our friendship. I can assure you, you'll never have cause to question it again.'

With a slow sigh, Robinia nodded, a ghost of a smile forming on her lips. 'I can understand why you did it. And it did provide valuable information. But I should've been kept in the loop. I thought the rage that used to build up inside you - the rage you found difficult to control - had come back to haunt us all.'

Spruce leaned forward, elbows resting on the table. His gaze flicked between Jasmine and Zander before settling on Robinia. 'The tunnels under Ruin,' he said, his voice filled with frustration. 'How many of them still exist? I remember them - at least, I think I do. But it's been so damn long since my child-hood, and after years under Control, my memories of that place feel like shadows behind frosted glass. If those tunnels are still there, they could be our way in. Our way to strike without Aconite seeing us coming.'

'I remember the smell of the cows,' I said, losing myself for a few seconds at the memory. 'The stench was awful. And the noise they made - they sounded as if their existence was so miserable. We had no idea what it was at first, but when we found out . . .' I shook my head, and a little laughter warmed my voice. 'Coral said if we ever brought about a rebellion, she would want to free the cows too.'

Robinia traced an invisible map onto the table with her fingertip. 'There are two entry points from the caves,' she began. 'One not far from Hazard Bay, another . . .' She stopped abruptly, her gaze snapping to mine. 'Believe it or not, from the Black Cave. The same one where you hid Mary.'

My breath hitched. 'The Black Cave.'

Robinia nodded. 'That tunnel was made by workers under orders of the first elite. It's how they shipped cloned cattle from the mainland onto the island and herded them below ground so no one would see.' Her lips curled into something that wasn't quite a smile. 'It was the reason that myths of draconian hybrids were spread, to keep children frightened, so they'd stay far from it. The myth was passed down over generations, lasting longer than the tunnels themselves.'

Spruce leaned back in his chair, arms crossed over his chest. 'Are the tunnels still passable? It's been generations since someone actually ventured all the way through.'

'There's only one way to find out,' Cooper said, with a fire in his tone that no one could miss. 'We need to locate Ash and Taxus. If we can't, we'll have to find something - anything - to get us to Ruin. And we need to do it fast.' He met my gaze, his eyes accusing without a single word spoken. 'The last thing we need is for Malus to have Coral and Spindle moved in preparation for him to hand them back over.'

Spruce threw in his own displeasure next. 'Now that we've settled on sending a party to Ruin, what's the plan for the hostage swap? We need a live feed showing his people on the move, and he'll want proof of life with Rowan. So, what's your strategy for handling this mess?'

My attention turned to Minx, who had been sitting still as a stone, her face blank. I had no choice now but to turn to her. 'Minx,' I said, my voice wavering. 'You've always had a likeness to Rowan. What if we could make you look ill - wrapped in blankets, barely able to move? We could put you in an awkward position, where the camera wouldn't pick up too much of your face, but just enough to fool them. There is just one thing we would need from you,' I paused, wondering how I would feel if it were me. 'You'd need to shave your head. Or, at least cut it really short.'

Minx's fingers threaded through her auburn hair, her gaze distant, as though weighing the enormity of what I'd just suggested. 'You know I'll do anything for our cause,' she said, in a voice full of conviction. 'Anything to see those who oppress us fall. But I hope, for my sake, that you can pull this off without asking me to sacrifice more than just my hair. What if he wants to see the stump you left Rowan with?'

'There's also the facial recognition system they have,' Spruce said. 'It could easily detect our lie.'

Robinia bit her bottom lip, as her mind raced with possibilities. 'Actually . . . it could work. If we cover half of Minx's face with old, dirty bandages - make it look like she got her head bashed in - we might just fool them. The mole above her lip, and that side of her face, could slip under their recognition systems if the other half of her face is covered.' Her gaze locked on mine. 'It's risky, but it's doable.'

A sly, calculating grin spread across Spruce's face. 'And with the old tech we've got down in the basement, we could dust off one of those outdated filming systems. Present them with screenshots that are fuzzy - just clear enough to give them something, but not enough to make them suspicious.'

Cooper's eyes burned with hope. 'We could use this old equipment to film the hostages getting into the vehicles. But here's the twist - instead of hostages, we load the vehicles with our fighters. If we play it right, we hit the capital and catch them off guard.' He paused, his expression hardening. 'The real issue now is getting the antidote for Control into their systems - either so it works . . . or fails completely. If Control's gone,

Malus's army might lay down their weapons. Our revolution could be far less bloody.'

Feeling more comfortable now that a plan was forming, I decided to chip in. 'So, we could have two possible scenarios, First, the antidote takes hold, and when we show up for battle, the soldiers and guards drop their weapons and surrender without a fight. Or, we're met with an army that shows no mercy - an enemy brainwashed to fight to the death.'

Robinia let out a whistled breath. 'So, let me get this straight,' she said, shaking her head. 'First, we head to Ruin. Take down Aconite without Malus catching wind. Rescue Coral and Spindle. Then get back . . . before the ten days are up. We need time to prep for filming and rally whatever fighters we can. It's going to be a tight schedule, to say the least.'

She glanced around the room, the enormity of the plan hitting everyone hard. There was no room for error.

I straightened my back, fists clenched at my sides to stop them from shaking. 'We won against the odds before,' I said, the words scraping out.

Orion's expression buckled. Every facial muscle tightened. 'Yes,' he muttered, 'And look what it cost us.'

The room fell into a sombre silence. No one knew what to say. It was Cooper who finally broke through the hush. 'The cost was unthinkable, and we both carry that weight. But Freya wouldn't want us to stop. Wherever her spirit is, I'm sure she's pushing us forward, not holding us back.' He took a deep breath. 'This is how we honour her. How we honour Nova. And every single one of those who paid the ultimate price. Because if we give in now.' His jaw tightened. 'Then Malus wins. And that, I won't allow - and if Freya were here, and she'd lost you - she wouldn't allow it either.'

Felix pushed himself up from his chair. 'If time is not on our side, we'd best get started. I'll begin by checking who's still fit to fight.' His gaze swept the room and settled on Spruce. 'Do you have a space in this facility large enough to hold a meeting? I'll have Falconer gather every woman and man still capable of combat.'

10

We travelled through the night, arriving at the docks in the early hours. The wind bit through our cloaks, carrying the scent of salt and damp wood. By the time the first light of day brushed the horizon, exhaustion had crept in.

We found shelter by the harbour, curling into the shadows between towering wooden barrows. Their rough, splintered edges pressed against our backs, shielding us from the worst of the chill.

The air reeked of fuel and stale seawater, the tang sharp in our throats. We didn't dare stir until the docks swelled with movement - merchants shouting orders, crates slamming onto decks, the creak and groan of watercraft shifting with the tide. Only then did we emerge, slipping into the crowd with our hooded cloaks drawn low to hide our hair. We became just another ripple in the endless tide of bodies, moving unnoticed. I couldn't help but wonder if this was the same path Mary had taken when she smuggled herself onto Ruin.

We agreed to split up, drifting through the pier like aimless wanderers, looking for any sign of our people - or a vessel we could take without raising alarm. Most crafts sat low in the water, heavy with supplies bound for the islands, their hulls creaking as they bobbed against the docks.

Every craft I passed might have been the one. Every shadowed figure in the mist could have been Ash. My pulse hammered as I swallowed hard. I sent a silent prayer into the crisp morning air. We had to find him. And soon.

After everything we had done - victory at the mountain camp, the burning of Omen's Keep, and the fear we carved into the heart of the elite settlement - the guards were thin on the ground. Perhaps Malus had grown complacent, convinced we were broken, our rebellion nothing more than dying embers. Or maybe he believed his victory was inevitable, that sooner or later, we would buckle. Our will eroded until there was nothing left for him to steal but our lives.

I strolled casually toward the brick well where we had left Larch. Aspen stood beside him, the perfect picture of a state medic tending to a man. Larch played his part well, slumped against the stone, the stump of his missing leg wrapped in fresh bandages.

Neither dared lift their heads - overhead, a drone passed with a low hiss, its unseen eye watching. One wrong move, one unguarded glance, and the system would lock onto their faces - feeding their identities straight to the government guards.

'We'll have to set sail on our own,' I said, watching as disappointment flashed across Larch's face. 'But we'll catch up with them - I'm sure of it. Ash has Taxus with him, and I know how capable they both are. They won't be alone. More of our people will have joined them by now, knowing that staying behind is a death sentence. It's only a matter of time before Malus uncovers their betrayal.'

Larch's gaze dropped, tracing the cracks between the cobblestones before he looked back at me. 'I'm sorry for the distance between us lately. I should be grateful - if it weren't for you, I'd never have known my son's name.' His voice quivered. 'Forgive me, Jasmine.'

His words were a melody to my ears. 'There's nothing to forgive.'

Astrid strode over and leaned above the well, cupping her hands to drink the slick, black rainwater. She didn't spare us a glance. 'Felix has managed to get a watercraft running in a junk shed at the tip of the pier. Don't all charge at once. Go in stages. Zander, Cooper, and Minx are already on their way. I'll go now. Then you, Jasmine.' She took another unhurried sip.

'How do you want to play this?' she asked Larch, knowing, as I did - a medic and an injured man might stand out more in the crowd.

'We'll go together,' Aspen said, without hesitation. His voice was calm, like he'd already thought this through. 'If a guard stops us, I'll tell them Larch is a patient I found struggling, and I'm helping him ease the cramp in his good leg by making him work it. I still have my cover intact, remember? If they scan my chip, it'll show I'm a medic on leave.' He glanced at Larch before continuing. 'If they check him, we're done. He has no chip. And worse - he carries the mark of the elite on his wrist. They'll wonder why he's dressed like a commoner, and that alone will be a red flag.'

I scanned the bustling pier with a sense of hope. The crowd moved in an active, organised rhythm - workers hauling crates, dockhands securing vessels. It was the perfect cover. 'At least it's busy,' I murmured, the energy of the docks feeding my confidence. 'We'll blend in.' I turned to Larch, giving his elbow a reassuring squeeze. 'We can do this.'

Astrid straightened, wiping a hand across her mouth. 'I'm off. See you all shortly.'

As Astrid vanished into the crowd, it was my turn. I kept my pace steady, eyes sweeping the pier for any sign of Ash. The salty wind tugged at my cloak as I walked; the sound of the pier buzzed in my ears - voices, creaking wood, and the occasional clang of metal.

I reached the shack at the end of the pier and jumped a cluster of smaller craft. My boots slammed onto the damp boards. I slipped once, but forced myself to keep moving. At last, I reached the watercraft moored at the end. My legs trembled and heart pounded, but I clung to the edge, breath catching with relief.

My friends were already in motion. Felix crouched low, checking the fuel lines, while Cooper assessed the hull for weaknesses. The craft creaked quietly beneath their careful hands, as if it, too, was preparing to flee.

The minutes passed, and there was no sign of Larch or Aspen. My nerves jangled. 'What could be keeping them?' I muttered, as the others grew restless.

Unable to stay still, I hopped back over the nearby craft and made my way to the doorway of the shack.

My blood ran cold. A few paces away, a guard's hand clamped tight on Aspen's shoulder. Aspen looked stiff, strained - but he wasn't fighting it. Larch limped towards me, his crutches dragging over the wooden boards with a grating scrape. His face was ashen.

'Oh no,' I whispered, my heart plummeting into my stomach. I rushed to Larch just as he hurled himself – crutches and all – onto the first craft. Grabbing him under the arm, I half dragged, half supported him across each one. At last, we reached our vessel. With a grunt, I hoisted him aboard. He slumped against me, limp with fatigue. Sweat glistened on his brow as he brushed it away. His breath rasped in short, guttural bursts.

'We got stopped,' he said, his voice trembling. 'But not for the reason you think. Someone collapsed in the town square - a guard spotted Aspen in his medic uniform. They asked if he could help.' He paused and shook his head. 'He had no choice but to let go of me, pushing me forward and advising I wasn't an emergency - just an injured man with cramp in his leg, nothing serious.'

I cursed under my breath, the frustration unbearable. 'I should never have agreed to let Aspen come with us. I could've managed on my own, carried the emergency supply of medication myself. Now, with him in this situation, we run the risk of being exposed - one wrong move, or one word from Aspen could be the one thing to bring us all down.'

'There's nothing we can do about it now,' Zander said, working the knots and loosening the tethered ropes. 'We need to move forward. Aspen knows what he's doing - he'll find a way to get back on track. You're overthinking it.'

I turned to Minx, the weight of another decision hitting me. Bringing her might've been a mistake too. 'We can't afford anything happening to you. You're our stand-in for Rowan, and we need you here.' I hesitated, reassuring myself I was making the right decision. 'You should head back. But on your way, see what you can find out about who collapsed - and where Aspen's at. Also, let Spruce know we've not found Ash.'

Minx embraced each of us in turn. 'If Ash manages to make contact, he'll know you're on your way.' With a final glance, she leapt over the watercraft, one smooth leap after another, before disappearing into the shadows of the shack.

Zander pushed our vessel away from the others with a long pole. 'Our stolen ride will raise suspicion faster than Aspen's little act, so stop fretting. It could be worse - he could only be pretending to be a medic.' He flashed a huge smile, his eyes mischievous. 'And if you're feeling ill, you can always lean on me.'

The craft swayed gently on the waves as it carried us further out to sea. Once Cooper judged the coast was clear, he fired up the engine. It spluttered to life with a low growl. 'Next stop is Ruin,' he said, with a grin.

* * *

We ran into trouble on the second day. The Pewter Sea, wild and unrelenting, met us with a ferocity that felt personal. Our craft was no match for the storm's fury, rocking violently beneath us. Its wooden frame groaned in protest as it strained against the ocean's wrath.

Each wave slammed into us with bone-shattering force, sending shockwaves through the hull, vibrating up my legs and into my bones. The sea was alive, a writhing monster of water and rage, determined to swallow us whole.

Black rain poured from the sky, cold and impenetrable, lashing our faces like a thousand whips. The world became a chaotic, blurred mess of darkness, water, and pain. Our hands slipped on the ropes, struggling to keep the craft from capsizing. My shoulders burned, and my muscles screamed with the strain. It seemed as though we were fighting a losing battle.

Thunder tore through the air. Lightning cracked the sky, illuminating the monstrous swells surrounding us. I saw Zander's face, pale with terror, his eyes wide with fear and exhaustion, a reflection of the storm's overwhelming power.

The storm wasn't the only thing breaking us. Our bodies shuddered from the relentless rocking of the craft. Astrid hung over the side, her body wracked with nausea, her face a ghostly silhouette against the blackness of the night. Cooper clung to the sides of the craft, his knuckles stark white, too weak to stand, his breath ragged from the struggle to hold on.

I gripped the railing with everything I had as another wave hit, slamming us sideways. The craft teetered for a terrifying moment, balanced on the brink of disaster, before it dropped back into the trough between waves with a sickening thud. The wood beneath us creaked, protesting under the strain of the water's assault. I could feel fear coiling in my gut as my breath came in short, sharp bursts. We had to survive. We had to make it to the island.

And then, through the storm's furious veil, I saw it - a jagged silhouette rising from the churning sea. A mass of rocks. At first, it was just a blur on the horizon, but with another flash of lightning, the outline sharpened. The coastline of Hazard Bay emerged, waiting to tear us apart. Our destination was within reach. But as our craft began to topple . . . so was death.

11

I barely had time to scream before I plunged into the sea. The impact tore the breath from my lungs. The black water closed over my head - suffocating, endless. My limbs flailed, panic thrashing through me as I tumbled in the darkness. Bubbles burst from my mouth, rising in frantic silver spirals towards the surface. My chest burned, muscles screaming for air as I fought against the pull of the deep.

Kicking hard, I followed the bubbles, arms slicing through the bitter water. My fingers brushed something solid - a splintered plank. I latched on, gasping . . . grateful I'd finally broken the surface.

Rain lashed down, blinding me. The wind howled across the water, tearing at my numb fingers as I clung to the wood. Waves swelled and dropped, dragging me closer to the unseen rocks at Hazard Bay.

Then - voices. Distant, muffled by the roar of the sea, but voices. My lips parted. 'Zander? Astrid?' Seawater spewed into my mouth, choking my cry. I strained to listen as the rain drummed against the surface. Gritting my teeth, I kicked hard.

I had to find them. If I was wrong - if the voices were only ghosts in the storm - I'd be lost. I'd be alone.

A blinding shaft of light sliced through the darkness, searing my vision. I flinched, squeezing my eyes shut against its piercing glare. The sea, once endless and shrouded, was suddenly stark, exposed. Was this a rescue - or something worse? Before I could react, rough hands grabbed me, strong fingers clamping around my arms. A gasp tore from my throat as I was wrenched from the water.

'I've got you,' a voice said - just as everything faded to black.

* * *

I woke to the violent lurch of the watercraft, my body jolting sideways as a wave slammed against the hull. My head pounded, my limbs ached, and the sharp tang of salt coated my tongue.

The low roar of the engine vibrated through the metal floor, almost drowned out by the wind howling outside.

This craft was large, far more powerful than the one that had capsized. Another wave sent a spray of icy water through a gap in the cabin door. I flinched, gripping the damp blanket wrapped around me.

It took a moment for my blurred vision to adjust. The dim cabin crammed familiar figures - each hunched against the cold, their eyes hollow. Somehow, against all odds, we remained. We had survived.

Then my gaze landed on the dark metal walls, the rein-forced panels, the insignia stamped in bold - the unmistakable symbol of Malus's warcrafts. My stomach twisted. This was no ordinary rescue. We were aboard a naval vessel used by Malus's forces to patrol the Pewter Sea. The craft surged forward, riding the crest of the storm.

I forced down the rising panic. 'Have we been saved - or taken?' I asked.

Everyone was too exhausted to move, their bodies slumped against the cabin walls, but in their eyes, I saw it - the quiet relief, the unspoken thanks to God that I was still here.

'Jasmine's awake,' Cooper cried, his voice ragged.

I noticed Larch, sprawled on a padded bench, his chest struggling to rise and fall. The craft lurched again, sending a fresh wave of nausea twisting through my stomach. My vision swam, the dim cabin blurring into shifting shadows and flickering light. Then - a face. Ash. He crouched beside me, his hand warm against my clammy brow.

'Jasmine, I pulled you from the water. It's okay - you're safe.'

I forced myself to sit. The world spun for a moment. 'Ash - it's really you.' I rubbed my eyes, just to make sure. 'But how . . . how did you find us. ?'

'You left before us. We only missed you by hours. This was a craft scheduled to patrol the outer islands. A few of the crew are our people, so we managed to commandeer it without too much trouble.' He sounded pleased, and rightly so. 'We have prisoners locked in the decks below,' he added.

I blinked, processing what he was saying. We had a naval vessel under our control, and Malus didn't have a clue. 'But how did you know where to find us, what route we had taken?'

His dark eyes twinkled in the dimness. 'I met Minx on the docks. She told me what happened with Aspen and that you'd stolen a craft from the shack. It was her who told us you were heading for Hazard Bay.' He paused, glancing toward the rain-slicked window as another wave hit. 'I knew it would be risky in the craft you took, so we followed the same path at full throttle, hoping to catch up with you.' His gaze flicked back to me. 'I'm glad we made it just in time.'

I pulled him into my arms without thinking. 'Thank you,' I

whispered, emotion tightening my throat. 'We owe you our lives.'

Ash pulled back slightly, a tired smile crossing his face. 'I made a vow to protect you - and I always will.'

'What is it?' I asked, sensing his dismay.

'I've updated Spruce, and he's aware Minx is on her way back. However, . . .' He hesitated. 'Aspen has been taken to the capital. Malus is clamping down on workers' leave. He's summoning all citizens back to their posts. It'll be difficult for Aspen to return to the outpost. Maybe impossible.'

A cold knot tightened in my stomach. This couldn't have come at a worse time. I pressed my fingers to the dull throb at my temple. 'But we need him - he's in the middle of making our antidote for Control. He's almost finished - it's ready . . . just untested.'

His voice grim, he said, 'We need to rule out any hope of that helping us now and prepare for the worst. It will be a bloodier war than we'd hoped.'

I exhaled slowly, glancing toward the others. 'We have no choice but to keep moving,' I said, forcing myself to sound like a leader. 'And we forget any hopes of a miracle.'

The vessel carved a path through the water, its bow groaning as we steered around the jagged outcrop of Hazard Bay. The storm had spent its fury, leaving behind a restless hush, the scent of rain and brine thick in the air. The first shards of dawn bled across the horizon, casting a pale glow over the shoreline - empty, save for ghosts of the past that lingered in my mind. This was the shore where Coral and I had found Mary. It was where our story began.

'How many able bodies do we have in total?' I asked Ash.

'Thirty men, plus all of you, Taxus, and me. There's also a technical expert on board who'll hopefully hide our tracks and keep us from both Malus and Aconite's watchful radar.'

Too few of us. Whatever lay ahead, we'd face it outnumbered. Our need for cunning had never been greater. Our only hope lay in Malus recalling many guards to the mainland, believing their resources were better spent there.

Taxus stepped onto the deck, his boots leaving smudges of oil and grime against the damp planks. His face, streaked with sweat and dirt, showed the marks of a man who had spent the night battling more than just the sea. He offered a lopsided grin. 'Jasmine,' he said, running a hand over his stubbled chin. 'I'm sorry your journey was rather bumpy, but who can predict the weather when crossing the Pewter Sea? You look surprisingly good, my friend.'

I wrapped my arms around him in a firm hug. 'Good to see you too,' I said, meaning every word. 'And I'm sure things would've been worse without you. If not for you lot, we'd be at the bottom of the Pewter Sea.'

'The water isn't deep enough for this vessel to take you ashore, so we're preparing to release the small rafts to get you there,' Taxus said, scanning the beach. 'I'm staying aboard. We'll head to the other islands to avoid suspicion. Ash has a radio to keep us updated on your progress, so we'll know exactly where to be when you need us.'

Larch hobbled through the small door and Ash moved to his side, offering an arm for support. It did my heart good to see the love between father and son.

'You should stay on board too, Larch,' I said, hating the fact I was separating him from Ash again. 'Your expertise will be more useful here. See if you can make contact with Spruce without detection.'

This was far more valuable to our survival than putting a laser gun in his hands. It wasn't just that he'd slow us down - this was safer. We'd already lost too many.

'Ash said there's someone who can shut down Aconite's systems. It makes more sense for him to take my place,' Larch said. He glanced down at the stump where his leg had been. He didn't speak, but somehow, he'd read my mind.

Then, as if already shifting gears, he moved his objective on. 'I'll focus on planting a false course on their nautical radar - make them believe this vessel is still on track in their charts.'

Ash squeezed Larch's shoulder. 'You've got this,' he said, quietly. 'You'll do a great job.'

Around us, the men moved with purpose, the deck alive with preparation. Weapons were checked and double-checked with sharp clicks of power cells locking into place. Lasers thrummed as they charged, their energy readings flashing green. Straps were tightened, holsters secured around waists, and final adjustments made.

Ash stuffed a few hand-held transmitters into a bag, zipping it shut. He slung the strap over his shoulder. 'These will keep us in touch if we need to split up.'

I took a look around, feeling the shift in the air - not just anticipation, but something stronger. A newfound confidence. I turned to Ash. 'You know,' I said, my voice lighter, 'I actually feel more hopeful about what we are about to do.' I let my gaze sweep over our fighters - strong, prepared, and ready. 'This mission suddenly feels possible.'

12

Stepping onto solid ground felt disorienting. The earth beneath my boots felt oddly foreign after days at sea. Yet, it was not just the stability that unsettled me - it was being back on the shoreline of Ruin.

Above us, a drone glided through the overcast sky, its sleek frame catching Ash's eye. He raised a hand to shield his gaze, the other hovering near the laser gun on his belt. The drone hovered, dipped slightly, then paused mid-air. After a moment, it rose and drifted away.

Ash let out a breath. 'That could've been a disaster. If it were one of Malus's drones, it would've opened fire. At least our operatives know we've arrived.'

We crept through the jagged mouth of the Black Cave, the air thick with the scent of damp stone and decay. I pressed a hand to my chest, willing my anxiousness to calm as we stepped into the tunnel. Shadows clung to the walls, shifting with the flicker of our torches. We followed the narrow passage into the cavern that had once hidden Mary.

Traces of Coral's time here remained - a seaweed bed, a hollowed rock for water, dark stains where black rain had pooled. A shiver ran through as I imagined her solitude - the endless days in damp gloom, surviving on insects and scraps. Then Spindle had found her, only for them both to fall into enemy hands.

The tunnel narrowed around us, damp rock rough beneath my fingertips. It reeked of salt, earth, and something old and sour. Dripping water echoed like footsteps, while torchlight cast twisting shadows over jagged stone. We pressed on, deeper into the cave's tightening grip.

I didn't know how long we'd walked, but then the stench hit - thick and rancid, clawing at my throat. I covered my nose. 'We're close,' I said. 'Up ahead is the labyrinth leading into Midpoint. One of the offshoots leads to the holding pen. That's where they're keeping Coral and Spindle.

A low, mournful groan drifted down the tunnel. We turned the corner - and there they were. Stalls upon stalls stretched into the gloom, filled with wretched beasts whose hooves restlessly shuffled on the concrete floor. They had never known daylight - only the cold iron bars and the reek of their own confinement.

Another corridor branched off, filled with the frantic clucking of hens crammed into wire coops, their feathers ragged from constant jostling. Further still, the shrill squeals of pigs, their bodies packed so tightly they had no room to turn.

And then, the worst of it. The slaughter room. The walls blackened by the stains of old blood. Metal hooks hung from chains overhead, swaying slightly in the draught. The floor was a shallow river of filth, congealed fragments pooling in the cracks of the uneven ground. The scent of death overwhelmed us - thick and metallic, mixed with the choking reek of disinfectant, as if someone had tried to scrub away the horror but failed. This was where it ended for them. Thankfully, no workers hovered, no one butchering. Maybe the slaughter only happened at a set time.

We pressed on, reaching the labyrinth I had spoken of. Here, we paused to catch our breath. The walls loomed high around us, their rough, timeworn surfaces swallowing the torchlight. Ahead of us, the tunnels splintered in every direction - darkened offshoots twisting into unknown paths.

I scanned the tunnels, my pulse quickening as my eyes locked onto the one I knew all too well. I had walked that path more times than I cared to remember, each step etched into my memory from my own trial in the Justice of Pax. Now, it would lead us exactly where we needed to go - the holding pen where Coral and Spindle were imprisoned. But I couldn't rush this. Timing was everything.

'So, how do you want this to play out?' Ash asked.

We froze as a soft shuffle echoed overhead. It was barely audible at first, but grew louder with each passing second. I tensed - we all did - ready for whoever was coming down those stairs. The footsteps drew nearer, and a figure slowly appeared at the bottom of the spiral staircase. Ash's hand went to the hilt of his laser, ready to strike. But as the figure fully emerged from the shadows, Ash paused. His grip loosened, and without a word, he stepped forward - extending his hand in a firm shake.

'Juniper,' Ash said, his voice low. 'It's good to see you.' He stepped back, held out his hand towards me. 'You'll remember Jasmine.'

His eyes glinted with admiration. 'How could I ever forget the heroine who defied Aconite and Malus in the Justice of Pax?'

'I'm sorry . . . but I don't remember you,' I said, studying his weathered face.

'I wouldn't have expected you to,' he said. 'I was one of the elders working in the kitchens. I used to see you sneak out food. I'd report it to Robinia, of course. But we never realised you were taking it to feed the woman, Mary. We thought it was just another part of your . . . wiring.' He hesitated, as if searching his mind for the right way to put it. 'Your way of defying the rules.'

I couldn't shake my nervousness. 'How did you know we'd be here?'

'We knew Ash was on his way, so were watching for him. We saw you enter the Black Cave from our drone and figured this is where you would make your entrance.'

'It's okay, Jasmine. Juniper's one of us,' Ash said, resting his arm on my shoulder. 'He's been with the Resistance on Ruin for years - long before either of us knew it existed.'

'I'm here to help. The others are above, waiting for your move. May I offer a suggestion?' Juniper asked.

'Yes, please.' I nodded. 'We're all in this together - and you know more about what's going on up there than we do.'

'Do you have any means of communication?' Juniper asked.

Ash swung the bag from his shoulder and lowered it to the ground. He unzipped it, retrieving one of our compact radios. 'Will these do?'

'Good,' Juniper said, then gestured towards a branching tunnel. 'Spindle and Coral are five minutes along that passage, held in the pen below the Justice of Pax. No guards are posted, but a live camera feeds their every move to the control room.'

'We already know,' I said, explaining that Malus had shown us a proof-of-life recording.

Juniper studied our group, weighing something up. 'Ash, take two of your men. Wait outside the holding pen until you hear from us that it's safe for you to move in.'

'I should go. I should be the one to free them,' I said, feeling how close they were - knowing, deep in my bones, I needed to see their faces.

Juniper and Ash shook their heads almost simultaneously, but Juniper was the one to speak. 'No, your place is in the fight above. You're the face of the Resistance. The others draw strength from you. If they see you standing at the front, they'll believe we can win.'

There was a spark of determination in Ash's eyes, his voice rich with promise. 'I'll bring them straight to you the moment we get them out.'

He leaned in and laid a kiss on my forehead. For a heart-beat, the world held its breath. It was just the two of us, bound by everything we'd endured, everything we'd sacrificed. When he pulled back, his fingers lingered against my cheek, as if memorising the moment.

'Be careful,' he said, his voice barely a whisper. 'I mean it. No reckless moves. No needless risks. We need you - not just now, but after. To lead us through whatever comes next.'

'Thank you, Ash. For everything,' I whispered, closing my eyes briefly and resting my cheek against his.

The torchlight flickered across his face, casting sharp shadows that deepened the worry etched in his eyes. His voice was low, with a slight note of hope. 'I'll be waiting for your signal. The moment you take control of Midpoint, I want to hear from you.' A flicker of a smile softened his lips. 'And don't keep me waiting too long.'

He gave my elbow a quick squeeze before stepping back, signalling to two of our men to follow him. With one last glance, he turned and moved out.

I watched them vanish into the branching passage. Every step he took away from me felt like one deeper into danger. 'Right, let's do this,' I said, turning to Juniper. 'How do you think we should proceed?

'As you already know, our guards patrol Midpoint in pairs. I'll approach a couple, tell them there's a problem down here in the slaughterhouse. We lure them in, knock them out, take the uniforms. Rinse and repeat until you're all in disguise.' He pointed to my head. 'The helmets will cover your hair, and the visors will keep facial recognition from flagging you.'

'What about the citizens? I don't want anyone hurt if things go awry.'

He smiled. 'Preparations are already underway. On my signal, members of the Resistance will spread word for everyone to gather at the Justice of Pax. It's the largest room in all of Midpoint. We'll lock in as many as it can hold - to keep them safe and stop them from reaching for spears and arrows.' He paused, his tone shifting. 'Let's hope it doesn't come to that. Ruin is made up mostly of babies, children and teenagers. The elders who work here are drugged on Control. Malus still believes the place is secure - untouched by outside influence. He also assumes that if anyone dared to rise up, the memory of your trial, and the price you paid, would be enough to silence them.'

'So, they won't be expecting any form of resistance,' I said, more to reassure myself than anything else.

There was a note of warning in Juniper's voice. 'We can't afford to be complacent. The last thing we need is for Aconite to alert Malus to the rebellion. If that happens - Malus will send an army.' He took one last glance at our group. 'Keep out of sight, with your torches off. Remember, we need to work quietly and quickly.' With that, he began to climb the stairs.

My gaze swept over Cooper, Zander, Astrid, Felix and Orion - each of them standing ready, braced for what lay ahead. 'Welcome to your first visit into one of our indoor cities,' I said, aware of how surreal this must seem to them. 'This is what we're fighting for - places like this, but for everyone. Free, safe townships. Just choice. Just freedom. Just the right to live without fear. And if we can somehow heal the Earth, we'll no longer need dome roofs to shield us from its wild, broken weather.'

Turning to the rest of the men - the naval soldiers who pledged their loyalty to the Resistance - I felt a swell of respect. They had freed themselves from Control's grip, and now they risked everything for our cause. 'It's an honour to fight along-side you,' I said. 'It's been a while since you stepped inside Ruin's Midpoint. This was where it all began for us - raised here without love or nurture, until we came of age. I'm sure the layout will start coming back to you.' I let my gaze meet theirs, making sure every word landed. 'Our objective is clear - we need to take control of their Operations Room, fast.' I searched their faces. 'Who among you is the technical expert Ash mentioned?'

One of the men raised his hand. 'That would be me,' he said with a crooked smile. 'Name's Cedar. Happy to be of service.'

'You're the most important person here today, Cedar,' I said, meeting his humble gaze. 'What you do with their operations will decide everything - whether this mission ends in a massacre with Malus's army coming for us - or if it runs smoothly. I'm counting on you to make it the latter. As soon as we take control, I need you to put the systems on a loop, showing that the daily operations of Midpoint are running as usual.'

'I'll do my best,' he replied, nodding.

I drew a steady breath and addressed the group. 'We'll be walking in pairs and will need to split up - but we can't afford to lose contact.'

The thought made my pulse quicken, although I tried not to let it show. 'Make sure you have radios, or at least stay within sight of someone who does. And thank you,' I added, hoping the sincerity in my voice was enough. 'Thank you for everything.'

I was about to say more when we heard them coming. Juniper's voice drifted down to us, calling for help to move some beasts, as the zapper in the slaughterhouse had run out of charge. We overpowered the two unsuspecting guards as they emerged, encountering no trouble, and continued the routine until we were all dressed in their uniforms.

Juniper ascended the spiral staircase ahead of us. As we climbed, my mind wandered back to memories that felt no more distant than a breath. I could still see Quercus, his dull eyes betraying nothing as he led me toward the holding pen. And there, I'd found Coral - her face pale, her body slumped in a cage.

More memories surged - Coral and I being dragged through Midpoint, beaten and bloodied. Ash had stood with Birch - Birch's hand resting protectively on Ash's shoulder. That was the moment when I believed Ash to be my Judas - the moment my love for him began to fade.

Then came Aconite - his twisted, sadistic smile as he stood over Coral and me, whipping the skin from our backs for nothing more than helping a lame fox.

But today, everything had shifted. Today, I was no longer the shattered captive. Today, I was the one in charge. I would claim vengeance - not just for me, but for Coral, for Salix, for Lily, for Willow, and for every soul crushed beneath their rule. Aconite . . . he'd learn what happens when you push someone too far. And once I had him, I'd hunt Malus down - like the monster he is.

13

We crouched in a line along the corridor. Ahead, the vast expanse of Midpoint stretched out, alive with the daily routines of its citizens. The familiar scene was both reassuring and suffocating - as though nothing had changed. Yet everything felt unbearably different. People moved in and out of buildings; some heading to their classes, others venturing out to trudge across the desolate landscape on assigned tasks. Some would be inside the Be Thankful Hall, while others worked in the gym.

Juniper, keeping his tone low, spoke to us all. 'Integrate into the walk lanes in twos. Stay in sight of each other. Head towards the Council Buildings. One of my assistants in the kitchens is working on cloning a chip that will get you into the Operations Room. I'll head straight over with it as soon as it's done. Once we have control over their systems, we can breathe easy. Remember - appear slowly, so it doesn't look suspicious.'

After he left, I turned to Zander. 'You partner with me. We'll go first.'

Pulling our visors down over our faces, we stepped out of the corridor and into the walkway. Our eyes fixed straight ahead toward the Council buildings. Elders strode among us with their deadpan eyes. A handful, robed in the distinctive insignia of the Council of Twelve, were scattered among the gathering, their garments billowing like emblems of power and command.

'This is where you grew up?' Zander asked, as he took in the lavish tiles adorning the floors and walls. I could imagine the wonder on the faces of all my friends. Compared to the dark, underground world of the caves, this place seemed like luxury - spacious, structured, almost opulent in its own sterile way.

My reply was simple. 'Yes.'

Yet, to me, it was far from a sanctuary. It was Hell, built on the false promise of order - a place where people were shackled by brainwashing, their freedoms suffocated by the drug called Control. The polished stone, the gleaming halls, the rigid structure and rules- it felt like a prison of another kind. It wasn't freedom; it was merely an illusion of utopia.

There was a break in the crowd as two guards strolled by, their complacency evident in the slow, assured pace of their steps. The ease with which they moved through the corridors confirmed everything Juniper advised - they feared nothing. The island, it seemed, was still wrapped in a false sense of security, unaware of the storm brewing on the mainland. I couldn't help but wonder - did they even know of the havoc we'd caused? Had Malus kept it a secret, not wanting the other islands to know how badly we'd struck them, how vulnerable they were?

As I walked, my gaze drifted to the bench where Ash and I had once sat. The moment was vivid in my mind - the first time I'd held his hand, the warmth of his fingers against mine, a fleeting connection. It was there that I'd looked into his eyes and, in an instant, realised who he was - Mary's grandson. A quiet ache spread through me, but I didn't stop. I couldn't. Not now.

And then I saw him - striding in my direction on the opposite side of the walkway, his towering figure unmistakable. Aconite. The sight of him froze the breath in my lungs. He was deep in conversation with one of the Council members, the very image of confidence and power. My heart pounded a staccato drumbeat.

The sight of him, so relaxed, so unnervingly composed, ignited pure rage deep within me. It was as if the world itself had stopped spinning, and in that moment, there was only him. The living embodiment of everything I despised - the architect of so much pain, suffering, and torment. The man whose hands had helped shape this island's misery.

Without thinking and without a word to Zander, I broke from our pairing. My heart hammered, each beat a roar in my ears as I moved toward him. Every step felt like it took me deeper into a storm, but I couldn't stop myself.

Aconite glanced down at me, his expression flickering with surprise at my sudden approach, though he quickly regained his composure. My pulse thundered in my neck, but I forced my voice steady, masking the rage simmering just beneath the surface. 'Sir,' I said, the words slipping from behind my visor. 'We've been sent to find you. There's been a breach on the island - poachers arrived by watercraft near Hazard Bay, and we need your guidance on operations.'

Aconite glanced down at me, his expression flickering with surprise at my sudden approach, though he quickly regained his composure. My pulse thundered in my neck, but I forced my voice steady, masking the rage simmering just beneath the surface.

He turned to the Council member with a dismissive wave. 'Carry on without me. I'll catch up with you at the city chambers once I've sorted this out.'

The Council member nodded, a subtle shift in his posture betraying his reluctance, before disappearing into the crowd.

Aconite's gaze shifted back to me, his eyes narrowing, assessing me like a predator. 'Why didn't you simply inform your commander?' His voice was calm, but there was a razor edge underlying it. 'Surely, a group of you should be able to head out and hunt them down?'

Zander lingered in the background, his uncertainty palpable, and I could feel the heat of his anger building. It was justified - this reckless act of mine had been a foolish gamble, one I hadn't fully thought through.

I wasn't even sure how to play this, my mind a blur of confusion, unable to grasp the protocol, the subtle steps, or the unspoken hierarchy that governed how the guards operated in situations like this. Once again, my anger had clouded my judgment, and now I feared I had jeopardised everything.

Aconite was sharp, calculating, always three steps ahead. If he caught even a whiff of hesitation, a glimmer of uncertainty in my posture or tone, he would pounce on it. I couldn't afford to let him see my doubt. I kept my back straight, forcing my shaking legs to keep me standing.

My mind raced, frantically sifting through memories of overheard orders and the way guards had spoken to their superiors. Should I ask for instructions, feign respect and deference? Or should I take a risk and make a suggestion? Stay silent and let him take control, as the chain of command dictated? Or - perhaps, just perhaps - should I pull my laser from its holster and end this in one decisive move?

Just as my fingers brushed the cold metal of the laser at my side, Aconite took control of the situation with unnerving calm. 'Come on, let's get this unfortunate situation sorted,' he said, his voice smooth and assured. It was as though nothing could disrupt the seamless order of things. 'They came in at Hazard Bay, you said?'

'Yes, sir. They've breached the shoreline there.'

'Come with me.'

He strode off and I matched his pace, forcing my heart to steady. Every muscle in my body tensed with the effort to appear calm. A quick glance over my shoulder confirmed my friends followed at a careful distance, their disguised forms merging seamlessly with the other guards moving through the bustling crowd. I could only imagine how furious they were at me acting on my own.

Aconite didn't spare me another look; his attention remained focused elsewhere. He believed me - for now. But fear gnawed at the edges of my mind. How long until he started asking questions I couldn't answer?

We arrived at a heavy steel door within the Council chambers, its surface smooth, cold, unmarked, and impenetrable. Aconite lifted his right wrist to the scanner, and it slid open with a faint beep.

I followed him, my pulse quickening, a knot of unease tightening in my chest. The moment I crossed the threshold, the door slid shut behind me with a finality that rang in my ears. I was on my own - cut off from my friends.

The room stretched wide. A cold blue light pulsed from hundreds of monitors, arrayed in curved rows that wrapped around the chamber like a digital embrace. The air was cool and filled with the static hum of electricity and the rhythmic clicking of fingers on keyboards. High-resolution monitors shifted between live feeds from every corner of Midpoint. Walkways, training yards, dormitories, even the busy pews of the Be Thankful Hall - nothing escaped their reach. Faces flickered in and out of frame, unaware they were being watched, measured, and tracked.

The workstations were positioned with military efficiency - sleek, angular consoles embedded into dark steel desks. A handful of elders sat at their stations, eyes glazed with focus, mouths murmuring to unseen voices through earpieces. Some worked with retinal overlays streaming data across their vision, others toggled between feeds with swift, silent gestures.

On the far wall, a pulsing map of the island glowed in crimson and gold, laced with layers of movement tracking, heat signatures, and drone paths. The island wasn't just watched - it was dissected, and controlled, manipulated in real time. Nothing moved without leaving a trace. It was a miracle we had managed to land undetected, but I guessed those in the Resistance here had a hand in that.

This was the epicentre. The very place where obedience was sculpted and rebellion erased on the island before it had time to spark. And I was standing in the centre of it. A sudden wave of nausea twisted through me. I was surrounded by enemies - every technician, every elder in this chamber would see me killed without hesitation if they knew who I truly was. They didn't look up. They didn't glance my way. But that didn't ease my fear of being caught. I could feel the tension crawl across my skin, as if the entire room knew something didn't quite fit.

Six guards stood at strategic points, lasers holstered but within easy reach. Their positions were no accident - calculated to cover the entrance, every corner, and every blind spot. They weren't relaxed, but they weren't tense either. Their vigilance was the calm kind, the sort that came from believing they stood in a fortress that was untouchable.

One of them, had his visor up. I noticed a scar running from his jaw to his ear. His gaze landed on me. For a breathless moment, I thought he might ask me something. But his eyes moved on, disinterested. I was just another guard. Another faceless cog in their perfect machine.

I prayed Juniper would have the key to the door soon. Every second ticking by saw the knot in my chest tighten. My mind raced, scrambling through possibilities - what to say once Aconite began to question me. What if Juniper didn't make it in time? What if the cloned chip failed? Come on, Juniper. *Please be close.*

I brushed my gloved hand over the hilt of my laser, not to draw it, but to remind myself I had some power left. If it all went sideways, I'd make it count. But still - I didn't want it to end in fire. Not yet. We needed control. We needed precision. I needed that door open.

Aconite turned to me slowly, his eyes narrowing with something I couldn't quite place - curiosity? Suspicion? Amusement?

'Welcome to the heart of Midpoint,' he said, his arm sweeping in a grand arc, as though he were presenting a masterpiece. Then his gaze fixed on the visor, as if he could see through it – as if he could see the depths of my soul through my hidden eyes. 'Now then,' he added, his tone sharp. 'Let's lift up your visor . . . and find out who you truly are.'

14

B efore anyone in the room could blink, I drew my laser and drove it against his neck. In the same motion, I kicked hard at the back of his knee. He buckled with a grunt, collapsing to the floor. I yanked him upright just enough to drag him back against me, using his body as a shield, my arm clamped tight across his chest.

'If any of you move, I'll kill him,' I said, jamming the laser beneath his jaw, pressing it hard into skin and bone. I could feel him wince.

The guards froze. Their hands hovered near their holsters, their fingers twitching.

'Listen carefully and do as I say,' I said, tightening my grip until Aconite gasped. 'Everyone of you - off your chairs. Kneel. Hands on your heads.'

I locked eyes with the guard nearest the door. 'You,' I said, nodding toward the keypad. 'Scan your wrist. Open it.'

He hesitated. I didn't. I pressed the laser harder into Aconite's throat. He gave a strangled gasp, his body stiffening. 'Tell him to do as I say,' I said, my voice deadly calm. It didn't even sound like me. It was alien, like someone else was speaking through me.

Aconite's throat bobbed, his bravado beginning to crack. With a reluctant nod, he gave the order. The guard slowly raised his wrist to the scanner. The door slid open. In a heartbeat, our disguised fighters surged into the room.

'Round them up,' I said, my command cutting through the flurry of movement. The elders and guards were herded into a corner. Weapons ripped from their holsters. Helmets torn off and thrown aside. Some faces hit me like old wounds - too familiar, too raw. But most were strangers.

I shoved Aconite into a chair, his body slamming into it with a dull thud. He glared up at me, his chest rising and falling with furious, rapid breaths. 'Who are you?'

I ignored him, calling out for Cedar. He appeared by my side, peeling off his helmet.

'Do whatever you need to do to sever communications with the mainland. And remember to create a loop to make sure all looks fine.'

Nodding, he positioned himself at one of the stations, his fingers blurring across the keypad. The screen flickered, lines of code flashing in rapid succession. Finally, he straightened, flexing his knuckles. 'It's done,' he said, glancing over his shoulder. 'Hopefully, it'll take them days to notice. I've masked a shutdown as a system glitch - a routine failure. With any luck, they'll think it's just another malfunction, wasting time trying to reboot instead of realising what's really going on. When they do reboot, recordings will be in place.'

Juniper appeared on one of the screens, heading straight towards us. Cedar zoomed in on his face, revealing the confusion in his eyes - we were nowhere to be seen.

'Go and fetch him, Zander.' I said, realising I still owed my people an apology.

Despite righting my wrong, the weight of jeopardising the whole mission still hungover me.

From the corridor, Zander's voice carried itself back to us, bright with mock reproach. 'You're late for the party, Juniper. What kept you?'

Juniper crossed the threshold, taking in the scene with wide eyes. 'How did you pull this off so quickly?' he asked, his gaze settling on Aconite.

Cooper didn't raise his voice or lace it with blame - just spoke in a dry, amused tone. 'Someone decided to take matters into her own hands. Again.'

All eyes shifted to me.

Aconite coughed and cleared his throat before fixing me with a stare sharp enough to cut through the visor like a blade. Then he asked agin, 'Who are you?'

I savoured his discomfort. The tables had turned, and he knew it. I could feel his fear rising - the weight of it pressing down on him. But I refused to satisfy his need to know, letting his curiosity stew a little longer.

Instead, I turned to Juniper. 'How are matters progressing with the citizens?'

He pointed to the cluster of monitors, their screens pulsing with movement. On them, figures moved in orderly lines - guided, not herded. Controlled.

'As you can see, they're heading toward the Justice of Pax. No panic so far. My people are dealing with the guards when the moments right - quick, and clean. No noise, and no traces. We've got operatives outside too, tracking those still out on tasks. We'll have everyone gathered soon.'

I turned my attention back to Aconite. He'd gone still – too still. His body was taught, shoulders tight as wire. His eyes locked on me - wide, and blinking at first. It was as if his mind struggled reconcile what it saw with what it believed. Without a word, I reached up and released the latch on my visor. It clicked softly, and the cool air of the room brushed my face.

Aconite recoiled as though I had physically struck him. '*You,*' he breathed. Just one word - his voice broken, disbelieving. His gaze scrambled over my features, desperate for denial - for proof that the past hadn't finally clawed its way back to him.

His hands clutched the arms of the chair as if to steady himself, knuckles white. He shook his head once, feebly. A tremor rippled across his lips. The colour drained from his face, his features hollowing, as though death had brushed its fingers down his cheek.

A slow, cold grin unfurled across my face. I took a step closer, then another, until the space between us was gone, and there was only me - only the girl he thought he'd destroyed.

Yes,' I said. 'It's me.'

He slumped back as if the chair had become his only anchor.

'I promised you I'd come back.'

'Jasmine,' he rasped, barely able to say my name.

'That's right.' My voice was steady. My eyes didn't leave his. 'It's Jasmine.' I let the name land on him - deliberate, unflinching. 'And I'm here to have my revenge. For Salix, Lily, Willow and Mary. And for every life you took. For every scream you buried under orders and experiments. For every night children were locked in cages and filth.'

He shrank away from me, his jaw trembling, his eyes glassy with something he'd long since forgotten how to feel - fear.

'I hope you're frightened, Aconite,' I said, my voice low and deadly. 'Because you should be.'

15

I stepped closer to the glowing wall of monitors. Row upon row of surveillance feeds rolled out in front of us - corridors, stairwells, the Be Thankful Hall, outer gates. All of it. Every security measure they'd trusted, every lock, every line of code - we had now hijacked. But it felt too smooth, too seamless. It was as if the system itself was waiting for us to crack it all open.

'Cedar,' I said, standing behind him. 'How do we find the footage of the holding pen?'

His fingers flew across the keyboard, tapping commands. Then - one of the squares blinked, and my breath caught in my throat. Coral. Spindle. Huddled together in the corner of their glass cages, pale and drawn, but alive. My heart slammed against my ribs, the force of it shaking my entire chest. I was seconds - just seconds - from them. I reached out, my fingertips brushing the glass of the screen, trying to close the distance.

Snapping myself from the trance, I reached for my radio. Static crackled through the line. 'Ash, can you hear me?'

'Loud as a bell.'

I drew a slow breath through my nose, forcing control back

into my voice. 'All systems are locked down.' My fingers tightened around the transmitter as I flicked my gaze to Cedar. 'What about the door to the pen? Do you need to open it for Ash?'

Cedar shook his head, eyes locked on the screen. 'He's good to go. The cages are open too.'

'I heard,' Ash said. 'We're moving in.'

'Bring them here, to the Operations Room,' I said, feeling too scared to be hopeful. 'But stay in character. One wrong move, and a single paranoid guard could blow this wide open.'

The monitor juddered and the feed shimmered with movement. It was happening. Ash appeared on-screen, flanked by the two men he'd taken with him - faces unreadable behind their visors, weapons raised. They swept into the holding pen, cutting through the gloom. Coral jerked upright, her eyes wild. Spindle followed a second behind, both of them frozen in stunned silence. Then - Ash yanked off his visor.

He opened both doors. Coral didn't hesitate - she bolted forward and crashed into him, her chained arms locking tight around his neck. Spindle clung to his back, fists tangled in Ash's jacket, holding on like he feared the world might tear him away again.

Tears streaked down their dirt-smeared faces. Their shoulders quaked, bodies rattled in shock. Not pain. Not punishment. Unexpected freedom. Unbelievable.

Ash bent his head, but I could see movement on his face. Whatever he said made Coral and Spindle lift their gazes, turning towards the camera as if it had just called their names. My breath caught again, sharper this time. They knew. They *knew* I was here. Watching.

The ache to reach through the screen, to drag them into my arms and feel the proof of them warm, alive, safe - was like a blade stabbing through my ribs. One hand curled into a fist, the nails biting into my palm. The other gripped my laser tight.

I locked eyes with Aconite and refused to look away. His gaze flicked between mine and the weapon clenched in my fist. Slowly, I raised the laser until it hovered inches from his skin. My thumb slid to the stun setting and the weapon snarled to life. A crackling blue current burst from the muzzle, spitting sparks and heat in front of his face.

He flinched, pressing himself as far back into his chair as possible, but held my gaze. Good. I wanted him to feel it - that creeping dread, that gut-punch realisation that power was slipping from him.'

'You're going to speak over the tannoy,' I said, fingers itching on the trigger, pulse snarling in my ears. 'Summon every guard to the gym. Tell them it's a drill, a briefing, an emergency - I don't care what. Just get them there.' The laser hummed a lethal beat in my grip. I stepped in, close enough to smell the fear on him. 'Do this - and maybe, just maybe - I'll let you crawl out of this alive.'

I seized him by the collar and yanked him towards the microphone. He planted his feet, spine locked tight - until I drove my fist into his back. He buckled, crashing into the desk, catching himself just before collapsing into the chair. A shudder rattled through him. His breath hissed, rough and ragged, as he dragged a trembling hand towards the controls.

His tongue darted over his lips. For a heartbeat, I thought he'd resist. But then his voice broke through the speakers - thin, brittle, and stripped of its usual arrogance.

'Guards,' he said, defeat hanging from every syllable. 'Can all guards in Midpoint make their way to the gym hall at once. There is news of new drills on the mainland that Malus wants you to be aware of.'

From my vantage point, sound was lost to me - I could only watch events unfold. On the monitors, guards across Midpoint froze mid-step, then turned, striding towards the gym. On other screens, workers set down their tools, teachers ushered students from classrooms, and cleaners wiped damp hands on aprons - all folding silently into the swelling crowd heading for the Justice of Pax.

My heart skipped a beat as the nursery unit emptied. Small feet pattered across the polished floor in neat pairs, wide eyes soaking in the sheer scale of Midpoint. For them - for all of them - this wasn't obligation, and it wasn't fear. It was an adventure. A break in the rhythm. Something new, strange, and thrilling.

On another monitor - Ash - still in disguise - led his procession towards the Operations Room. Behind him, Spindle and Coral, shackled and stooped, shuffled forward, boxed in by his two men. The crowd scarcely glanced their way. No suspicion. No hesitation. We drifted through their world like phantoms - unseen, unnoticed.

Ash had worked on Aconite's special projects, but this room - this level of clearance - I doubted he'd ever set foot in here. 'Go meet them,' I said, turning to Cooper.

I tapped Cedar's shoulder. 'Once the guards are inside the gym, lock the doors. Do the same with the Justice of Pax. No one gets out.'

'You'll never get away with this,' Aconite spat, his face blotched red with barely restrained fury.

I couldn't help but laugh. 'Oh, Aconite, but I already have. Not just here - on the mainland too. Judging by the pitiful state of your security, I'd wager you've no idea about the chaos I've unleashed. I'm guessing Malus kept that little detail to himself - too humiliated to admit to the other island leaders he's lost control of Omen's Keep and one of his settlements.'

'There will be reprisals. You'll pay for what you've done today,' Aconite said, his tone shifting - less rage, more reason. As if he thought he could talk me down. 'You understand that, don't you?'

I nodded, eyes burning with hate as I locked onto his.

'We've lost more than you could ever comprehend. And we're ready to lose everything, because the life you offer us . . . it's not a life - it's a sentence. The people from the caves, and the Resistance fighters - we're united. We'll die on our feet before we kneel to your one-world doctrine.'

He swept a hand towards the monitors, his voice rising with conviction. 'The life our ancestors built saved humanity. From the depths of ruin, we forged a civilisation - a sanctuary. Look at what we've created.'

He paused, his eyes narrowing as he searched my face for a flicker of doubt - a crack he could exploit. 'Surely,' he said, almost pleading, 'Somewhere deep in your heart, you can see it. You understand why it matters. Why I did what I did. What all our gracious leaders did.' His voice carried the desperation of someone clinging to the last thread of justification, trying to drag me into his web of twisted logic.

His words bounced off me. 'You lied. You enslaved us . . . for generations,' I said, my voice laced with bitterness. 'Pax was nothing but a story - a convenient fiction to keep us beneath your boot.'

I stepped closer, fury fuelling every word. 'It was people like you who destroyed humanity - bringing it back from the ashes to use it for your selfish gain.' My voice dropped. 'But when you're gone, we'll rebuild something better. Fairer. No more tyrants. No more thrones built on fear.'

I met his gaze - mine unflinching. 'You'll be the example - the face of everything we tear down.' I leaned in until there was barely space to breathe between us. 'You call what you did to me punishment?' I said, my voice like ice. 'That was nothing. What's coming for you . . . will make your nightmares feel like lullabies.' I let silence hang for a few seconds. 'Be afraid, Aconite, because you'll pray for death by the time I'm finished.'

The door slid open, and my heart jolted. Ash stood in the threshold, framed by the corridor's pale light. He stepped inside, followed by Coral and Spindle – their faces drawn, eyes shadowed with exhaustion. For a long, breathless beat, I couldn't move. Couldn't speak. The noise, the tension, the chaos around me - all of it bled away, until only they remained. Coral and Spindle. Alive. Free.

Ash moved quickly, snatching a key ring from the scar-faced guard's belt. He found the right one and freed their wrists. I watched as Coral and Spindle cradled their arms, rubbing at the raw skin - relief and pain flickering behind their eyes. The mood shifted, the tension finally cracking. Before I could think, I was moving. The three of us colliding , wordless and trembling, held together by something that ran deeper than blood or loyalty.

As we broke apart, my eyes caught movement. Ash. He stood just beyond us, watching - still, unsure, as if he didn't want to intrude. Empathy stirred in me. I lifted my hand and reached for him. An unspoken invitation.

For a second, I thought he might retreat - and he did, just a half-step. Hesitation flickered across his face. Then, as if some quiet force within pushed him forward, he moved. One step. Then another. And just like that, he was with us. The circle closed. A stillness settled over us, not awkward, but full of all we had shared to survive. We didn't need words. In that moment, we were whole again. All of us, together.

We all stepped back, the space between us thrumming with something I can only describe as pure, undiluted love. I reached for Coral, cupping her sweet, beautiful face in my hands. Her skin was cold beneath my fingers. I searched her sky-blue eyes, willing the light to return to them.

'Not a single day went by that I didn't think of you,' I whispered. 'My brave, beautiful sister. My heart's ached for this moment - for you. Just to see you again. To know you'd made it through.'

Coral's eyes shimmered with unshed tears, her hands trembling as she placed them over mine. 'I never stopped thinking about you either,' she said, her voice fragile. 'Through every bit of darkness, I held onto the thought of you . . . of us, and the memories of Mary.'

She leaned her forehead against mine. 'To know you're here, safe and with me, Jasmine . . . it's more than I ever dared dream.'

A quiet, but unshakable conviction settled between us. I almost sobbed the words. 'We're together again. And nothing . . . nothing will ever tear us apart.'

Spindle's eyes shone with warmth as I turned to him. Despite everything he'd endured, there was a softness in his gaze - a bittersweet smile tugging at the corner of his lips. His face held a tenderness that sent a sharp ache through my heart.

I reached for him, my hand trembling slightly. 'I waited for your sign while in the caves,' I said, my voice catching in my throat. 'I cursed you, every single day, until the waiting became unbearable. I didn't know you'd gone after Coral.' I faltered, searching his face for forgiveness. 'Thank you,' I whispered. 'For trying to bring her back.'

Spindle's smile deepened as he rested a hand on my shoulder, the touch sending a current of longing through me. A promise he didn't need to say aloud. 'I'd do anything for you.' His gaze shifted briefly to Ash, and for a moment something dimmed in his eyes - acknowledgement, perhaps. The past of what once had been, and his need to respect it.

But then his eyes found mine again, and there was no mistaking the truth behind them. The softness, the fire, the love that had grown between us. His cheeks flushed, just slightly, but he didn't look away. 'We would all do anything for you - every last one of us.'

I turned to face Aconite, satisfaction flooding through me. 'This,' I said, my voice thick with emotion. 'This is what love is. The bond we share. The strength we draw from one another.

What we build from love, from respect, from true equality - there'll be no limits to it.' I stepped closer, letting the truth fall. 'Your world is almost gone, Aconite. And your legacy - it's already dead.'

I glanced at Ash. 'Take some of our people and escort the prisoners to the holding cells. Get them ready for transport. We'll hold them as prisoners of war.'

Ash nodded, moving quickly with a few of our men. They hauled our captors to their feet, bound their wrists behind their backs with zip cords, and began lining them up to file them out. I turned back to Aconite, my voice turning to ice. 'Except him. He stays - for now.'

Aconite's jaw tightened, but he said nothing. He didn't need to. The slight narrowing of his eyes, and the way his shoulders slouched - it was the last grasp of a man realising the walls were closing in.

I turned to Cedar. 'Can you see to it that our prisoners are secured from here?'

'They won't get out,' Cedar said, firmly. 'Not a chance.'

I faced our fighters. 'Sweep the compound. Round up any stragglers - citizens or guards.' I paused, letting my gaze rest once more on Aconite. 'I need to send a message to the people of Ruin. One they might not yet understand - not while Control still clouds their thoughts.' My eyes shifted to the screen showing those already gathered in the Justice of Pax. 'But once they're free, they'll never forget it.'

16

We stood rigid before the glowing wall of monitors. Our eyes fixed on the live feed from the Justice of Pax. The grand hall - the iron heart of order, the citadel of obedience - now throbbed with a restless energy. The crowd was a crush of bodies - citizens jostling shoulder to shoulder while the Council of Twelve cloaked in their pompous robes, looked around them. The wonderment of what was going on was visible on their features. I could almost hear them ask their neighbour, '*Are you sure Aconite wanted us here?*'

Thousands of faces turned towards the vast, elevated stage. They had gathered to hear the voice of command, to absorb the authority of their Supreme Leader, Aconite. But he didn't appear. Seconds stretched into minutes. Hope shifted to doubt. A low ripple of unease stirred through the crowd. The stage remained empty. The discomfort deepened.

I pointed to the microphone. 'Speak to your people, Aconite. Tell them the Resistance has taken over the Island of Ruin.'

He flinched - his fear growing. The mighty voice of the State, silenced by the girl whose back he had once flayed.

I stepped closer, savouring his unease as a slow curl of satisfaction tugged at my lips. 'Introduce me,' I said. 'Tell them you're handing over the care of their existence to me - to the girl you condemned to the mines for a crime of compassion. Say it clearly. Say it was a crime to help an old woman, dragged half-dead from the shores of the Pewter Sea.'

He looked at the microphone like it might bite. 'I don't . . . I don't think I can.'

I slapped his head forward. 'Tell them how sorry you are,' I said, my voice laced with iron. 'Tell them how wrong you were. That you let Malus twist this world so far that mercy became treason. That we grew up believing kindness deserved chains.'

Those gathered in the hall grew restless. Some twisted in their seats, impatience flickering in every glance, every twitch. 'The citizens are waiting.' I grabbed his head with both hands and forced him to look at the monitor. 'Say it - or I'll have one of my people fetch a knife and cut out your tongue.'

He stared at the microphone, his jaw tightening. He knew there was no path left but the one laid before him. Slowly, as though each movement cost him a sliver of his pride, he leaned in. The static crackled. His voice, once a thunderclap in the halls of command, came out dry, and trembling at the edges.

'Dear citizens. You may wonder where I am. I'm being held prisoner in the Control Room by Jasmine.' My name caught in his throat. 'Jasmine, who was tried in the Justice of Pax for the crime of helping the woman from the caves. She has asked me to publicly apologise for this act . . . and wants me to hand over control of our Midpoint into her hands.'

I listened, lips pressed into a fine line. His words rang hollow, each one devoid of regret. 'Is that it?' I asked. 'Is that all the apology I'm going to get?'

He didn't answer. He didn't need to. I already knew. There hadn't been a trace of remorse in his tone - not a single note of sincerity. But then, what else had I expected from a man who had help to build a world where kindness was a crime?

I moved forward, took the microphone from the desk, and held it close - close enough for those listening to hear the breath in my lungs. On the screen, the crowd rippled with confusion - faces wide-eyed, looking around, straining to make sense of what was unfolding.

'Citizens,' I began. 'You've just heard the last words of a man who ruled our island with fear and called it order. You've heard his apology, such as it is. Now you'll hear the truth - from the girl he buried alive in the depths of the mines.'

Beside me, Aconite shook. Whether it was fury twisting through his bones, cold dread curling in his gut, or the slow, choking realisation that his reign was rotting beneath him - I couldn't say. And I didn't care. His trembling was just background noise now, the last vibrations of crumbling power. I kept my focus where it belonged.

'Can those in the Resistance please make your way forward to the stage, so all can see our brave and active members.'

At first, there was only stillness - then, movement. I watched, blinking against a sting of emotion I hadn't prepared for, as they stepped into the light - one by one, then in clusters. Figures I had overlooked during my time here. Cooks in food-stained aprons, cleaners with tired eyes, dock workers with calloused palms and sun-leathered skin. People I'd passed a hundred times, never knowing they had risked everything for freedom in the shadows.

Barely able to tear my eyes from the sight of them - our people, our quiet revolutionaries - I turned to Juniper. 'I had no idea,' I said, my voice filled with awe. 'How did you manage all of this without anyone knowing?'

Juniper smiled. His eyes gleaming, but not with arrogance. 'Most of the citizens here are children - teenagers - all caught up in their own drama. As for the elite on the island, they never really looked at us, believing we were so numbed down by Control - that it made our work with the Resistance less difficult. Much easier than our comrades on the mainland. However, from here, we watched and waited for signs. We listened. And when needed, we passed notes in laundry baskets and messages in soup pots.'

I looked at the screen again, my heart swelling with gratitude. There they were - hundreds strong. Elders. Labourers. The forgotten. The overlooked. And yet, here they stood - not broken, but defiant. Every one of them had conspired in secret, daring to plot beneath the very noses of our oppressors. They had laid the groundwork for our rebellion. And now, they stood tall - shoulders squared, heads high. No longer invisible.

'I don't want anyone to be afraid,' I said, speaking clearly into the microphone. 'From this day forward, those standing before you will be your guardians. Not rulers. Not watchers. Guardians. They will care for you, and protect you, until the war is won.'

I paused, letting the silence stretch just enough to let my words settle. 'For those of you still on Control - your weaning begins immediately. You may start to feel things you haven't felt in a long time. Fear. Joy. Grief. Hope. Let them come. You are not broken - you were drugged into obedience. That ends now.'

On screen, the crowd had stilled. Every pair of eyes locked on the platform. The restless shifting had ceased. I could only hope that the words I spoke offered some comfort amid the confusion .'

'To the rest of you - this is your Liberation Day,' I said, my tone rising a little. 'A day to rejoice. There will be no guards watching you. No elders noting your every move. And in the world we're building, you will have the chance to become whatever you want to be. Free will is yours again, with one caveat - use it with care. Your freedom only ends where another's harm begins. When we win this war - and we will win - a new government will rise. Laws will exist, yes, to keep peace, to protect the vulnerable. But they will never again shackle your rights. We will not repeat the sins of our past.'

My eyes fell on Coral, seated quietly on a nearby chair - she looked frail, but her presence was fierce. 'Children of Ruin, and all of you here today, I want to finish by honouring Coral. She stood beside me when we were sentenced in the Justice of Pax. They sent her to Mortem, marked her for sacrifice - and still, she endured. She carried me through more than you will ever know. When I was ready to fall, she lifted me. When I wanted to give up, she pushed me forward. She reminded me that belief in yourself is the first act of rebellion.' I drew a breath, fighting to hold back my tears of gratitude. 'And now, I ask of all of you - what she once asked of me - to help make this world better - not just for the elite - but for all of us.' I looked out over the sea of faces on the monitor, old and young, stunned and stirring. 'Today, we stand on the edge of two roads - Ruin or Redemption. And I hope, for all of our sakes, that you choose redemption.' My eyes found Coral's once more. 'Thank you.'

Ash strode in, several of our men at his back. 'All prisoners are secure,' he said. 'They're ready to be taken with us when we leave.'

'Thank you,' I replied, offering a tight smile that didn't quite reach my eyes. Relief, yes - but I still had a feeling it was all going too easy. I turned to Juniper. 'Keep everyone locked inside the Justice of Pax for now,' I said. 'No one leaves until we're gone. This is for their own safety as I'm sure some will rebel at first. Confusion breeds panic - but treat them with strict kindness. Let them know we are not here to replace one form of cruelty with another.'

I then turned to Aconite. He remained slumped in the chair, every inch of him seeming smaller. 'Now,' I said, cold and calm. 'You need to address the guards in the gym. Tell them to lay their weapons down in front of them, then move to the far wall and face it.'

He glared at me - saying nothing.

'Do it, Aconite. Don't make me ask you again.'

Once again, all eyes were fixed on the monitors - the feed showing the gym. The guards obeyed Aconite's order. Some paused, but none defied him. One by one, they laid down their weapons, turned, and walked to the back wall - facing it.

I didn't look at Aconite. I didn't need to. Whatever power he'd once held had drained from the room the moment they obeyed. Once they were all in position I turned to Ash. 'Take your men, and round them all up. Put them with the others.'

'What about him?' Ash asked, nodding towards Aconite.

'He's served his purpose for now. Get him out of my sight.'

Ash addressed everyone in the room - not just his men, but all of my friends too. 'Alright, you heard the boss - let's get moving and get this done.'

They moved immediately. No hesitation. No wasted time. Then Ash's focus shifted, his stance easing as he stepped toward Coral. His hand rested gently on her arm. 'Come with me,' he said, his tone light. 'We'll get you something to eat from the Be Thankful Hall. You look like you need a good feed.'

His gaze flickered briefly to Spindle, lingering a moment too long. 'I daresay you two have some catching up to do,' he said, keeping his tone casual.

There was something just beneath it - a ghost of something held back. Not quite jealousy. Not quite indifference. Perhaps acceptance. It was a kind gesture - one that must've cost him. I didn't miss the look that passed between them. Guilt in Spindle's eyes - for feeling the way he did about me. And in Ash's, a sadness. A sadness for what had been. For the love I once held for him . . . but no longer did.

And then it was just us. Spindle and me. I finally exhaled. My body gave way, trembling as the adrenaline drained from me. I stumbled, but he was there - his arms steady, strong - catching me like he always had. He pulled me in, holding me against his chest. His lips brushed the top of my head, slow and respectful. Then down, the faintest trail to my neck, where they lingered - tasting the moment, the reunion, the ache of time lost. And then his mouth found mine.

The kiss was urgent but careful, a blend of hunger and hope. It wasn't a question. It wasn't an apology. It was an anchor. A way back to something that was meant to be. The world fell away - the war, the walls, the fear. For that one beautiful moment in time, there was only us. And in his kiss, I remembered what it felt like to be wanted, to be chosen. To be home.

17

Once again, the watercraft rolled beneath my boots, the briny wind slashing at my face as a few of us gathered near the helm.

Taxus hovered over a battered map splayed across a bench, his finger dragging along the serrated outline of the island and the sea. 'We intercepted a naval vessel on its way to retrieve Spindle and Coral for a hostage exchange.' His voice rose over the thunderous crash of the waves. 'We killed our engine and sent out a distress call, luring them in. They never saw it coming.' He glanced up, his dark eyes locking onto mine. 'We have control of the vessel now, and it's circling Ruin in case something goes wrong and we need to go back to fight. But it won't be long before the rest of Malus's fleet realises something's amiss.'

It was another triumph. We now commanded two armoured warcraft, their crews disarmed and at our mercy. But the true battle waited inland, buried deep in the heart of the capital, far beyond the Pewter Sea's grasp.

Victory on Ruin had ignited a fire in all of us - we had seized control, planted our stronghold, and left the island in the steady hands of the Resistance. But there was no time to revel in success. We had to move forward, to weave the next deception. Malus needed to believe Coral and Spindle remained his captives. We had to assemble a crew, craft the illusion flawlessly, and lead him straight into our trap - which we were still working on.

Inside, Coral sat by a porthole, her gaze lost in the endless stretch of the Pewter Sea, the moonlight casting silver ribbons across the waves. I grabbed two flasks of Cooper's celebratory moonshine and made my way over to her. With a smirk, I handed her one.

'Here, take a sip of this and tell me it's not gut rot. But hey, at least it'll make you feel good. For a little while, anyway.'

She lifted it to her lips, took a cautious sip, then winced, coughing violently. 'Definitely gut rot,' she said, a glint of amusement in her eyes. 'Before you start apologising - don't,' she said, firmly. 'In this life, we're dealt a hand of cards. It's how we play them that matters. And so far, you've played yours well. By the grace of Mary's God, you'll keep doing so.'

She paused, studying me, then smiled. 'Ash told me everything - what you've done, your success - and Malus's retribution. You've come so far, Jasmine. Further than any of us ever dreamed. Never feel guilty,' she said, her tone sincere. 'Like you said, It's ruin or redemption. And I'm with you - all the way - to redemption.' Her fingers tightened around the flask, her gaze fierce as she met mine. 'Whatever comes next, we face it together.'

I leaned in, wrapping my arms around her, holding her close as the scent of salt clung to us both. Her tenderness, her strength, it grounded me. 'I won't apologise. But I'll tell you this, like I have before, and I'll keep telling you until my last breath - you are one of the bravest, kindest, and cleverest people I know. You are family to me. Always.'

Coral pulled back, her hands still gripping my arms as she

studied me. 'So,' she said slowly, dragging out the word. 'What's the story with you and Spindle?' She nudged me playfully, her smile widening. 'He told me he was in love with you. I've got to admit - I never saw that one coming. You both hated each other back on Ruin.'

She reached for my hand, giving it a squeeze. I let out a small laugh, my gaze drifting towards Spindle, where he sat deep in conversation with Ash and the others.

'Neither did I, to be honest,' I said, shaking my head. 'It sort of crept up on me. But one thing I know for sure - I am in love with him.'

The words felt both terrifying and exhilarating. I turned back to Coral, my voice quieter now. 'I'd love to be his wife. To have his children. But that's a wish for another day. Another time. When the war is won. When we are all free.'

A lump settled in my chest as I watched Coral, her laughter bubbling - so full of life, so full of hope. But inside, a quiet fear ate away at me.If only Aspen could find a cure . . . so this condition didn't kill me from the inside out. Perhaps when we freed him from the capital, I could have him work tirelessly on finding that cure.

I couldn't tell Coral about the state of my health. Not now - not when we'd only just found each other again after so long. She didn't need to carry that burden, not when we were finally on the brink of something better. I watched her, forcing a smile, determined to keep the secret locked away form her for as long as I could. So, I change the subject. 'What do you think of us capturing Aconite?'

* * *

The watercraft rocked gently as we approached the shore. The salty breeze ruffled my hair while the sharp tang of the sea blended with the earthy scent of land ahead. It had been unanimously agreed, that apart from Aconite, the prisoners would be confined to the naval craft's hold - a sweltering cavity buried deep within the vessel's belly.

Members of the Resistance, their covers still intact, would continue to man the helm and occupy key stations, maintaining the illusion of routine. We could only hope this deception would be enough to evade Malus's suspicion.

As the hull scraped against the dock with a low, groaning protest, we moved quickly. Dressed in the leathers and helmets of the guards, we adjusted straps, fastened buttons, and checked each other for any signs that might betray the ruse. The fabric smelled of sweat, remnants of those who had worn them last. With our gear slung across our shoulders and nerves pulled taut beneath the surface, we prepared to disembark.

We slipped away in staggered groups, threading through the pier and slipping past the city's edge, heading for the vehicle we'd hidden deep in an abandoned junkyard. Aconite moved with us, cloaked in a long, slate-grey mantle that covered his boots, the hood casting his face in deep shadow. Beneath the heavy folds, the tape binding his hands and mouth remained hidden.

Zander and Cooper marched beside him, Cooper's laser pointing discreetly at Aconite's side. From a distance, they looked convincing - two guards escorting a subdued prisoner to some grim, undisclosed fate. All we could do now was pray the ruse held long enough to get us where we needed to be.

Sleep was, once again, a stranger - with my body exhausted and my mind unwilling to rest. Every shadow looked like a threat, every whisper like it might carry Aspen's name. I kept imagining his face - and worried for his safety. Had he been discovered? What were they doing to him? The outpost came into view - familiar, yet hollow without him.

Minx was already waiting in the tunnel, pacing. The moment we stepped out of the vehicle, her face lit up - not with

joy exactly, but with the raw, unfiltered relief of someone who
hadn't dared to hope too hard. She darted towards us, eyes
scanning, counting. 'Thank goodness you're all okay. I was terrified you'd be discovered on the way back after achieving so
much.'

Zander and Cooper stepped out on either side of Aconite.
He moved stiffly beneath the cloak, bound and hooded, yet still
managing to carry an air of disdain. Minx's eyes locked onto
him the moment he stepped into the light. She put her hands
on her hips, head tilted slightly as she took him in. 'So,' she
said, voice cool as steel. 'This is the evil monster who ruled over
you for so long.'

He looked smaller - almost insignificant. I nodded,
watching as they guided him towards the lift and the cell where
he'd be held. 'That's him,' I said, letting out a sigh. 'As much as
I'd like to see him dead, for now he's a bargaining chip - and we
might need him more than I want to admit.'

'When you're ready, Spruce will see you in the Operations
Room,' Minx said.

Just then, Orion emerged from the vehicle. He spared Minx
a brief glance before lowering his gaze. Saying nothing, he
moved past us with hunched shoulders.

Minx watched him go, concern darkening her features.
'How's he been?' she asked, her voice laced with worry.

'Quiet,' I murmured. 'Hardly said a word during the whole
mission. Ash and Cooper said he played his part, but he was
like . . . more machine than man. I think his grief is swallowing
him whole.'

Minx pressed her lips into a thin line. 'Maybe he should've
come back with me instead of throwing himself into the fight.'

I shook my head. 'He was adamant. Said he needed to be
with Cooper. Honestly, I think he's just gutted he didn't get to
kill anyone.'

Minx's brow furrowed. 'After losing Freya and Nova, I get it.

But still . . . he should talk to someone. Try to work through it - before his grief eats him alive.'

Felix strolled over. 'What are you two whispering about?' he asked, grinning. He pulled Minx into a tight hug.

She exhaled softly, giving him a weary smile. 'Orion. We're worried about him.'

His expression saddened slightly. 'Aren't we all? I'll keep an eye on him. It'll take time for him to get over what happened.'

'He should go down to the medical bay and visit Jaz,' Minx said, rubbing her chin. 'They were close once. Maybe talking to her will help. I believe she's making progress.'

I sighed, knowing we had so much to do. 'I should take time to visit.' A leader who didn't show care for the wounded was no leader at all. 'Coral and Spindle need urgent medical attention,' I added. 'They barely ate on Ruin. We don't know the full extent of what they endured.'

Felix glanced toward the lift, watching Orion disappear. 'Let's hope Jaz can get through to him,' he murmured. 'Before he loses himself completely. Freya would not want that for him.'

* * *

You could almost taste the tension in the Operations Room. Spruce jabbed a finger at a cluster of coordinates on the map spread across the steel table. 'What if we sent two buses?' he said, looking up at me. 'One here, loaded with fake hostages as a decoy - while the real transport, carrying our fighters, heads for the capital.'

Across the room, Robinia's face tightened. Her hands gripped the arms of her chair, knuckles bone-white. 'If Malus gets wind of our coordinates, he'll be watching with drones. If he even suspects a trap, he'll turn the whole exchange into a massacre. We all know exactly what he's capable of.'

Zander leaned forward, his hands pressing against the table. 'Then we give him something real to believe in.' He smiled at Spruce. 'I think you could be on to something here. The decoy bus carries the weakest of our prisoners - those where we have nothing to gain by holding them. Meanwhile, the real bus, hidden under blackout tarps, is loaded with our best fighters, weapons primed, ready to strike at the heart of the capital. We need to cause as much destruction at several locations as possible. Is there any way we can have access to any of the other indoor cities?'

Felix shot me a worried look. 'And Minx? What if Malus wants to see Rowan's stump. Minx is willing to shave her head but we can't ask her to chop off her hand.'

My stomach coiled as I faced her. 'Are you still happy to play Rowan, sickly, dying - wrapped in blankets, face half turned away. Surely, we should be able to set the illusion so well that Malus won't blink.'

We were all silent. It was Larch who broke it. 'We need our strategy soon. It won't be long before Malus realises he's lost Ruin to the Resistance. He'll be expecting that vessel we took to arrive soon - with Coral and Spindle. When it doesn't come in the next few days, he'll start asking questions. And when he does, he'll make contact.' His gaze swept over all of us. 'So whatever plans we make - they need to be made fast. Our people on Ruin need to be ready for an attack. If we can move before he does, we take the element of surprise again and keep them safe.'

A murmur of agreement rippled through the room. The clock was ticking, and this time, it wasn't just survival at stake - it was the war itself.

Then a thought struck me, sending a jolt of adrenaline through my veins. I straightened, my eyes locking onto Larch. 'What if we contact Malus first?' The words tumbled out, faster than my own doubts could catch them. 'Why wait for him to realise what's happened? Could we hack into his communications - turn the tables and appear on his screens in the capital. We could then perhaps demand a meeting on our terms?'

Larch's brow furrowed as he considered it. Around the room, heads lifted, turning to me with curiosity . . . and unease. I could see it in their eyes - *What crazy road is she taking us down now?*

18

Spruce leaned back in his chair, arms clamped across his chest. His eyes narrowed. Across the table, Robinia tapped a restless rhythm with her fingers, her gaze flitting to Felix, who gave nothing away. Even Cooper - my usual shadow in any madness, stared at the floor. His silence speaking louder than any protest.

'It's not as reckless as it sounds,' I said, my voice disguising the panic rising in my gut. 'We're already running out of time. But if we strike first, we seize the momentum. We force him to react, to second-guess us, instead of the other way round.'

Larch gave a dry chuckle. His features looked a little guarded, but his eyes told a different story. Calculating. Hooked. Maybe even convinced. 'Let me get this straight. You're suggesting we breach his system . . . and call him?'

'Exactly,' I said, a thrill racing through me at the thought. 'We pretend we're still playing by his rules - only this time, we initiate. Catch him off guard. Maybe even feed him a line of false intel. What if we used the craft meant to bring Coral and Spindle to the mainland as bait? Send it out, empty. Then detonate it offshore - just before it reaches the mainland. He'd assume they were aboard. He'd think he'd lost his prisoners and his crew.'

I let the silence stretch for a few seconds, the idea hanging in the air. 'The possibilities for chaos are endless. Like we said, we strike in multiple locations and hit him hard. Force him to divide his forces. We bleed Malus's army from within.'

Minx let out a low whistle. 'You've got nerve, I'll give you that.'

A smile pulled at the corner of Larch's mouth. 'Alright,' he said. 'Let's see if we can pull it off. By the time I figure out how to make a call - you better have a solid plan in place.'

He pushed back his chair and stood. 'Spruce, I'll need to consult with a few of your technical analysts. We can't afford to get this wrong.'

'Take whoever you need,' Spruce said, with a nod. 'And keep us in the loop.'

After some back-and-forth over a few issues, and in desperate need of a break, I decided to head to the medical bay to see what was happening.

* * *

The medical bay reeked of antiseptic - and something heavier. Fatigue, maybe. Or the lingering trace of too many close calls. I should've come sooner. In those first chaotic hours after the convoy rolled in, the medics must've been drowning - too many bodies, too few hands. I could picture the frenzy, a desperate fight against time, infection, and death.

And yet, somehow, they'd carved out calm from the chaos. Beds lined in neat rows. Bandages clean and tight, IV drips feeding life-saving solutions. Against all odds, our medics had brought order and clam.

As I walked past the narrow rooms lining the corridor, the true cost of Malus's cruelty revealed itself - row upon row of narrow beds filled with the broken, the grieving, and those barely clinging to life.

In one room, a mother cradled her child, swaddled in blankets. She rocked slowly, whispering words meant for the child alone. The baby's tiny fingers twitched weakly against her chest, breath shallow, fading. I thought of Nova, asleep forever in the cold hard ground.

Across the hall, an elderly woman lay unmoving, her face etched with the sorrow of too many partings. A girl - no more than Coral's age - sat beside her, gripping her frail hand.

I kept walking. More rooms. More lives torn at the seams. A boy, perhaps ten, stared blankly at the ceiling, his leg trapped in a crude splint. His fingers clutched the edge of his sheet. In the next room, a child - maybe five - lay curled beside her unconscious father, her small chest rising and falling in time with his fragile breaths.

Then, as I reached the next doorway, I stopped. Orion sat hunched over Jaz's bedside, his broad shoulders shaking from silent sobs, his fingers tightly laced through hers.

Jaz noticed me first. Despite the paleness of her face and the weakness of her body she still managed a faint, tired smile. 'Hi,' she said, her voice hoarse. 'Orion told me of your success. I'm so pleased.'

Orion straightened, dragging a hand across his tear-streaked face. 'Jaz was telling me how proud Freya was,' he murmured, his eyes unfocused. 'That I was part of your inner circle . . . fighting for our freedom.'

I swallowed hard and stepped into the room. 'She told me the same. She said you'd shown real courage - especially going into the pit to prove it wasn't you who stole my medication.'

Perhaps mentioning that particular time had been a mistake. An awkward silence settled between us. Jaz's boyfriend, Klin, had been the one to betray me - to twist the knife - and she'd paid the price for trying to warn me. Klin had thrown her into the pit to silence her, to stop her from exposing his plan to kill me. He'd cast her aside like she was nothing.

But what Klin hadn't accounted for was Rowan. She'd stepped in, shielding me from his spear. She'd taken the blow meant for me. Given her life so I could keep mine.

The memory scorched my thoughts. The disbelief in Rowan's eyes as the weapon struck, the dull thud of her body hitting the ground - it still echoed in my dreams. And Klin? He was gone - crushed beneath the rubble when Malus unleashed his fury. It should have felt like justice. But justice couldn't bring Rowan back.

I hesitated, searching Jaz's face for any trace of anger - any wounds the past might've left unhealed. But she only sighed, shifting against the pillows. 'I didn't know,' she said, her voice tinged with regret. 'Not until it was too late. But things are clearer now.' Her eyes found mine. 'I hope you don't doubt me anymore. Once I'm back on my feet, I'll prove it to you. You'll see the fierce fighter I really am.'

For the first time since the mountains fell, Orion smiled. A real one - genuine, unguarded. 'Fierce?' he said shaking his head. 'You were a menace. Nearly blew your fingers off making those explosives.'

A breath of laughter escaped her. 'I knew what I was doing.' She shot back.

Orion arched a brow. 'Oh really? Because I distinctly remember you singeing off half your eyebrows before you got it right. And then there was the time your hair caught fire.'

His grin widened as he turned slightly towards me. 'Jasmine, have you ever wondered why one side of her head's shaved while the other's all long and multicoloured?' He smirked, throwing Jaz a sideways glance. 'It was never about fashion. She was just making the best of a very bad burnt-hair day.'

Laughing, Jaz shook her head. 'I was starting a rebellious trend.'

The teasing was a small thing, but it mattered. For the first time in what felt like forever, Orion wasn't drowning. He was here - with us - moored to something other than grief.

'I'd love to hear more of your adventures, Jaz,' I said, relief settling in my chest. The tension that had hung between us - doubt, betrayal, the seeds of mistrust - was gone now.

Jaz offered a tired, but unmistakably genuine smile. 'I'll hold you to that.'

I nodded. 'Good. We're going to need every fighter we can find. And if your speciality is explosives.' I tilted my head, letting the idea form. 'I might have a job for you sooner than you think. So long as you promise not to blow yourself up in the process.'

Jaz winced slightly as she pushed herself further up the bed, eyes glinting. 'No promises,' she said, with a sly grin. 'But I'll do my best. How soon do you need me?'

Orion glanced between us, his features bright with amusement. 'Brilliant. Just what we need - our resident lunatic back playing with fire.'

I grinned, folding my arms. 'What can I say? It's a useful skill in wartime. Get yourself strong - we'll talk soon.'

Jaz smiled. 'Thank you. I can't wait to get started.'

Leaving them in peace, I stepped into the corridor, the overhead lights bright against the sterile walls. I walked quietly until I reached Coral's room and eased the door open. Her colour had returned, the sickly pallor of starvation replaced by a warm, healthy flush.

'I really shouldn't still be in bed,' she said, plumping her pillows to sit up straighter. 'I feel fine now I've had proper rest. So.' Her eyes met mine. 'Tell me. What part do I get to play in the Resistance?'

I brushed a finger gently along her cheek. She was still a

child, but her eyes held the knowledge of someone far older. Ruin had forced her to grow up too quickly - hardened by pain, sharpened by survival. And yet, beneath all of it, she was still Coral. Brave, clever, and willing to fight for something greater than herself.

'We've time to figure out where you're most needed,' I said, taking her hand, silently promising I'd never let her face danger alone again. 'But first, tell me what happened to you after the trial?'

Coral's smile slipped. Her fingers tightened around mine. 'They took me straight from the Justice of Pax and put me on a watercraft bound for Mortem.' She hesitated, eyes flickering as the memory surfaced. 'It hit trouble near Hazard Bay - crashed hard. The woman they'd sent with me was a leader in the religious order, meant to oversee my sacrifice.' She paused, staring past me. 'She unshackled me. If she hadn't, I'd have drowned.'

I stayed silent, letting her speak at her own pace, though my thoughts raced. A wreck. A near-drowning. Another soul caught in Malus's cruel grip. She'd endured far more than I'd ever imagined.

'I made it to the Black Cave,' she said, her voice dropping to a whisper. 'Hid there for what seemed like forever. Lived on insects and black rain.' She gave a dry, humourless laugh. 'Not exactly a feast, but it kept me alive.'

The image of her alone in that cursed place - cold, starving, and clinging to life - twisted in my gut.

'Then Spindle found me.' A trace of warmth lit her eyes. 'I was so relieved. But guards must've tracked his craft. They ambushed us. His men had orders - if he didn't return by a certain time, they were to leave without him. But Spindle.' She shook her head, her grip tightening around mine. 'He told me to have faith in you. Said you were uniting the Resistance with the cave dwellers. That you'd never stop - not until we were safe.'

A wave of emotion surged through me. Spindle had believed in me, even when I hadn't believed in myself. Even when everything had felt impossible. 'And he was right,' I said, as I held her gaze. 'I did come for you. And I always will.'

Then - pain. Sharp and sudden, it lanced through my right temple, white-hot and blinding. I gasped, pressing my fingers against my skull, trying to rub it away. But the pressure only throbbed harder beneath my touch.

'Are you alright?' Coral asked, her eyes narrowing as she took in my distress.

I forced a smile, shoving the pain to the back of my mind. 'I'm fine,' I said, though even to my own ears the words rang hollow. 'Just a headache creeping in. I'll grab something for it.'

Coral didn't look convinced, but she didn't press the matter.

'Get some rest,' I said, squeezing her hand one last time before rising. 'I'll pop back tomorrow.'

She watched me as I moved to the door, her gaze thoughtful, almost searching. The pain still pulsed behind my eye - low and rhythmic, a reminder that time wasn't just running out for the Resistance. It was running out for me too.

19

Silence filled the room, save for the slow, steady rhythm of Spindle's breathing. I lay on my side, my head propped on my arm, watching him as he slept. The dull light cast soft shadows over his face, tracing the square line of his jaw, the faint creases between his brow, and the gentle rise and fall of his chest. His short crop of sandy hair suited him.

I reached out, barely letting my fingers graze the curve of his shoulder, afraid to wake him, afraid to break whatever delicate spell had settled over us. The world outside still raged - war brewing, plans forming, time slipping through my fingers - but here, in this fleeting moment, everything had stilled.

I had never known a touch that wasn't meant for survival. Never let myself believe I could have something that belonged only to me. But tonight, I had allowed myself to feel, to exist beyond duty, beyond war, beyond the ticking clock inside me. Tonight, I had made love.

A sadness settled in my chest, because if I was being honest, I knew with all my gut I was going to die. He wouldn't want to believe it - not truly. And I wouldn't let him. Not yet. Because, for now, I wanted to stay like this, memorising every detail.

I knew my condition would have him slip away from me. The memory of him - that precious spark - would become nothing more than a fading shadow I'd grasp at in the dark, always just out of reach. The life I longed to make with him could never happen.

He must have felt me watching. Slowly, his eyelids fluttered open. He turned, his body shifting toward me, his hand reaching out to gently cup my face. His touch was warm and tender.

'I love you so much, Jasmine,' he murmured, his thumb brushing over my cheek with a softness that made my heart ache. 'But please understand, I can't show this to you in front of Ash. Don't be angry. He's my best friend, and I know he's still in love with you. I can't see him hurt.'

His words pierced through me - love and sacrifice, a bitter twist of loyalty to someone who could never truly understand the depth of what we shared. I wanted to scream at him, to demand he proclaim our love to the world, but I didn't. Instead, I forced myself to appreciate his feelings on the matter, lying beside him, feeling the comfort of his love surround me.

'I love you too,' I whispered, placing my hand over his, holding it against my cheek a little longer. 'And it's okay. I understand.' I sighed. 'I don't want to hurt Ash either. I've forgiven him for the lies he told in the Justice of Pax. He's tried so hard to make up for them. I'm glad he has Larch, and that's kept him focused. But I agree . . . we keep what we have for when we're alone.'

A look of relief spread across his face. He exhaled deeply, his eyes meeting mine. 'Thank you. It will make everything much easier.'

'Robinia was going to tell me how she got you in with the Resistance when the time was right,' I said, my curiosity rising. 'Sadly, the time never came. But now I have you here, all to myself, indulge me. Tell me your story.'

He shifted, pulling me closer until I was half lying on top of him, my head resting on his chest. His lips brushed the crown of my hair, the sensation both tender and intimate, as his hand trailed along the length of my scarred back. I shivered with delight.

'It was so long ago,' he said, his voice faltering. 'Can you remember our nursery years, when Robinia was one of the Commanders watching over us?'

I nodded, my chin brushing gently against his chest.

'She beat me black and blue for reaching out to comfort you,' he said slowly, as though reluctant to dredge up the past.

'When that memory resurfaced, it explained a lot,' I said, feeling and hearing his heartbeat against my ear. 'I thought that was the reason you hated me so much.'

He chuckled softly, the sound carrying a hint of awkwardness. 'I didn't hate you, Jasmine. You annoyed me. Probably because I was told to spy on you for the Resistance.'

'You were spying on me?'

'The Resistance was interested in you because of the negative effects of Control in your system. The more I spied on you, the more I thought you were trouble. Plus, I was always jealous of Salix and Ash. You always got on so easily with them, and if we'd been friends back then, it would've made my orders to keep track of you a lot easier.'

He sighed, shaking his head slightly as if gathering his scattered thoughts. 'I'm going off-topic. Back to Robinia. At the time of the beating, she was on Control and wasn't part of the Resistance yet. She beat me so badly that day, I ended up in the medical bay. Robinia was seriously reprimanded, but after that, she took out her anger on me even more and made my life hell. That's one thing about Control. I don't know if you've noticed, but sometimes it doesn't suppress cruelty. Some of the Section Commanders could be truly horrific.'

His hand tightened slightly on my back. 'The medics used

to interfere with our memories, so we'd never remember the experiments. Like you, they thought I was special. Because no matter what they did, I remembered everything. No matter how much they tampered with my brain, they couldn't make me forget. I grew up thinking I was crazy - and I mentioned it to Salix once.'

'What did Salix say?'

'He told me I should take something for my night terrors and that is all they were.'

'Robinia told me you were special too,' I murmured, piecing things together.

'Gradually, Robinia started being nice to me. I think I was about year ten at the time, and I quizzed her about it - asking if she was being kind because of how badly she'd been treating me. Did she feel guilty? We built a relationship from there, and she began grooming me for the Resistance.'

A tremor ran through me, both from the intimacy of his confession and from the horrifying memories he must carry from his childhood.

'Then she told me something really freaky,' he continued, his voice rising slightly. 'That she'd traced my bloodline, and I was her half-brother. We both share the same mother from the breeders coupling.'

The connection between them was deeper than I'd ever imagined - a bond forged in secrets and blood. 'Why didn't she tell me?'

'Perhaps she felt it wasn't her story to tell. She might have been scared of your reaction, knowing it was her who ordered me to spy on you. We all know what you're like when you go off on one.'

It was said in jest, but I felt the truth behind it. I punched him lightly on the chest, the playful gesture offering a small release from the seriousness of his memories. He chuckled, shifting his position and pulling us so we were facing each other again.

Before I could say a word, he leaned in, his lips finding mine with a passion that caught me off guard. I was lost to him once more - drowning in the sensation of his touch, the tenderness of his embrace, and the pull that had always been there, waiting for us to finally give in.

* * *

I stood at the head of the Operations Room, surveying my war cabinet. Every face was tight with focus, eyes trained on me, waiting for the next command. The plans we'd painstakingly put together over the last few days were now on the verge of execution - as careful and precise as we could make them. I drew in a long breath, trying to calm the nerves churning in my stomach.

'Before we proceed,' I began. 'Are we all in agreement with the plans we've made and the way we intend to carry them out?'

The room was still, but every head nodded in unison, their expressions resolute.

'What's the status on the naval craft that's supposed to hold Coral and Spindle?' I asked, turning to Larch.

His gaze met mine. 'We sent a message saying they'd run into troubled waters, and their arrival will be delayed,' Larch replied. 'Those who took it seemed satisfied and didn't appear to suspect anything. We've also heard from Ruin. Malus contacted Aconite to check on the transportation of Spindle and Coral. Aconite was released from his cell and forced to cooperate. As far as we know, they don't suspect anything's out of the ordinary.'

'Was Malus not suspicious about Aconite's surroundings?'

'We had Juniper send a recording of the Operations Room

on Ruin, overlaying it onto the background when Aconite returned Malus's call,' Larch replied.

'Good thinking,' I said, relieved all details were being properly processed and thought through.

My eyes moved from one face to the next. 'If only we had word from Aspen. I'll worry he'll be caught up in the fighting.'

Robinia put my mind at ease. 'He'll be in a medical facility. We're not targeting civilians, so he'll be fine.'

'I hope so,' I said, nodding, but my mind kept racing, piecing together the next steps.

'We still have all the guard uniforms,' Felix added, his voice full of optimism. 'So, if we can get in and out of Midpoints, we're good to go.'

'I've got Cedar working on that,' Larch confirmed, glancing over to where Cedar sat. 'He's copying locking mechanism formats as we speak. If they work, we'll be able to breach any indoor city.'

Astrid was next to speak, her voice filled with confidence. 'I've already uploaded the footage of Minx pretending to be Rowan onto our server. It's old and grainy, but hopefully Malus will think it's the best we could do.'

I looked around at them all again - each one an essential piece of our operations. My mind was made up. This was it. 'Okay,' I said, the finality clear in my voice. 'It's now or never. Let's get Malus on the screen and give him the surprise of his life.'

Larch worked quickly, his fingers flying across the controls as he patched into Malus's systems. We could see the lines of code streaming across the screens, a digital web pulling tighter. The room was silent, and thick with anticipation. Every breath felt louder than it should have been. Hearts pounded. We were seconds away from confrontation, and no one dared look away. Then, Malus appeared.

He looked momentarily stunned to see me, his expression

tentative before he gathered himself, smoothing it away with cold precision. 'Jasmine, what a surprise. How nice of you to call. I see you've managed to tap into the line.'

I couldn't help the slight smile jerking at my lips. 'It wasn't too difficult, since you already placed the line in our system,' I replied, letting a thread of mockery slip through. 'Sorry if I've interrupted your precious schedule, but time is of the essence.'

His eyes narrowed, and I saw unease in them. He was rattled - exactly as I needed him to be. 'I'm sending you the footage we took of Rowan,' I said, my tone cold. 'She's deteriorating quickly, so I thought it best to move things along.' I could imagine the cogs in his brain turning. 'When will you have Spindle and Coral ready for the swap?'

A muscle twitched at his temple. He wasn't ready - but the pressure was on. 'They are on their way. I'll have them soon.'

'Good. You'll receive a live feed of the hostages being loaded - we can manage that from where they're being held. According to my systems, the film of Rowan should be with you now. I'll be in touch soon.'

Before he could speak again, I cut the feed. The screen snapped to black. This wasn't just the end of a call - we'd forcefully booted Malus's connection from our systems. Cedar had overridden the code with a single line of brilliance.

A rush of exhilaration surged through me as the screen stayed black, leaving Malus in the void of his own confusion. I could almost feel his rage through the severed connection - sharp, immediate, and utterly satisfying. For the first time in a long while, I allowed myself to bask in the thrill of control. The balance had shifted, and it was him left scrambling in the dark.

20

W e filmed as the women and children from the settlement climbed into one of our transport units, the scientists from Omen's Keep following close behind. The children who'd been experimented on were separated, loaded into a different vehicle - kept well clear of the ones who had harmed them.

'Are you sure, when we show this to Malus, he'll believe it's a live feed?' I asked Ash.

He adjusted the lens, his eyes never leaving the screen. 'We'll find out soon enough.' Hopefully. He believed Astrid's footage from Minx. I think we would have known by now if he felt it was false. It's uncanny how much she looks like Rowan. I often wonder if they were related somehow. I guess we'll never know.'

'Rowan was so brave, Ash. Braver than I ever gave her credit for. I wish I hadn't spent so long hating her. I just hope, wherever she is now, she knows I'm grateful - for all of it.'

Ash's eyes lost focus, clouding with memory. 'After we left Ruin, and Control took hold of her, she was a shell - as if the real Rowan had already gone. She looked straight through me, like I was a stranger.' He paused, a sadness in his tone. 'But before that, Rowan was a force. Stubborn. Fierce. She never backed down, never gave in. I don't think any of us realised what we had in her until she slipped away.'

The tunnel still throbbed with movement - boots striking concrete, hushed voices, the rustle of fabric against cool air. More women and children shuffled forward, eyes scanning the gloom. Their faces held no trust, only a brittle kind of hope - the hope of going home, of being free.

As the final group boarded, a knot of guilt twisted in my gut. I watched them intently - mothers pulling their children close, shielding them with thin arms - and I couldn't help feel what we were doing was wrong. They weren't being freed. They'd be driven in circles for two days while we staged the illusion, then sent back to the very walls they feared.

We didn't beat or starve them. They were given food, water, warmth. But the deception - the hope we dangled and then tore away - was its own kind of cruelty.

Some of the scientists stood rigid, reluctant to board, their hands trembling, their eyes darting back and forth. Panic clung to them. The grip of Control had slipped, and they were becoming more aware of the deception and tyranny of their once beloved masters.

Ash stood behind them all, the camera steady against his shoulder. He tracked every step, every glance, every false promise. Focused. Detached. Preparing for the right moment to feed it all to Malus.

Ash adjusted the lens again, a faint smirk pulling the corner of his mouth. 'Do you think you'd ever shave your head again?' he asked, trying to keep his tone light.

I gave a soft laugh. 'This probably sound silly, but I think it gives me strength,' I said, running my fingers through my crop of thickening curls. And for the record, we didn't shave all of Minx's hair. We just cut it really short. Even Malus would realise that hair grows. Larch felt it would help deceive the facial recognition technology too.'

I stole a glance at the faint shadow of hair dusting his scalp. Once, I would've longed to reach out - just to feel it between my fingers. 'Yours is coming along nicely,' I said. 'It's dark - just like mine.'

The vehicles were full. Cooper and Zander, our drivers, revved the engines - the low growl echoing through the tunnel as the vehicles crept toward the surface.

'Where's Felix?' I asked, glancing down the tunnel. 'He's meant to be driving the buggy with you.'

As if summoned by the mention of his name, Felix stepped out of the lift and hurried towards us. 'Sorry - Jaz couldn't find the ammunition room, so I took her down, and introduced her to the team. Got her settled in.'

'She must be keen,' I said. 'I told her I'd take her once you lot had gone.'

The three of us leapt into the sand buggy. Felix gripped the wheel and fired the engine to life. We shot forward, bouncing violently as we burst from the tunnel's lip into the blinding glare of daylight - a harsh contrast to the low, artificial glow behind us.

I squinted against the brightness, raising a hand to shield my eyes. 'Why have Malus's drones never found us?'

'We're too far from their base,' Ash replied. 'And with the air thinning, he probably assumes no one could survive this far out from the main grids.' He paused, then added, 'But if he even suspected we were out here, he wouldn't waste time with drones - he'd send soldiers.'

Felix crunched the gears, accelerating. 'Or he'd conjure one of his earthquake tricks,' he muttered.

The isolation - the inhospitable silence of this place - was our greatest shield. It made us invisible to anyone not already looking. But still, a knot of unease pulled at me.

'If Malus digs into the old records - finds the outpost, even a trace - it's over. The Resistance won't stand a chance.'

Felix brought the buggy to a halt, the engine ticking beneath us. 'Alright, Jasmine, this is your stop. I promised Spruce we'd drop you off within walking distance. We'll circle around filming for a few days and then head back.'

As I jumped out, I spotted the medical bag on the back seat. 'Are you sure you have plenty of inhalers?'

Ash chuckled, nodding. 'Stop worrying, we'll be fine. The inhalers are just a backup.'

I rubbed my arm instinctively, the memory of the injection resurfacing - that first sharp sting, followed by the burn and the dull, lingering ache. It was the price we paid for a single, easy breath. 'What about water and sustenance packs?'

'All in the vehicles,' Ash said.

Before I could question them further, they drove off at speed, the buggy tyres kicking up plumes of dust as they followed, filming the two vehicles ahead. There were no landmarks - nothing to betray our location. Just mile after mile of scorched orange dust and barren desert. Like much of the mainland now, settlements and Midpoints were rare, isolated pockets of life clinging on in a wasteland.

Only when the vehicles shrank to a dot on the horizon did I turn back towards the tunnel and the lift. For a moment, I let the looming threat of war slip from my mind. Instead, my thoughts drifted to the Earth - scarred, broken, and gasping for life. How could we ever make her heal again?

* * *

I found Robinia hunched over her breakfast, chewing thoughtfully as she scanned a data-pad. Seizing the moment, I grabbed a herbal tea and some bread and slid into the seat beside her.

'Have you found anything on the *Star in a Jar* project?' I asked.

She swallowed and set the pad down. 'I've done some digging.' Her eyes shone as she met my gaze. 'I'm ready to give you a full report whenever you've got time.'

'How about now?'

'Sure.' Robinia tapped the pad, symbols flickering beneath her fingers. A file blinked open - lines of technical data streaming across the cracked screen. She selected one, and the report expanded.

'The official name for *Star in a Jar* was Solar Ignition and Amplification Junction.' With another tap, the display on her tablet shifted, bringing up schematic drawings etched in a faded blue colour.

I squinted at the sketches - an underground labyrinth buried beneath what was once the great salt flats. A forgotten place, entombed beneath layers of rock.

Robinia continued, almost in disbelief. 'They carved it into the bones of the earth. Hundreds of metres down, shielded from satellites and prying eyes. No windows. No surface entrances. Just tunnels, airlocks, and walls thick enough to withstand a thousand meltdowns. They called it Solis Core.'

A chill traced the length of my spine. 'And what about the machine they used?'

Her lips thinned as she flipped to another schematic. 'It was designed with a view that it would hold the Sun's energy. Once harnessed, they thought they would be invincible with the power it would radiate,' she said. 'They fed it hydrogen, forced it to burn - but the core was unstable. It needed constant monitoring, constant corrections. The whole project failed because it was never truly ready to control the sun.'

Robinia's fingers hovered at the edge of the screen. 'It was as if they were trying to build a star beneath civilizations feet,' she murmured.

My hands tightened around the warmth of my cup. 'Do we have any engineers who could look into this? See if there's a way the machine could . . . reverse the damage?'

Robinia exhaled slowly. 'We didn't even know it existed until you told us to start digging. I think we'd need to pull every resource we have - maybe even question the scientists we've taken into custody . . . now that Control seems to be leaving their system.'

She hesitated, then tapped another command. The screen flickered, revealing fragmented reports - warnings, shutdown protocols, messages buried deep beneath layers of the capital's classified seals. 'Everything I've got came from a hack into the central archives,' she said. 'We don't have the knowledge to rebuild something like this. Not now. It would take years - maybe decades.'

She passed me her monitor and I studied the image of the machine. The dials, the buttons, the tubes - twisting like veins. It was like nothing I'd ever seen. A monstrous construction, both intricate and brutal - a creation of steel and circuitry, built to hold the uncontainable. It appeared ancient and advanced all at once. The control panels were littered with cryptic symbols, warnings scrawled in faded ink beside switches that had once held the fate of the world in their grasp. At its centre sat the core - an enormous, coiled reactor like the heart of some mechanical god.

My eyes fixed on the screen. 'I don't want to copy or rebuild it.'

Robinia frowned, studying me. 'If you don't want to replicate it, why have me look into it?'

'Because we use this one. We figure out how it operates, and we see if it can be reactivated.'

She blinked, the shock written clear across her face. 'That's impossible. There's no way we could use this machine.'

I frowned. 'Why not?'

She shook her head slowly. 'Because sending someone inside would be sending them to their death. Even if we somehow gained access - if it's even still there - the radiation alone would kill them.'

The words landed like a slap. 'But the facility was sealed.'

She shook her head. 'You have to remember - this machine caused a meltdown. The chemicals it spewed into the atmosphere, the radioactive waste it dragged back into itself . . . You'd be risking another End of Days. That chamber - it'll never be safe. Not in a million years.'

A shiver ran through me. 'Still - look into it,' I said, clinging to the fragile hope that this might be the key to healing our world. 'Speak to the scientists when they return. If Control really is fading from their systems, they might be willing to help.'

Robinia didn't respond. She simply stared at the schematic, her jaw tight.

'No matter what,' I said, with a confidence I couldn't explain, 'There has to be a way.'

21

I leaned heavily against the edge of the splintered
workbench, its jagged grain biting into my palms as I
pressed the heel of one hand to my temple. The dull throb
behind my eyes pulsed, threatening to unfurl into a full-blown
headache. I turned inward, shutting everything else out for a
moment, breathing through the pressure, willing the pain to
settle.

The ammunition room reeked of bitter gunpowder - an iron
tang that clung to the back of my throat and coated my tongue.
Shelves lined the walls, cluttered with old tools, twisted wires,
and crates marked with faded warnings.

Across from me, Jaz sat cross-legged on the cracked
concrete floor, surrounded by torn cloth and spools of fuse
wire. 'Are you okay,' she asked, seeing my discomfort.

'I'm fine,' I said, waving it off. 'The smell in here's just
hitting harder than I expected.'

Her nimble fingers assembled the miniature explosive
charges. She wrapped each one meticulously, the cloth bound
tight with sturdy knots. Those movements - calm and auto-
matic - looked as if she were folding napkins rather than

bundling fragments of destruction. Despite the throbbing pressure in my skull, I found a shard of focus in watching her work; every knot, every twist of wire edged us closer to being ready.

'How many are good to go?'

Jaz pointed to bundles carefully stockpiled in a corner. 'Enough to punch through a few of your settlement walls. But if you're asking whether it's enough to stop an army? Not even close. We'll also need timers for the smaller electrical charges I've put together. Those will be the best ones to take out the watercraft.'

I nodded, dragging my focus back through the fog of fatigue. 'Then we make every single one count,' I said, glancing over at Minx and Larch. The two of them were hunched over a table, heads close together, mapping out where the charges would hit hardest. 'They'll let us know how many we'll need.'

Larch looked up. 'Jasmine, do you have a minute?'

I strolled over.

'The capital's still our main target,' he said, tapping his plans with a marker. 'We can't let Malus keep his grip here. But . . .' He slid the marker towards the coastline. 'We need to hit the docks first. If we time it right - detonate the watercraft - it'll set off a chain of explosions across the pier. That kind of chaos will pull Malus's attention away from the capital. Once his forces start to mobilise, we make our move and take over the city.'

Minx cut in. 'It all comes down to precision. The charges have to hit infrastructure, not civilians. Same with any of the settlements. We sever supply lines, collapse key routes - but we do not touch the sectors where ordinary civilians' dwell.'

'It looks like you've got everything under control here,' I said, heading for the door. 'I'll check back in a little while.'

I walked a few paces down the corridor and into the next room. A group of men gathered around a rusted table, maps and blueprints spread across it. These were our infiltrators –

the men who would slip into the Midpoints wearing stolen guard uniforms.

They would plant explosives in the basement of each indoor city. All charges would be secured with wire to its mounting point - a concrete beam or metal strut - and fitted with a small timed detonator. The plan, however, hinged on Cedar completing the microchips to grant them access.

Their hushed discussion fell silent as I entered. Eyes lifted, waiting. I rested a hand on the back of a chair. 'Minx and Larch are finalising where the devices should be placed,' I said. Once the targets have been established, you move quickly - plant the charges, and the pulses, and get out clean.'

A gaunt man, his face etched by hard years, nodded towards the map. 'If Cedar can't get the chips working, we can still enter through these passages,' he said, tapping the maintenance route of the sewers. 'It'll take longer, and we'll need machinery to cut through thick metal grills, but it's doable. I doubt surveillance cameras will be buried in the sewage.'

A wave of nausea washed over me. Just the thought turned my stomach - our people slithering through muck, wading knee-deep in rot and refuse. 'Let's hope it never comes to that,' I said. 'But thank you . . . for being ready and willing.'

Leaving them to their preparations, I turned into the corridor once again and found Astrid approaching from the other end. 'How's it going?' I asked, falling into step beside her.

'Spruce is in the main hall,' she said. 'He's briefing the fighters from the caves - explaining how the indoor cities operate, how the tunnels run beneath the outpost, and where the choke points are. For some of them, it's all unfamiliar. They don't trust it.'

I raked a hand through my hair. 'They trust the mountains - the open sky, and solid ground underfoot. But this? These Midpoint walls must feel like a trap.'

Astrid nodded. 'Exactly. They think if Malus triggers

another earthquake, these places will become tombs. Spruce is trying to reassure them, but you know how it goes. Words only go so far.'

I stopped, turning to face her fully. 'Then we need to make sure Malus never hears a whisper of our plans.'

Moving from room to room, I checked on progress, measuring what still needed doing, refining the timeline in my head. Every piece had to fall into place - each step, each delivery, each charge needed to be set with accuracy.

Eventually, I reached a smaller room at the end of the corridor. Its only light came from an old lamp, its flicker casting long shadows across a cluttered table. Inside, Spindle bent over a map so worn the edges curled. His eyes scanned its blank terrain, seeking paths for our vehicles to slip through unnoticed - roads once patrolled by soldiers he used to command.

I paused in the doorway, watching him work and feeling my admiration for him grow. His brow furrowed with focus, his jaw tight, a shadow of a stubble on his skin. He still wore his camouflage uniform - its government insignia torn away - a phantom of a past life.

As if sensing my presence, he looked up, his eyes locking onto mine. A mischievous grin spread across his face. 'Have you come to check on my work, or just to enjoy the view?'

I stepped into the room. 'Maybe both,' I said, arms folding across my chest. 'But mostly, I need to know if we're ready.'

His gaze dropped back to the map. He tapped a section with two fingers. 'If we stick to these paths, we'll ghost right past them. But like everything else, it all depends on timing. One wrong move, and we're the ones being hunted. And with the number of explosives . . .' He glanced up at me, mouth twisting wryly. 'I don't fancy going out in a blaze of fire before we have the chance to light theirs. We'd blow ourselves to dust before making a dent.'

I nodded, stepping closer, my fingertips brushing the edge of the table. 'Then we make sure there are no wrong moves.'

For a heartbeat, he hesitated - his usual swagger giving way to something quieter. Then, with effortless calm, he moved away from the table and crossed the small space between us.

He stopped just short, reached out, his fingers finding mine. Calloused and warm, his thumbs brushed gentle arcs across my knuckles. When he met my eyes, there was no trace of bravado - just a solemn look I'd come to trust more than any plan.

He leaned in, his breath brushing my skin. Without a thought, I lifted my face to meet his. When our lips touched, the world faded. And once again - it was only us.

'I love you,' I whispered, the words falling easily as we broke apart. It was as if those words had always belonged to him. He made me feel stronger - like I could lead, survive, and win. But more than anything, I loved the way his eyes softened when he looked at me. Because in them, I saw it - no fear, no doubt. He loved me back.

'I know you won't like what I'm about to say,' Spindle murmured, his hands tightening around mine.

A knot twisted in my chest before he even finished. 'Then don't say it.'

'When the fighting starts, you should be here - in the outpost.' His eyes searched mine. 'You can still lead. Still command. But do it from here.'

I pulled my hands free. 'You want me to hide,' I said, my tone flat.

He shook his head. 'No. I want you to live.' His hands found my arms, his grip soft, grounding. 'You think being in the thick of it proves something, but Jasmine . . . if we lose you, we lose everything. The Resistance needs a leader who makes it to the end of this fight. You need to be ready to rule the new world we are battling for.'

He paused, his eyes pleading. 'Please. Don't be angry with

me. Whatever time we have left - I don't want to spend it quarrelling.'

I offered a smile, swallowing the surge of emotion, my fingers grazing the stubble on his cheek. 'I need to be in the capital when it falls - when Malus's grip finally breaks.'

'Then let me be there too,' he said, his voice low, caring. 'Let me stand beside you. And I'll protect you with my life.'

I looked at him - really looked - and for a moment, I saw the boy he used to be, the man he'd become, and the battle-worn fighter standing before me now. I hated how right he was. I also hated that part of me that wanted to stay back and let someone else charge the frontlines for once. But that wasn't who I was.

'I don't need a protector.' My voice wasn't cold - just certain, steady. There was no anger in it, no bitterness. Just the calm resolve of someone who had learned, through pain and misery, how to stand on her own.

'I know,' he said simply. 'But that doesn't mean I wouldn't give my life for you.'

There was no drama in his words, no desperate plea for recognition. Just truth - raw and unguarded. He wasn't offering protection out of pity or duty, but something deeper, forged in shared fire and silence. He understood I didn't need saving. That was never the point. It was about standing beside me, even when I chose to walk through the storm alone.

A moment stretched between us, heavy with all the things we hadn't yet spoken aloud. Our shared hope for something beyond this war, the fragile dream of a future built not just on survival, but on love that would never fade. A life together. A family of our own. That unspoken promise beat between us, aching to be real.

I reached for his hand again, threading my fingers through his. 'Then stay close,' I whispered. 'No heroics. No lone missions. We go in together and we walk out together. Deal?'

His face lit with love, faith, and the fragile gleam of hope. 'It's a deal.'

A gentle rap on the door and Astrid's voice cut through our quiet. 'Jasmine, do you have a minute?'

I held his gaze a moment longer, clinging to the promise between us, then slowly let go of his hand. The world was calling again, but with Spindle by my side, I didn't feel alone.

22

I lingered outside the reinforced entrance, my palm hovering inches from the keypad as my breath caught in my throat. Beyond it sat the man who had once ruled Ruin with an iron fist - Aconite. Now my captive. It took every ounce of will not to storm in and snatch the life from him. I inhaled deeply, forced the fury back down and punched in the code.

Inside, he slumped in shackles, his wrists chained to the table, while the harsh strip lighting carved every gaunt angle of his lined face. He looked like a statue cracked by the march of time - smaller, older, no longer a ruler, no longer feared.

'You don't look so powerful now,' I said, keeping my voice calm.

A faint smile pulled at his cracked lips. 'And you don't appear the frightened little girl I once knew.'

'I was never scared - at least, not for myself.'

He looked at me with disdain, his eyes shimmering with scorn. 'Others were always your weakness. That bleeding heart of yours, no matter how hard you tried to bury it under rage and revenge.' He chuckled, low and hollow. 'It'll undo you. It always does. You'll never be able to save everyone. They will all die in the end.'

'Yet, here we sit, and now it's you wearing the chains.'

'Chains can be broken.'

I changed the subject. 'Do you remember the incident with the fox?'

He didn't answer.

'You flogged both Coral and me for showing it mercy. Compassion. You called us weak.'

'Mercy and compassion,' he scoffed. 'A sickness we couldn't afford. It spreads. It softens. It destroys.'

'You called compassion a disease. But that's what made us strong. What's kept us human. It was in that moment you made me realise I would fight to the death to bring about a better world. A better way of living for all people.'

He shifted in his seat, the shackles clinking softly. 'I guess it made you more defiant. That's why we watched you. Why we feared you.'

'I know you feared me?'

He nodded slowly. 'You cared. Even when it cost you. That kind of strength - the kind that doesn't break - to us, it's danger-ous. Even Control couldn't tame you. If it had been up to me, we would have put you down a long time ago. But others insisted - they wanted to study you and chart your progress.'

I pulled a folded sheet of paper from my pocket and laid it on the table. It was a register Robinia had found, listing all the names of the children who had been experimented on. 'Let's talk about this,' I said, tapping the paper. 'You do realise that all those involved will be charged with crimes against humanity. There will be a lesser sentencing and more understanding for those working under the influence of Control. But those of you who have all their faculties intact . . . there will be no escaping justice.'

He only grunted.

'Omen's Keep. I bet you'd have loved to have sent me there?' Lucy knew children were going missing on Ruin. She reported it. Was that why you had her cleansed - partly to silence her, and partly to get back at me?'

Aconite glanced sheepishly at his feet, as if the scuffed toes of his shoes might offer a better excuse than his tangled tongue ever could.

'To be fair, you weren't in charge. Not really,' I said. 'Neither is Malus. You're both puppets. Your strings are pulled by people we've never seen. Who are they?'

He looked up at me, his eyes sharp despite the hollows. 'You wouldn't believe me.'

'Try me.'

Silence stretched between us. I leaned in, my tone hushed but lethal. 'Coral. Spindle. The children. The experiments. The Star in a Jar. You think I'm just chasing ghosts? I'm going to take down everyone involved. Now you either help me, or I'll do worse to you than a simple cleansing. I can see it in your eyes. You're terrified. And so you should be.'

A look of acceptance passed over his face. 'They call themselves Keepers,' he said, then paused as if recalling more. 'Or, it could be Curators - I'm not sure. They don't live in Midpoints. Not even in private settlements. They exist above it all. Beyond consequence. You'll never find them.'

'Names.'

'I don't have them. I never did. They use numbers. Codes. I was given directives, not identities.'

I studied him, his expression unreadable. 'Is Malus a high-ranking figure in their hierarchy?'

Aconite tilted his head. 'Not even a knight,' he murmured. 'Just a pawn to move and sacrifice. The board's far bigger than you think.'

'Was Malus handpicked for the role?'

'What role?'

'To stand before mankind pretending to be the true leader of their one world government.'

He chuckled, it came out as a rasping sound. 'He was groomed from an early age. They called him the Knife. He was never meant to think. Just to cut.'

'And you?' I asked. 'What did they call you?'

He lifted his chin, pride colouring his voice. 'The Gatekeeper. I kept order on Ruin. I was the one who made sure every last one of you reached your potential.'

I shook my head. 'And now look at you. They'll abandon you. Once they realise their reign is crumbling, they won't lift a finger to save you. How do you feel about that?'

There was a long pause. The kind that stretched just enough to feel deliberate—calculated. His voice, when it finally came, was low and measured, almost coaxing.

'You'll never win, Jasmine. You don't understand the scale of what you're up against. They're not just powerful - they're entrenched. Every system, every shadow, every whisper in the dark answers to them. You think you're leading a revolution, but all you're doing is playing into their hands. Why don't you give up now? Walk away from this madness. I'm sure there's still a path back - a way to reintegrate, to be part of the world again. We could help you. End this before you lose everything.'

'No,' I said, my tone holding a venomous edge. 'They gave you a whip and called it authority. You were nothing to them. Simply, a vicious bully snapping at the helpless – just to please your masters.'

That silenced him. Not because he lacked words, but because mine had stripped him bare. The truth remained, they would not waste time saving him. And he knew it.

'Once the war is over, you'll stand trial. Not in some hollow spectacle like the Justice of Pax - no pomp, no pretence. This will be a true reckoning. A tribunal shaped by those who represent all of humanity, not just the victors. Your fate will rest in their hands. But don't mistake fairness for mercy. You'll be found guilty - I've no doubt. And there'll only be one outcome waiting for you at the end.'

I rose to leave, my thoughts a storm I couldn't calm. Something was shifting in me - I could feel it. I didn't need to kill him. Not anymore. He didn't hold that kind of power over me now. But just as I reached the door, his voice caught up with me.

'There is . . . one place. One lead. I can't say for certain whether it even exists. A rumour, a whisper, little more. But if it proves genuine - if it leads you to what you're after - then perhaps you'll consider sparing my life? A gesture of mercy in return for a sliver of truth?'

I froze mid-step.

'They call it Ashes of Eden,' he said. 'A vault. Or a lab. Or a sanctuary. I don't know. But whatever it is, they always feared it falling into the wrong hands . . . according to Malus.'

'Where?'

He shrugged. 'I'm not sure. Somewhere beyond a place called the Archipelago Island. Apparently, there's a tower that looks as if it touches the clouds. Malus is the one you should ask. He's the one with your answers.'

I didn't turn back.

* * *

Outside the cell, Robinia was waiting. 'Well?'

I felt the colour drain from my face. 'This could all end in disaster before we even begin.'

Robinia tilted her head. 'Why. What did he say?'

'Most of the time he talked in riddles. We need to dig into their systems.' I said, my mind racing. ' See what you can find on something called Ashes of Eden, or an island named Archipelago. There's supposed to be a massive tower there.'

Robinia gave a slow shrug. 'Doesn't ring any bells. I don't recall anything in the documents I've looked at so far.'

'Aconite could be lying, planting seeds to distract me. But somehow . . . I don't think he is.'

'So, what do you intend to do?' Robinia asked.

'We need to rethink everything. The capital's not the be-all and end-all. But where to begin - I've no idea.'

23

'We don't have time to make changes to our plans,' Spruce said, arms folded tight across his chest, his voice clipped.

My war cabinet stood visibly on edge, the operatives at their stations equally unsettled. They traded uneasy glances, eyes flicking toward the two of us, as if waiting for something to snap.

Spruce pressed on. 'We've set a course in action. Second-guessing now will only scatter our strength.'

'At least you're telling us this time,' Zander said, his tone edged with reproach. 'The mission on Ruin could've ended in disaster when you went off-script and approached Aconite on your own. Once plans are finalised, we need to stick to them.' He shook his head. 'I'm sorry, but I'm with Spruce on this one.'

I leaned forward, fingers braced on the edge of the table. 'Then maybe it's time we stopped making plans that box us in.'

Cooper let out a low groan. 'You helped make those plans - you don't get to ignore them when it suits you.'

Keeping my tone calm, I said, 'Do none of you get it. We're not dealing with just Malus and the capital. There's a full system behind the regime - one that might adapt faster than we can. We can't afford to win this war and then be taken over by an enemy we don't even know. There has to be a way they can be defeated too.'

Spruce stayed firm. 'But we can't afford wild detours. We do what we can now and worry about what comes later.'

'This isn't a detour.' I held his gaze. 'We can't win this war by playing catch-up, Spruce.'

'She's right,' Spindle said, without a flicker of doubt. 'You might not like hearing it, but Jasmine's the only one talking sense. We can't keep dragging ourselves through war after war. We need to take the whole system down in one clean strike.'

The mood in the room shifted. I saw their resolve begin to crack - the smallest crease in a brow, a sliver of uncertainty in their eyes. Their features softened with the look of defiance giving way.

'I'm not asking you to throw everything away,' I said, pressing the point. 'Just take a look. Assign someone - Cedar, maybe. Let him dig into it. If it turns out to be nothing, fine, we move on. But if it's not . . . we might be sparing ourselves a world of heartache later.'

Spruce raised a hand. 'Fine,' he said, rubbing the bridge of his nose. 'I'll put Cedar on it. But I swear, Jasmine, if this pulls focus from our primary mission – then that's on you.'

'It won't,' I said, already turning towards the door. 'Because we're all going to keep it on course. No one's losing focus. Not on my watch.'

* * *

The sky hung iron-grey, the wind tugging at our clothes as we crouched behind stacked containers at the edge of the docks. Spindle moved with the ease of someone stepping back into familiar danger, following Ash along the pier.

They had memorised the locations for planting explosives, and now Spindle and Ash surveyed each spot, calculating and assessing the true feasibility of the plan.

Wrapped tightly in cloaks, hooded against the chill, they looked like any other citizen trying to stay warm against the biting wind, blending in with the workers as if they belonged there.

'Look over there,' Jaz whispered, pointing toward a small watercraft moored at the far end. 'Is that the one secured to take us out?'

'I think so,' I said. 'Its tied to where we were told.'

'It looks smaller than I expected,' Cooper muttered. 'I hope it's safe enough to carry us and the explosives.'

Zander leaned in, his voice low. 'Larch and Cedar have the watercraft coordination running like clockwork. I'm confident the transport they've arranged to get us there will be fine.'

'What about the prisoners below deck?' I asked.

'They've been moved to our other craft.' Zander said. 'Cedar's rerouted the comms, so any transmission from the crew will appear to come from Malus's vessel - and not from the one Ash took. Larch will also be able to reroute messages, making it appear as if all is operating as normal. He'll think Coral and Spindle are still aboard, bound for the mainland.'

I rubbed the back of my neck, eyes locked on the grey smudge of the horizon. 'What worries me most are Malus's systems,' I said, annoyed at myself for dwelling on the worst scenario. 'If they're monitoring vessel movement and realise it's anchored, they'll know something's off. The whole plan could unravel. We won't get another shot.'

'That's why we have to move fast,' Cooper said, his jaw clenched. 'I just wish we had radio contact with the team planting explosives in the capital. They know what they're doing, no doubt about that - but still, one slip-up and it's all over.'

'At least we know the microchips have done their job,' Zander said. 'No Midpoint is beyond our reach. Though, some of our fighters would still prefer to lure the enemy outside and fight in the open.'

His words lingered with us, a thread of reassurance amid the tension. No one replied - we all knew how fragile success could be. Final checks were made in silence, minds focused, muscles braced.

Then, as night settled over the jetty, we sprinted forward, keeping low and melting into the shadows until we reached the small watercraft. With just a handful of us and bags full of explosives, the space was tight.

We bobbed along with the waves, the small craft rocking gently as we paddled away from the pier. The dark water sloshed against the hull, the moonlight catching on the ripples. Eventually, Cooper turned on the engine, its low hum swallowed by the wind, as we followed the nautical routes Larch had mapped out. Then, through the gloom, the outline of the vessel emerged. It floated like a ghost ship - silent, still, and waiting.

We climbed single file, like a line of insects scaling a sheer surface, each of us clinging to the thin steel ladder bolted to the ship's hull. Salt and sea-spray coated it, the rungs biting into our palms with every shudder of the waves below. The cold metal stung through our gloves, and the wind tugged at us as if trying to pry us off one by one.

My muscles burned with the effort; my boots slipping more than once on the narrow steps. No one spoke - we couldn't afford to. Just the sound of our breath, ragged and shallow, and the soft clink of gear brushing against the steel. The top of the climb felt impossibly far, like we were reaching for something that didn't want to be reached.

We made it, the deck groaning beneath us, echoing into the stillness as we set about our business. I followed Jaz across wood and rusted metal, past hatches and coiled ropes, until she led me down into the bowels of the ship. As we descended, the air grew thick with oil, salt, and something metallic. Down here, everything felt claustrophobic.

Jaz crouched beside a bulkhead, unzipping her pack. 'We lay them here,' she whispered, carefully setting out the first charge. 'It will bring about a chain reaction. One detonation, and the rest go off in sequence. By the time Malus's people get here, this vessel will be nothing but scorched memory.'

I nodded, crouching beside her as she handed me a charge. 'What if they go looking for bodies?'

She glanced up, her eyes cold. 'Then let them look. By the time they realise there's nothing here, we'll be tearing the capital apart.'

We worked in silence after that, the only sounds were the faint creak of the ship and the soft click of each charge sliding into place. The darkness swallowed our movements, but every step felt like defiance. Every step was one step closer to our goal.

Once we were sure all charges were in place - tucked into bulkheads, behind support beams, beneath the deck plates - we made our way back up to the top. The cold night air slammed into us, taking our breath as we climbed back down the ladder, disappearing into the swell of sea below.

We slipped into the watercraft and pushed off, waiting for the moment it would be detonated. The lights of the distant shoreline flickered in the mist, guiding us back to the mainland.

* * *

We met Spindle and Ash at the abandoned junkyard near the pier. I saw the relief in their eyes when they realised we'd made it back safely. But I kept my focus steady, masking the wave of relief I felt for Spindle. 'How did you get on?' I asked.

Spindle glanced at Ash before answering. 'It's done. There's a chance the explosives could be found before we're ready, but like everything else we've plotted so far, we don't have a choice.'

Cooper pulled out a small tablet that Larch had given him and tapped in the vessel's coordinates. 'Let's hope this Integrated Bridge System works. It was a nightmare to install, but I think I got it.'

'What does it do?' I asked.

'It should allow Larch to take control of the craft from the outpost. Lift the anchor and send it slowly forward to shore.'

'We can't worry about it now,' I said, afraid of how much could still go wrong.

Is everyone accounted for?' Zander asked, his gaze sweeping over the group. 'Good. Let's get back in the vehicle and head to the outpost. The last thing we need is a drone zooming past and clocking us standing around like targets.'

* * *

Back in the Operations Room, the air buzzed with urgency. Spruce stood by the central table, arms folded, eyes scanning the layout of the capital displayed on the large plasma screen. As I approached, he glanced up, keeping an air of calm.

'So far, so good,' he said, nodding towards the display. 'Our people made it inside the capital and several settlements without a hitch. The microchips cleared them through the scanners, and the guard uniforms did the rest. They slipped into the underground passageways and moved undetected beneath the streets.' He looked me in the eye. 'No alarms. No complications. Everything is going exactly to plan - for now.'

24

L arch sat, hands poised above the keyboard, his knuckles pale. He shot a glance over his shoulder, the muscles in his jaw ticking. 'It's ready,' he said. 'We're patched into Malus's system.'

Everyone exchanged that look - the kind that said everything. This was it. We were initiating war.

I nodded. 'Put him through.'

The screen flashed, distorted for a beat, then stabilised into chilling clarity. Malus's face filled the frame. The faint vibration of interference buzzed in the background, and for a moment, we just looked at each other.

'Are Spindle and Coral on their way?' I asked.

A pause. He tilted his head, as if weighing how much to give away. 'The last I heard, yes. But the Pewter Sea's been unpredictable these past few days. Storm surges. Magnetic fluctuations. You understand.' A smile crept across his face.

'Then contact your crew again. Find out when we can expect the craft to reach the mainland.'

He raised an eyebrow, intrigued. 'You seem rather confident.'

I turned toward Larch. 'Please patch the live feed through.'

Larch's fingers flew over the console. Within seconds, the screen split - Malus feed on one side, and what we hoped he would think - live footage on the other. His smile faltered as he watched two large transport vehicles slowly fill with our hostages - vacant-eyed, their movements slow and mechanical.

His expression barely shifted - just the faintest twitch at the corner of his mouth. His eyes revealed nothing. Whether he'd swallowed our deception or was simply playing along, I couldn't tell. His silence felt like a blade waiting to fall. Eventually, he said, 'You're in an underground bunker.'

'Of course,' I said, my voice cold. 'Where else would we be? We've got bunkers buried all over the mainland. And don't fool yourself - you'll never find us.'

The film flowed into a new scene. Two buses crawling across the scorched, cracked plains, dust billowing in their wake.

'As you can see, the hostages are on their way. I'll ask you once again - when can we expect Spindle and Coral?'

Malus steepled his fingers, his gaze steady. 'Let me reach out to my crew. I'll find out their position and relay an update. I presume you'll be in touch.'

'I will,' I said. 'Very soon. And when I do, I'll give you the co-ordinates for where your people can be collected.'

He opened his mouth, but I cut in before him, my tone steel-edged. 'One more thing. I want Coral and Spindle placed into a vehicle. No trackers. No chips. No chemical markers. You show me the live feed of them - safe, unharmed, and unmarked - and only then will I give you the drop point.'

Malus was silent for a long moment. Behind his eyes, something darker stirred - a flicker of calculation, annoyance, perhaps even respect. Finally, he gave a shallow nod. 'Very well. But if you deceive me . . .'

I held his stare. 'I don't need to. You've already underestimated us. You made that mistake before and I know you're watching. You won't make it again. As for me, I won't risk another earthquake on innocent people. So, you have my word.'

'And as long as you keep it, those still living in the mountains will remain unharmed - for now.'

I motioned to Larch to cut the call and the screen snapped to black. Silence rang in the Operations Room . . . it was deafening. My breath came out in a hard, deliberate hiss as my fists unclenched. The fear I felt throbbed fiercely, but I shoved it to the side.

Larch turned to me. 'Malus seemed happy with our filming. If he saw it was a trick, I'm sure he'd have said.'

'Yes,' I replied, glancing at the others. 'But it all seems to be going too easy. Something's bound to go wrong at some point. So, we need to be ready.' I scanned the room, spotting Cedar. 'Any luck with the Ashes of Eden? Or Archipelago Island?'

'Nothing yet,' Cedar said, not looking up. 'But I'll keep on it. It would help if we had more intel.'

Robinia leaned against the doorway, arms loosely folded. 'I suppose I could entertain Aconite for a while. Who knows, he might enjoy my company and let something slip.'

* * *

The container creaked as Spindle and I ducked inside, the door screaming on its hinges as I closed it.

'Welcome to our junkyard headquarters,' Coral said, grinning as she rushed over, pulling both of us into a tight hug. She took a step back, sweeping her arm wide. 'What do you think?'

I took it in. The container looked as if it was barely standing on the outside. Its metal sides patched with sheets of salvaged tin, and black tarpaulin flapped where the wind sneaked through. But inside, Coral had made a real effort - string-lights from scavenged bulbs, a makeshift planning table built from pallets and crates, with maps pinned up alongside hand-written notes.

A pile of blankets and a single camping stove were tucked into one corner, a handheld radio resting beside them. It was created for Jaz, Spindle, and Ash, who would be staying the night.

'It's beautiful,' I said, with a smirk. 'In a post-apocalyptic - it might crumble on us at any moment - kind of way.'

Coral laughed. 'Don't knock it - it's the finest strategic bunker within a twenty-mile radius of this dump.'

I grinned, but something in my chest tightened. For all the jokes and cobbled-together charm, this would be our base while away from the outpost. 'You've done well,' I said, my tone sincere. 'Seriously. It's perfect.'

'A few drones have flown past, but we're keeping out of sight,' Coral said, her tone calm. Almost too calm.

Movement stirred outside - the crunch of gravel, followed by the soft scuff of footsteps. Spindles's hand drifted towards the laser tucked in his belt. Coral froze. The hinges gave a familiar groan as the door creaked open. It was Jaz and Ash.

They stepped inside, Jaz full of confidence, her chin high, her eyes scanning the container like she already owned it. The guard uniform still clung to her awkwardly, but she wore it like armour - confident as ever. 'Is this what you call five star?' she said, turning to Ash. 'Next time you promise a lady a room, make sure it's worth her while.'

Coral let out a breath. 'Next time, knock. Or rattle some-thing. Spindle was ready to zap you.'

Jaz grinned. 'We were keeping you on your toes,' she said, placing her pack carefully on the floor and crouching to unzip it. It revealed the rest of the explosives wrapped in faded towels and foam scraps. 'These should be enough to line the rest of the pier,' she said, checking the charges. 'If we space them evenly between the explosives already there, the whole thing blows up.'

'We'll lay them late tonight, or in the early hours,' Ash said, more to Spindle than the rest of us.

'Once the naval vessel goes up, the army will move in,' Jaz said. 'They'll seal off the area from civilians, leaving just military personnel, and hopefully Malus. If I time the pier bombs for, say, two hours after the initial vessel blast, that should be enough time to cripple their responses.'

'Hopefully the citizens will stay away,' I said.

Spindle's gaze flitted between Jaz and Ash. 'The explosions will cause mass confusion, which should clear a path for the three of us to make our way to the capital and take up the fight there.'

'So, we begin to hit the capital and the settlements once the pier's down.' I said, trying to keep my voice steady. 'All explosives there are centred around government buildings, so hopefully it'll minimise civilian loss. Once our fighters are in place, Larch will fake a call, making sure Malus knows his vessel is a few miles from land.'

We'd been over this plan so many times in the last few days - each detail, every contingency. But talking it aloud again brought me a sense of comfort. There was something grounding in hearing the words, even if they were always the same.

'Will you be okay driving back?' Spindle asked, his gaze landing on me. 'Remember to keep to the routes I gave you. Those are the least patrolled. Don't risk getting caught.'

'I'll be fine,' I said, with forced confidence. 'I know the routes. And if anyone tries to stop me, I'll make sure they regret it. Besides.' I placed a hand on Coral's shoulder. 'I have my co-pilot here to keep me right.'

Spindle didn't look convinced. His frown deepened. He started to speak, then thought better of it, pressing his lips into a tight line.

'Can you do me a favour, Jasmine, and keep an eye on Orion?' Jaz asked. 'He's doing better, but I'm worried he's on a suicide mission.'

I nodded without hesitation. 'I'll keep him close. He won't do anything stupid while I'm around.'

Jaz's lips tightened. 'He's desperate for vengeance and will do anything to have it.'

'I'll keep him safe,' I said, more firmly this time.

We stood in silence looking at each other for a few minutes.

'Right, time for Coral and me to move out,' I said, the pain of leaving Spindle lodging deep in my heart. 'Take care, all of you. Tomorrow will be remembered as the day we took back our freedom. The start of a new era.' I paused, steadying myself against the wave of vulnerability I could feel rising. 'I don't need to tell you to be careful. I trust you will be.'

I looked around the container, meeting each of their eyes. These were the ones who would make it happen. The ones who would launch the first strike, igniting a war I hoped would be the last.

We group-hugged, a moment of solidarity before the chaos would unfold. Without another word, I pulled away and left the container, Coral at my heels. The door creaked shut behind us, but before it could fully close, I heard Ash's voice, 'You should go to her. Say a proper goodbye.'

The words barely registered before Spindle's hand was on my shoulder, pulling me back, his body pressing against mine as he took me in his arms. I didn't have time to process what was happening before his lips found mine. His kiss was long, urgent, and filled with a raw passion that caught me off guard. It was everything I expected - fierce, desperate. When he finally pulled away, our foreheads rested against each other, with my heart drumming in my ears.

'Just . . . be careful,' he said, his voice cracking. 'As soon as I'm finished here, I'll make my way straight to the capital - straight to your side.'

I nodded, not trusting myself to speak. The last thing I wanted was for him to see me stumble or cry.

25

A sharp tone pulsed from the speakers - crisp, clinical. Then Larch's voice cut in. 'Jasmine, the line is now live. I've masked it to make it appear as though its coming from the naval craft. One of our operatives on the other vessel is posing as their Command.' He hesitated for second. 'We're just waiting for Malus to pick up. You'll be able to listen in on the call.'

My heart leapt into my throat. Every operative fell still. No one dared breathe.

A gruff, sea-worn voice came through the speaker next. 'This is Command. We're a few hours off the coast. A storm battered us earlier, but we steered wide. Our craft is intact. The prisoners are with us. All alive. No injuries. We'll make landfall in under two hours.'

Malus's voice came through with a reply. 'Copy that. I'll have guards and transport waiting.'

The line went dead - abrupt, chilling. Malus had ended the call.

'What does he mean he'll have guards waiting?' I asked, my voice filled with frustration. I thought he'd perhaps be there to meet them himself.'

'Let's put ourselves in his mindset,' Spruce said. 'He's not planning to meet our demands - not really. He'll stay in the capital, and likely send out drones to track the vehicles he thinks is carrying the hostages. He's probably betting he can locate them before he needs to show you a live feed of Coral and Spindle's release. He might appear at the docks after the pier blasts.'

I couldn't help but wonder why Spruce thought heading to a blown-up pier was a clever strategy. 'That doesn't make sense,' I said, screwing up my face. 'There are only two chances - he either greets the vessel as it arrives - which we now know he won't - or heads there directly once the vessel explodes. He's not going to waltz straight into the eye of a storm. Once the pier goes up, he'll realise it's war and hunker down in the capital to take command.'

Orion turned his laser over in his hands, his eyes fixed on it, already picturing the moment it would fire. 'It doesn't matter where he is,' he said, venom dripping from his tone. 'I'll find him.'

Approaching him quietly while the others planned, I kept my voice low. 'Orion,' I said, 'Are you okay?'

He didn't look up. His eyes were firmly fixed on his weapon. 'I'm fine. Why wouldn't I be?'

The answer was too quick. Too flat. 'Listen,' I said, stepping in front of him. 'I know this battle means everything to you. But don't let it consume you. Don't let grief turn into martyrdom. I need you to make it out alive. No heroics. Promise me.'

He finally met my gaze, but his stare was hollow. 'I hear you,' he said, placing his laser back in his belt. 'We should get our guards outfits on and get moving, if we want to be at the capital when it all kicks off.'

Spruce handed out the comms units. 'Keep the frequency on Level Twelve - it's the least likely to be intercepted. Make sure your teams give constant updates. No radio silence unless you're compromised.'

'Thanks, Spruce,' I said.

'I'm only doing my job.'

'For allowing me to go and fight. I know it wasn't an easy decision, but I'm glad you have faith in me.'

Spruce gave a faint, uneasy smile before glancing away briefly, as if weighing his words. 'I should've had faith in you sooner. I made things difficult at the start. I know that now. Back then, my loyalty was with those who held power before you. I didn't realise they were leading us . . . down a dark path.' His eyes flickered bak to mine, but he struggled to hold my gaze. 'You made me see it. And, I'm sorry it took so long.'

He stepped past me and raised his voice to the room. 'Our people are spread across the settlements and inside the capital. If things go sideways, the know to scatter and regroup. Juniper's crew on Ruin has been briefed. They're ready to fight if it comes to that. Head to your positions. Safe speed. I'll contact Jaz when it's time to blow the vessel.'

I turned to Robinia. Her face was drawn and unreadable. 'Is there still no word from Aspen?'

She shook her head. 'I'm certain he's holed up in a medical facility somewhere and unable to get a message through. Don't worry - we haven't targeted any residential zones. Aspen's smart. He'll know what to do when the bombs go off.'

'Let's hope you're right,' I said, offering a silent prayer for his safety. 'Let me know if you get anything out of Aconite. I have a feeling its important so press him hard. Do what you need to do.'

'I'll head down to speak to him as soon as you've gone.'

Spruce approached, a compact monitor in his hand. 'Take this,' he said. 'You'll be able to see what's happening on the dock. I've linked it to a transmitter - one of our drones will feed you a live stream. But don't switch it on until the moment comes. The frequency could attract attention from Malus's drones. Once it's live, you'll have real-time visuals of the action.'

We said our farewells with handshakes, tight embraces, and nods that carried a thousand unspoken truths - the kind of goodbyes you say when you're not sure who'll come back. One by one, we broke away to our vehicles.

Mine was cramped. Cooper sat beside me, fingers drumming against the door. Zander leaned against the window, half lost in thought. Astrid adjusted her belt, her shoulders rigid. Minx toyed with her knife, flipping it between gloved hands. Felix stared out at the barren land, lips moving silently - perhaps a prayer, or a list of names he refused to forget. And Orion sat behind me. Quiet. Unreadable.

Apart from Orion, we'd been prisoners in the mines together - broken, beaten, and starving. That version of us had no weapons, no freedom, and no voice. Now, we were rebels - sharpened by loss and forged by purpose. Each of us carried something heavier than a weapon. We carried hope - the kind of hope that sets the world on fire.

I turned the radio to the frequency Spruce had given me, static crackling to fill the silence. I waited, straining to catch even the faintest whisper of a voice, hoping it would be Spindle.

Our vehicle sat among a line of armoured trucks in the compound just outside the capital's Midpoint. From the outside, we looked like any other group of guards preparing for their shift.

After what felt like forever, the first voice crackled through the radio - Spruce's. 'Jaz, you're good to go.'

Seated in the back, the others gathered close as I poured up the monitor Spruce had given me. Our drones fed through the grainy, slightly distorted - but clear enough - images to the screen. We could make out the docks and, on the horizon, the naval vessel crawling forward. A pang of relief hit me - Larch's system to manoeuvre the ship was working. We were off to a good start.

My heart dipped as I watched the civilians going about their daily routines. There seemed far too many. All I could hope for was that, when the vessel blew, they would run and take cover. Hopefully the army would arrive quickly and cordon off the scene.

'I don't understand,' I said, my voice trembling. 'The vessel should've exploded by now. What's the delay?' I looked up, scanning my friends' faces for answers none of us had.

We waited, each second dragging longer than the last. When the delay stretched into minutes, I grabbed the radio. 'Jaz, do you read me? What's going on? Talk to me.'

It was Ash's voice that cut through the static, thick with frustration. 'Something's wrong with the detonator. Jaz is working on it. Spindle's helping her.'

'They need to move fast,' I said, trying to hide my worry. 'Do they know if it's an isolated issue, or are all the explosives compromised?'

'We're not sure,' Ash replied, his panic rising.

In the background, we could hear Jaz's muffled voice. Then Ash came back to us. 'No,' he said. Jaz thinks it's the distance. The signal to detonate isn't reaching. The craft is too far out - it's too weak to trigger the charge.'

Silence - but only for a minute or so. Ash's voice came back. 'Wait . . . where are you both going?'

'What's happening?' I asked, keeping my voice calm, even though I wanted to scream.

'They've gone,' Ash said. 'Jaz took off, and Spindle's chasing her.'

Five minutes later, movement jerked my attention to the monitor. A figure dressed in the black leather of the guards sprinted down the pier towards a moored watercraft. I wasn't sure if it was Spindle or Jaz. I squinted, trying to make them out, but their face was hidden beneath their helmet. They slammed into a trader loading goods onto the craft, sending him tumbling onto the stone steps.

They seized the rudder, yanking the craft into motion, steering it out of the harbour and into the Pewter Sea. Though we couldn't hear them, shouts rose from the shocked crowd - pointing, yelling, panicking.

Guards swarmed the scene from every direction. Then drones appeared, their shape silhouettes cutting through the sky. Armed to the teeth, they bore down on the watercraft. Laser fire streaked the air, bright and deadly. The craft ducked and weaved in a blur of zig-zag movements, every twist and turn a desperate bid to escape the deadly pursuit.

Malus's naval craft gained on the fleeing figure, and again I could imagine the sound of their engines howling, warning lights blazing, and a voice over a loudspeaker yelling for them to stop. But they didn't slow. Instead, they accelerated, heading straight for the helm of our targeted vessel.

The blast tore through the air - a monstrous wave of heat and light that engulfed both craft, leaving behind nothing but flaming husks. Smoke billowed upwards, thick and fast, coiling into the sky like a black scream. I froze. My heart pounded, throat clenched tight. Every part of me rebelled against the sight. It could've been Jaz. It could've been Spindle. Spindle . . . my Spindle - gone.

The firestorm was breathtaking - golden at its heart, bleeding into oranges and deep, furious reds. Apocalyptic. Like the sea itself had caught fire and dragged someone I loved down with it. I stared at the screen, willing it to rewind, to take it back - to show me a different ending. But it didn't.

The shockwave struck a second later, a brutal force that made the monitor shudder. It crashed outward in all directions, flattening waves, tossing debris like sand in a storm. A roaring wall of sound cracked through the radio like thunder splitting the sky, the speakers distorting under the sheer force of it.

Bits of wreckage rained down, flaming scraps falling into the sea with hollow, hissing splashes. The naval craft was gone. Obliterated, taking those in pursuit with them. Nothing but fragments now, charred metal and burning ruin.

We could see the faces of those on the docks. We could only imagine their gasps, and cries. Some dropped to their knees, the sight too much. Others simply stood, frozen by the sheer scale of it - as if the explosion had ripped not just through the vessel, but through reality itself.

And then, far too soon, without our detonations, the pier blew. Whether it was the heat fanning in from the sea or a domino reaction, I couldn't say - our chain of explosions tore through the timbers and stone on the pier, sending flames roaring skyward in a frenzy of heat and destruction.

26

I slammed my fist against the console, my voice erupting into the radio, ragged with panic. 'Ash, you need to move - now. Get out of there. The whole place will be crawling with Guards.' My throat burned, heart jackhammering in my chest. 'Who crashed into the vessel? Was it Spindle?'

Silence cracked back - no reply. Just dead air. Dread twisted in my gut, cold and sharp. I pressed the transmit button again, harder this time, like the force alone might bring them back. 'Ash, come in - do you read me? Please.'

The static hissed in reply - thin, cruel, a sound meant to mock. Ash remained out there. Alone. I couldn't reach him. I couldn't reach Spindle or Jaz. One of them had sacrificed themselves, and I had no idea which.

Then - just as I was about to scream his name again - Ash's voice burst through the static, breathless and rushed. 'I've found him. He's okay.'

Relief surged through, but before I could respond, the signal fractured again. I could hardly contain my panic - then another voice cut in, rough and familiar.

'Jasmine, it's me, Spindle.' His voice was raw, haunted. 'I

tried to stop Jaz. She said she needed to detonate the craft herself. I told her I'd go - that I'd handle it.' He gulped back a breath. 'When I followed her, she hid behind a pile of junk . . . then hit me over the head with a plank.' His voice racked with disbelief. 'Knocked me clean out. I should've worn my helmet . . . I'm so sorry.'

I pressed the radio to my lips, barely able to breathe. 'It's not your fault. I'm so glad you're okay,' I whispered, the words catching in my throat. 'I thought I'd lost you.' The silence on the line that followed wasn't empty - it was full. Full of everything we didn't need to say. For a second, the chaos faded, and all that remained was the fragile relief of still having him. 'Get moving. I need you here.'

'We're on our way.'

My voice shook as I jabbed the comms switch. 'Spruce, did you get all that?'

'We watched the whole thing on the plasma. Malus will know we've deceived him. He'll no longer waste resources on trying to find the hostages or sending scouting parties to the wrecked craft. He'll concentrate all efforts on securing the capital. We've lost our element of surprise.' He paused, just long enough for the weight to settle. 'We need to keep our strategy on track. No delays.' Then, louder - so everyone within reach of the comms could hear - he declared, 'The time is now. The battle is on.'

His voice rang out like a war drum spurring us all into action. The first explosion ripped through the capital with a thunderous roar, turning the dawn-stained, domed sky into a blaze of fire and smoke. Windows shattered. The shockwave rolled outward, rattling the bones of every building and every soul. I watched from the entrance to the capital, breath catching as flames licked the rooftops and smoke spiralled into the air.

We stormed through the breach, marching on scorched

ground with our lasers primed and ready. Guards and soldiers scrambled, their orders lost beneath the roar of detonation after detonation. We opened fire - bursts that cut through the mayhem. Panic erupted. Civilians scattered in every direction, shrieking, ducking behind market stalls and overturned benches. The capital, once a place of order and fear, had become a warzone.

Chaos surged through the streets. Sirens blared, echoing off glass towers and marble façades, swallowed seconds later by the next eruption. Another fireball bloomed, this one closer to the Ministry's west wall, flinging debris across the square.

Blinding laser shots split the smoky air, crackling. Sparks skittered over the paving stones as volleys of return fire tore from the government's defensive line. Their shots should have been wild - disjointed, desperate. We had struck first, and we had struck with devastating force. However, the enemy seemed to pin-point us with accuracy when we should have blended in. The chaos, the roar of battle swallowed everything, and when I finally paused for breath, I realised we had been torn from our group. I stood in the swirling smoke, with only Felix and Minx at my side.

Spruce's voice crackled in my earpiece. 'You need to take out their communications tower and then head for the Council buildings. That's where they'll hunker down. If Malus is in the capital, that's where he'll be.'

'Copy that,' I replied, ducking behind a fractured wall as a blast sent bricks raining down from above. The ground trembled beneath us, but we pushed forward. I turned to Felix and Minx, crouched beside me. 'We move on my count.'

Felix and Minx's heads dipped in silent agreement.

'Okay,' I said. 'Three - two - one - Go.'

We edged out from our cover, only to snap back almost instantly, hearts racing as a barrage of lasers tore through the air around us. We were pinned. A group of soldiers had seized a commanding position above us, their relentless hail of rapid fire forcing us to inch back with every shot.

The thrum of their weapons rang in our bones, the force of their fire driving us further into cover. We were unable to move. Each blast zeroed in on our position, a constant pressure that threatened to crush us under its weight.

Then, out of nowhere, Orion materialised - he strode forward with his visor up. Perhaps he wanted those who he fought to see his face, to know his anger. I had been so consumed with worry for Spindle and Ash, still reeling from the shock of Jaz's courageous bravery, that I'd lost track of him when we plunged into the fray. But now he strode forward, fearless - his weapon roaring in his hands. His rattling shots shattered the foundations of the balcony where our enemies had entrenched themselves. It sent chunks of debris spiralling into the air as their position began to crumble under his assault.

As the balcony gave way with a thunderous crack, Orion staggered back, his body jolting from the impact of laser fire. Blood seeped from his torso, soaking through his black leathers. He dropped to one knee, clutching his side as a violent cough racked his chest. Then came the splatter, a crimson spray from his mouth that painted the ground red.

Before I could so much as breathe, Felix launched himself into the open, charging towards Orion's crumpled form. He reached him in seconds, hands struggling to drag him clear. A searing bolt tore through the void, slamming into Felix's shoulder. He jerked, staggered, and then another blast caught his leg. He dropped beside Orion with a guttural cry, his body twisting in pain. I started forward, heart hammering, but Minx yanked me back hard.

'No,' she hissed, her grip like iron. 'They'll pick us off one by one. We need to find the shooter. Take him out - then we move.'

I peeked out from our hiding place, scanning the chaos. A

cold spike of fear gripped me, as I searched for Cooper, Zander, and Astrid. Smoke curled through the air, dense and biting, but there was no sign of any of them. I dared a glance from behind the wall - just a sliver - and a laser beam screamed past my cheek, so close it singed the edge of my visor. I ducked back.

'This is hopeless,' I muttered, yanking up the visor to wipe the fog from my eyes. 'I've lost Cooper. My earpiece is dead - I can't hear Spruce or anyone. Do you think . . . do you think they're okay?'

'They're probably holed up somewhere, same as us,' Minx said, checking the battery on her laser. 'They'll be fine. Cooper and Zander are tough. They'll be giving as good as they get.'

'How can they tell us apart from them? I thought we'd be invisible, blending in with the guard uniforms. But the moment they see us, they open fire. They're supposed to think we're one of them.'

'We don't have time to worry about that now,' Minx said, her words tumbling out quickly. 'I need you to edge out a little more. I'll be right behind you - I promise - but I've got to pinpoint where that laser's coming from. Just a little, all right? I don't fancy wearing your brains.' She gave a tight smile, then added, 'And please . . . put your visor back down.' As she snapped her own shut with a sharp click.

I edged out just far enough to glimpse the carnage. Flames licked at the crumbling buildings, throwing jagged shadows across the shattered cityscape. The air reeked of smoke and blood. I heard Felix groan. He had dragged himself halfway over Orion, his body a desperate shield against whatever fresh horror was bearing down on us.

The laser cracked . . . ruthless, savage. Minx yanked me back, dragging me behind cover as the beam tore past. She sprang up, firing in short, furious bursts of white-hot light. A shot grazed her arm - she jerked, gritted her teeth - but didn't stop. Then, silence. The laser fire ceased. Smoke hung heavy. We held our breath, listening.

'I think I got him,' Minx said, clutching her wounded arm, pulling back beside me. 'Give me a few seconds . . . then edge out again.'

'Are you hurt bad?' I asked, as she nursed her arm.

'It could've been worse. Okay, I'm ready,' she said with a quick nod. 'Let's finish this.'

I peered out a little further this time. Nothing. No shots. No movement. The silence was almost deafening.

'I think we're good,' I muttered, hope sparking in my chest.

We moved cautiously forward, our steps hesitant at first, but our confidence slowly building as we closed the distance to Felix and Orion.

Felix writhed, gasping through his visor. We dragged him back - no strength left, only fear. Felix groaned, a horrible, broken sound. I ripped off his helmet. His face twisted, unrecognisable. His skin felt slick, burning hot and ice-cold all at once

'It's all right,' I said. A lie. A desperate, stupid lie. 'Aspen . . . we'll find him soon. He'll fix you.'

Orion didn't move. Didn't breathe. He lay too still. Too pale. 'Orion, I said, lifting his head and holding him to me. 'Wake up . . . you need to wake up . . . now.'

Felix gritted his teeth, the words scraping out of him. 'He's dead.' He lurched, reaching out for Orion, but fell back with a cry. 'He did it for them,' Felix choked. Tears and blood and pain, all tangled together. 'Said . . . we've to finish the job.'

27

We remained behind the safety of the fallen brick - a charred overhang of stone shielding us from the worst of the ash that still floated like a curse through the city. Felix lay propped against the rock, his breathing shallow, blood soaking through the makeshift wrap Minx had knotted around his thigh.

She also took her leather jacket off and cut a chunk with her knife making a padded compress. 'Here, hold this tight against your wound,' she said, pressing it against his shoulder. Felix winced but didn't argue; his fingers trembling as he obeyed.

Sweat began to bead at his temples. 'I can manage,' he mumbled.

I crouched beside him, brushing dust from his brow with the sleeve of my jacket. 'We'll make you as comfortable as we can,' I murmured. The words tasted bitter. Too much like good-bye. 'Minx will stay with you, until I come back.'

Minx said nothing, her jaw clenched tight as she folded the remains of her jacket and set to work on her own wound. When she finally looked up, her eyes were fierce - and shining with unshed tears. 'You're not going alone.'

I glanced towards the horizon, where the capital's spires jutted sharply agains the skyline. 'I have to. The longer we wait, the more chance they'll reinforce their lines. If I can get through now - slip into the outer rings - I might still have a chance to reach the Council buildings before the next wave arrives.'

Minx stood, the heels of her boots grinding into the stone. 'That's suicide. Malus's men will be pouring in from every direction. There could be traps, ambushes.'

'I know,' I cut in. 'But we can't afford to wait. If we do, our forces will have to pull back - and we'll lose everything we've gained. I need to try and find the others.'

Felix stirred, his voice barely a rasp. 'You both should go.'

Minx dropped to her knees beside him, grabbing his hand. 'You need to hold on. Don't you dare close your eyes. Try to focus and stay alert.'

'I'll be fine,' Felix said, even though his lips were pale with a bluish tint. 'You have to keep going.'

Then - a sound. Distant at first. The crunch of footsteps. I reached for my weapon, Minx doing the same, our shoulders stiffening.

A voice rose above the dust. 'Jasmine? Is that you?'

My heart twisted. 'Cooper?' I shouted back, stepping out from under the outcrop.

Zander, Cooper, and Astrid emerged through the haze, a dozen of our fighters flanking them. Their relief was palpable, eyes wide, faces streaked with grime.

'Thank goodness we found you,' Astrid said, racing forward. Her eyes scanned our ragged group. 'What happened?'

I exhaled, my shoulders sagging. 'We got split after one of the explosions. The ground tore open behind us. We darted for cover, and in the chaos . . . we were scattered. We spent the last hour fighting off small units of Malus's soldiers.'

Cooper's eyes settled on Orion's still form behind us, crumpled in the dust and half-shielded by Minx's jacket. His jaw twitched. Moving slowly, almost reverently, he knelt beside him. 'God, no,' he murmured, trembling.

'I'm sorry, Cooper. I should never have let him out of my sight,' I said, my voice cracking.

Cooper placed a shaking hand on Orion's forehead. 'He was my responsibility too. But he charged off when we were pinned down. I don't know how he managed it, but he caught those holding us back from behind. Took them all out. Waved at me afterwards . . . then vanished into the smoke.'

'He did the same for us,' Felix said, his voice hoarse. 'They caught me when I tried to pull him back from their range of fire.'

Astrid crouched beside Felix, her eyes flicking over his injuries. Her fingers brushed the edge of his wounds. She let out a slow breath. 'They got you pretty bad,' she said, her tone filled with concern. She leaned in closer to him, her eyes locking onto his. 'You're tough, my friend - you've got this. You always do.'

'I'm fine,' Felix said. 'Please . . . get moving.'

'We're not leaving you behind,' Minx said, glancing around. 'Is there anything we could use as a stretcher?'

He shook his head slowly. 'Don't be foolish. I'm not going to make it . . . not on a stretcher. I'll stay here with Orion. Keep him company until you return.' He coughed, blood spilling from his lips in a thin, dark line. 'Go . . . before I get angry and decide to drag myself up and beat the living daylights out of you all.'

Another group of our fighters emerged from the smoke, their helmets discarded, weapons held high in defiance - grim, determined, battered, but alive. They moved as one, a force borne of desperation and grit.

'Jasmine.' The voice cut through the mayhem, and I turned to see Falconer, his face streaked with dirt but his eyes burning with intensity. 'Some of our fighters managed to climb over the rooftops. They're pushing forward. The battle's still raging.'

'I'm so glad you're all okay,' I said, overwhelmed by the strength and bravery they'd shown.

Falconer nodded, his gaze hardening. 'We should keep pressing forward. I don't think their soldiers have ever known real battle. They've only ever been in those small skirmishes out in the wastelands. They've never faced something like this - not a fight of this scale. It works to our advantage.' He looked behind him, as if searching. 'Many of our men are still catching up. They're scavenging weapons from the bodies of our enemies - taking what they can use.'

I looked at them all - Falconer and his fighters, Cooper's raw grief, Minx kneeling by Felix, Astrid and Zander weary and dumped. A silent battle of hope and despair. We couldn't give up.

'Then we press forward,' I said, my voice firm. 'But we split up. I'll take a small group and move ahead. The rest of you circle back and regroup with the main force. Get Felix to safety. See if you can find the medical facility - and find Aspen. Quickly.'

'If you're going into Malus's den,' Astrid said, grimly, 'you'll need more than a prayer. My last contact with Spruce said all forces are being redirected here. They've secured the other settlements we attacked. He feels we should retreat and head back to the outpost.'

'I've got something better than prayers,' I replied. 'I've nothing left to lose.'

I knelt beside Felix one last time, my heart thudding

painfully. I brushed the damp curls from his brow and kissed his forehead. 'You're not going to die, do you hear me?'

He reached up, his fingers trembling as they touched my cheek. 'Be safe.'

I swallowed hard and rose to my feet. There was no time for goodbyes. 'Find the rest of our fighters,' I said to Astrid. 'Try and make contact with the outpost, and let Spruce know our position. We won't be retreating today . . . and not ever.'

Steeling myself, I crept to the edge of the outcrop and scanned the city ahead. Smoke billowed through the alleys, fires crackled in the ruins, and bodies lay twisted in the dust. But the streets were quiet. At least the citizens had found shelter.

I stepped into the open, Cooper and Zander beside me. Ahead, Falconer's men moved, disappearing down a side lane. Suddenly, laser fire cracked - sharp and unexpected.

'Down,' I shouted, dragging Cooper behind a burnt-out vendor cart, the beam pinging off the metal. Cooper returned fire, but it was no use - we were outnumbered, and they were closing in fast.

'There.' Zander pointed to an open doorway a block further down. 'Move.'

We bolted across the open space, adrenaline during, ducking behind benches. The factory door groaned open to reveal rows of sewing machines, threads dangling and fabrics half-stitched beneath needles.

'They left in a hurry,' I said, as we took off our helmets and looked around. 'Probably when the explosions started.'

Chairs were left at odd angles, one still rocking slightly as if the worker had just leapt up and run. A flask of tea sat untouched on a side table. The overhead lights flickered, prob-ably due to power outages.

I slowed, breathing hard, and picked up a square of cloth from one of the desks. The fabric was coarse, regulation grey, stitched with the unmistakable crest of the government. 'They were making uniforms to send to Ruin,' I murmured, turning it over in my hands.

Zander leaned in beside me. 'So, they'd make them here and send them over with traders.'

'Time's ticking,' Cooper said, standing guard at the doorway. 'They'll be sweeping this zone next.' He pointed to the ceiling. 'Here. This looks like a vent shaft.'

We dragged a table beneath the vent. Cooper stepped up, rising onto his toes as he reached for the ceiling grid. With a grunt, he gripped the edge and hauled himself up, bracing his boots against the wall for leverage. The grid gave way, crashing down with a clatter, and Cooper dropped back onto the table with a thud.

'Are you okay?' I asked.

'Yep,' Cooper replied. 'I'm good. Just bruised my pride.' He shifted, rising again. 'Zander, boost me up.'

Zander jumped onto he table and cupped his hands. Cooper stepped in, and with a spring, Zander launched him upwards. Cooper grabbed the edge and hauled himself through the opening.

'Okay,' he called down. 'Your turn, Jasmine.'

He leaned back and reached for me. Zander gave me a shove up; Cooper caught my arm as I scrambled into the shaft. I saw Zander leap next, his wrists gripped by Cooper and me as we hauled him in. Breathless, we crouched together in the cool, dark metal.

The ventilation shaft was just wide enough for us to crawl on our hands and knees. The metal beneath us was cold, clanging softly with each shift of weight. A sudden gust from the air conditioning system tore through the shaft, slicing through our leathers and biting at our sweat-slicked skin. The air reeked faintly of oil and something clinical - sterile.

We moved in silence, ghost-like, slipping through the lungs of the city.

'When did you last have contact with Spruce?' Cooper asked, from up ahead.

'I lost him when we were under fire,' I said. 'I'm shocked that he would want us to retreat. Doesn't he realise we don't have a choice anymore.'

'He was trying to reroute the signal when I was on to him - then nothing,' Cooper replied.

Zander muttered behind me. 'It was probably Malus blocking our signals. He knows we're scattered. He'll do his best to keep it that way.'

'Have the other settlements really fallen?' I asked, trying not to dwell on those who had sacrificed their lives.

'According to Spruce, they have,' Zander said. 'He sounded certain.'

Silence followed. Only the sound of our movements echoed in the narrow ducts, the dull thump of knees against metal, the soft scrape of palms, and an occasional grunt. The ducts groaned faintly around us, but we kept going.

I knew this fight wasn't going our way, but I would make sure we kept moving, because what else was there? Surrender was never an option, no matter what Spruce would demand of us. I'd bleed out on these streets if it meant shaking the very foundations of Malus's regime.

We had already torn holes in his strongholds, cracked open the illusion of his power. Chaos had erupted in the heart of the capital - proof that they could be touched, that they could suffer. We might not win this war, not today, but our story wouldn't end here. It would spread like wildfire, passed from whispered secrets to deafening screams. And one day, someone would finish what we started. Because where tyranny digs in, resistance claws its way back. Always.

28

The metal shaft opened into a wide junction - an eerie crossroads of rust-stained ducts. We crouched just inside the mouth of the tunnel, every breath tight with caution. Shafts split off in every direction, each one yawning into shadows.

Cooper glanced from one tunnel to the next, his brows furrowed. 'Which way?' he asked, his voice taut. 'The last thing we need is to double back and crawl straight into a patrol. We need to keep pushing toward the Council buildings. Toward the control rooms.'

Zander leaned forward, bracing his hands on his knees. 'Pick one and move. We'll know we're close when we hear voices.' He scanned the junction, unease creeping into his voice. 'But doesn't it strike you as odd? Not a single civilian in the levels below. No whispers. No footsteps. Nothing.'

I nodded slowly. 'Do you think there's a protocol? Somewhere they've been told to go to in the event of an attack. Maybe a lockdown bunker or the equivalent of our outpost.'

'Or,' Cooper muttered, 'They knew we were coming. Something feels off.' He shifted, his shoulder brushing the cold duct wall as he glanced around. 'We need to blow a hole in the glass roof. The smoke's choking the city . . . it needs an outlet. Why the hell build an indoor city anyway? It's stupid.' Frustration simmered beneath his words.

'To be fair, those domes were built to protect us,' I said. 'You had caves - we had climate-sealed cities. That's why I wanted to unharness the sun. To give the Earth back its balance. I'll never get the chance now.'

Zander gave me a light thump on the back. 'Hey. Don't spiral. This isn't over. Not yet. We're not done until we say we are. My father believed that. He believed in you. And so do I.'

I thought of Saxon then, the man who had once supported me in the darkest days. Now it was his son grounding me, bearing that same quiet strength. 'He'd be proud of you,' I said, meeting Zander's eyes. 'Proud of all of us.'

I turned toward the tunnel that dipped slightly downwards. 'This city . . . it feels bigger than the schematics Robinia showed us. Maybe there were expansions no one recorded.'

'It wouldn't surprise me,' Zander muttered. 'Power breeds paranoia. I bet there's an entire complex of buildings - just for the ruling class.'

The ducts narrowed, forcing us onto our elbows. Machinery whined - more than ventilation. It felt like surveillance - heat sensors, systems hunting the unwanted. My mind raced with dread.

A faint glow flickered ahead - a grated vent. I froze, signalling the others. 'Movement,' I whispered.

We pressed our ears to the duct floor. Distant voices filtered upward - commands, footsteps, the occasional groan of metal doors opening and closing. We crept forward, until we reached the grill.

Below us, a medical ward stretched out - rows of bandaged, bruised soldiers lying motionless on narrow cots. Medics moves swiftly, but the vacant, unblinking faces held my attention. Control's grip was absolute. I searched for

Aspen among the medics but found no sign of him. He had to be close.

We pushed on, reaching another junction. This one opened above a narrow corridor. As we peered down, our eyes caught the red motion sensors - strung low across the floor like a deadly web, their warning lights flickering ominously.

Zander's jaw tensed. 'We must be close to something important,' he said. 'They wouldn't bother with such high-tech security unless they're guarding something vital.'

We slithered forward, every movement a silent prayer that the metal beneath us wouldn't give way. No one spoke. We had no plan for what waited ahead - only the certainty that whatever came next, we had to make it count.

I heard him before I saw him - his voice laced with venom, rising to meet us, sharp and cutting. Peering through the grill, we realised we were now level with the walls, no longer above the rooms as we had been before.

Malus sat at a sleek, polished conference table, surrounded by his Council. But their eyes weren't on him - they were fixed on the massive plasma screen mounted to the far wall. It showed no faces, only the emblem of the regime. From that dark void, the true voices of power emerged - the Puppeteers. The ones who pulled every string from the shadows. Their power absolute.

'We are not impressed.' A voice boomed from the screen.

'We've tried,' Malus said. We've looked at every past code, scoured every backdoor. But their firewall . . . it's like their entire communications network has vanished. There's nothing to trace, nothing to breach. Our technicians think the only reason we found them at all was because they got to us first.'

Another voice crackled through the screen, its accent subtly different. 'Perhaps they're using outdated systems. Did it not. Occur to you to search the pre-End records? To locate bunkers that may have survived? There are likely still shelters breathing beneath the dust.' The voice sharpened, frustration bleeding through. 'Our scanners swept the islands - a task your patrols should should have handled. Do you know what we found?'

'What?' Malus asked.

'Ruin has fallen and Aconite is gone. They must have him as one of their captives.'

Malus blinked, stunned. 'Ruin . . . fell to her?' The words scraped out, dry and disbelieving. 'How?'

Another voice, this time a woman. 'You were outmanoeuvred. While the Resistance cultivated numbers within your walls - Jasmine, united the tribes in the caves turning chaotic upstarts into soldiers.'

A new voice cut in, taunting Malus. 'Old bunkers. Old tech. Revived right under your nose. What shame you bring upon us.'

Malus turned from the screen, his jaw set, his hands trembling. 'We can rebuild,' he said, trying to maintain a show of confidence.

'No,' the woman said. 'They've taken over all the settlements. The capital is under attack. It won't be long until it falls.'

Then came their decree. 'It has been decided that we wish to start again. We will release the Ashes of Eden. And from it, a new world will rise. Something new - untainted . . . for the next generations.'

The words struck cold. I glanced at Zander, then Cooper. My throat tightened, dry as dust. *Ashes of Eden* - the phrase Aconite had given me. Now, I feared it more than ever.

Malus rubbed his chin. 'We'll need time. To evacuate our wives . . . our children.' His voice was unsteady, showing a crack in his usual composure.

Murmurs rippled behind the screen, low and unsettling. Then the woman's voice cut through again, cold and calculated. 'And water vessels to transport breeders. Pick only the best . . . those with track records of producing more than one child at a time. It will take slaves to build a new world for our ruling class to govern.'

A male voice came next, mechanical in its tone. 'Remember we have cloning pods. These artificial wombs can enhance growth. Look at how successful we were with the other girl . . . Coral. These pods will prove useful, but they must be transported carefully.'

'Surely, there must be another way,' Malus argued, his voice shaking slightly. 'We've built so much . . . to just throw what we have away. Creating a new world will take decades. We can recover from this. Re-group, fight back.'

The voices came together as one, their reply chilling. 'Our decision is final. We end this world and start again.'

Malus paled, his lips barely moving as he whispered, 'How long do we have?'

The woman's reply came - cold, and final. 'That depends on how quickly we intend to erase the old one. Begin planning, and we'll let you know. If you're not ready by then . . . you'll die a painful death with the rest of the masses.'

The screen blinked out, plunging the chamber into an oppressive hush. Malus turned slowly, his eyes scanning the faces of his Council. They sat motionless, their spines rigid, fear on their faces. Their eyes - wide, glossy with rising panic - conveyed everything.

'You heard our masters,' Malus said, his voice strained. 'Begin the evacuation plans. Select only the most productive breeders - and enough guards to ensure order during transport.' He paused, allowing the seriousness of the situation to sink in. 'Return to your homes. Have your families ready to move. We no longer govern. We obey.'

I could hardly breathe. The air inside the shaft felt thinner, as if the declaration had sucked the oxygen from the world around us. I stared at Malus below - a man who, for all his power, looked suddenly small.

Chairs scraped back from the polished floor. They rose, moving stiffly, as if their bodies had aged in the space of a single command. No one met Malus's eyes as they filed out in grim procession.

One man stepped into place beside Malus, his voice dry. 'Do you wish me to record the pending genocide as the will of Pax for the indoctrination of future generations?' he asked.

Malus didn't spare him a glance. His gaze remained fixed ahead, cold and unreadable, as though the other man didn't even exist. 'Write what you must,' he said, his voice flat. 'As long as it fits into our masters' narrative.'

29

Z ander's hand gripped my arm. 'We need to move. Now.'

But I couldn't. My eyes stayed fixed on the room below, even though it offered nothing but symbols, empty and impersonal. The faceless voices behind it had already sealed our fate - cold as iron, sharp as frost. *Ashes of Eden.* It wasn't a code name. It wasn't a bluff. It was a purge. It was a weapon for genocide.

'They mean to wipe everything out and start again,' I whispered, my voice cracking. 'Reset the world . . . and rebuild.'

Zander leaned close. 'Then we burn this place first with them in it - before they evacuate to wherever it is they're going to go.'

Cooper crawled up beside me, his face a mask of stone. 'We need to find the chamber. The one where they're keeping it. If it's biological, it'll need containment.'

Zander pulled out his pocketknife and pried open the grill. We climbed out of the hole and dropped down, landing as quietly as we could.

Cooper pointed at the door. 'Stand guard,' he muttered.

Without waiting for a response, he and Zander moved to

inspect the room. None of us knew exactly what we were looking for. We were reaching, grasping at any clue, any scrap that might unravel the mystery or tell us what to do next.

'There's nothing here,' Cooper said, irritation creeping into his voice. 'Let's climb back up.' He gestured to the hole we'd dropped through. 'We'll stop at each gridded vent, assess the rooms, and if they're empty, we'll take a look. See if we can find anything useful.'

I nodded, feeling the familiar sensation of tension settling in my chest. The plan was simple, but it felt like another endless crawl through the dark, searching for a sliver of hope.

The crawl seemed longer this time. The metal beneath us shuddered, trembling with faint vibrations that carried up from the world below. We must have veered off course, because the path ahead led us to a fork. We turned left. The duct constricted again, the air growing thick as the walls pressed tighter around us. Zander reached the next grill and peered through. I slid up beside him, my heart pounding, each beat thudding in my ears.

We had the view of a sealed corridor stretching out before us - unlike any we'd passed before. On one side, thick glass partitions lined the walls, each one fogged from within, as if condensation distorted the shapes behind it. A technician in a white bio-suit moved behind the glass, their silhouette faint and blurred by the mist. Along the far wall, towering steel canisters loomed, massive and foreboding. They were connected to a network of pipes that snaked upward, disappearing into the ceiling like veins.

Zander exhaled slowly, his voice barely a whisper. 'I think we've found it.'

A screen near the centre of the room flickered casting an eerie red glow. Pulsating symbols flashed on the display - *Ashes of Eden*, followed by *status: secure*.

'Yes, this must be it,' I said, a cold wave of dread washing over me. 'It's definitely some kind of biological lab.'

'They could aerosol it,' Zander murmured, his eyes scanning the scene. 'Inject it into the ventilation systems, or disperse it across the islands. Or drones could carry it. The weather towers too.'

I pointed to another sign on the wall. 'Those symbols . . . they're for dreams. This must be where they are decoding our thoughts.'

'What the hell do we do now? Cooper asked. 'We can't risk blowing it up. We'll only release it quicker.'

They turned to me, wordless, expectant - their belief in me a pressure I could feel in my bones.

'We disable it,' I said, my voice calm. 'We find the override and shut it down before they have the chance to use it.'

Cooper hesitated, a flash of doubt crossing his face. 'None of us have a clue how to do that.'

I wasn't going to let that stop me. 'We go down there, get as much information as we can, and head back to the outpost. Cedar will know what to do.'

'What world are you living in, Jasmine?' Cooper asked. 'Those freaks behind the screen know we're hiding out in underground bunkers. It won't take long for them to find our position. We don't have time for Cedar to figure it out. We need scientists who know this stuff . . . people we don't have. We're goosed.'

I swallowed hard. 'We have to try. Zander said earlier that Saxon would never give up. He was your mentor too. We can do this.'

'Just so long as we're not walking into that misted lab,' Zander muttered, casting a wary glance at the men in the biosuits. 'I'm in no rush to be their next chemical test subject.'

'No, just in the space below,' I replied.

Once again, we slipped the grill and dropped down. I stood

watch again, every muscle tense. My eyes darted between the narrow hallway, and the glass room where the lab technicians worked. Zander moved quickly, emptying a bag filled with face masks, and began filling it with tablets and small electronic filing pens.

Cooper rifled through a small box with computer discs. 'These might hold information too,' he said, dumping the box in the bag. He took a final glance around. 'We need to head back to the fight. See how many of us are still standing.'

We climbed back into the ducts and pressed on, the bulge of the bag digging uncomfortably against my ribs. I could sense it - we were almost there. Then, in the distance, I caught the faint sound of energy weapons, followed by the constant crackle of laser fire. We quickened our crawl, drawn toward the pungent scent of scorched air and the metallic bite of an ongoing battle. The smell surged toward us, guiding our way.

Back in the factory room, the silence hit like a wall. Nothing had changed. The clothes still waited to be stitched, and our helmets sat untouched, exactly where we'd left them.

I grabbed mine, turning it over in my hands. 'There's something I can't shake,' I said. 'How did they know to open fire on us? We're dressed as guards - we should've passed unnoticed. So, how did they know we were the enemy?' I glanced up, the unease tightening in my chest. 'And Spruce said we'd lost ground, told us to pull back to the outpost. But according to what we heard back there, we were the ones winning. None of it adds up.'

Zander looked at me, his expression sceptical. 'Confusion is common in the midst of battle.'

A nervous tic tugged at Cooper's brow. 'It's possible they've been monitoring their own people, watching for anyone out of place. A uniform won't hide you if they've already pegged you as a threat.' He paused, eyes narrowing. 'And let's not forget - this isn't just any facility. It's a high-security capital city.'

I wasn't convinced. 'We need to stay alert. Something about today doesn't feel right. What if the detonators Jaz used on the vessel were tampered with? And the pier - whatever triggered that blast, it happened far too soon. None of it adds up.'

Zander sighed heavily. 'If there was a traitor within the Resistance, Malus would've discovered the outpost ages ago. Today went sideways - badly - but I don't buy that it's because we've got a mole among us.'

Cooper gave me a quick pat on the back. 'We'll piece it together later. Right now, if we don't move - we might not get the chance.'

We slammed on our helmets and moved quickly, weaving through ruined buildings with eyes sharp for danger. Soon, we stumbled into a firefight. Laser beams shot from the alley ahead, but they hadn't noticed us, focused instead on our fighters in the street further down.

We struck swiftly - Zander's clean shot dropped the first, Cooper took the second, and I finished the last before he could react. The bodies hit the ground lifeless. Nerves raw, we carried on.

The battle roared on, relentless - a cacophony of screams, laser fire, and the bone-jarring rumble of detonations. We fought through it all, step by step, until finally, the gunfire faded. One last echo . . . then eventually . . . silence.

A strange stillness fell over the city. We had regrouped, breathless and bloodied, throwing our arms around the fighters who remained. Helmets removed, our faces were smeared with ash, our eyes wide with relief. The government forces had vanished - retreated, fled into the smoke. Maybe to regroup. Maybe to smuggle Malus out before we could corner him. Either way, the city was ours - for now.

'How's Felix?' I asked, pulling myself free from Astrid and Minx's embrace.

Astrid's expression dimmed. 'Not good. We've made him

comfortable in one of our vehicles. He's holding on . . . but only just.'

I nodded grimly. 'We need to find Aspen. Malus has already slipped the net, so we don't have much time.'

Turning to Zander, I gestured towards the still-smoking streets. 'Take a few people with you - see if you can find where the citizens are holed up. We need to round them up, let them know it's safe now. Try to bring some kind of order for them.'

Zander raised an eyebrow. 'That's going to be a challenge. They're under the influence of Control. They won't trust us.'

'We have to try, but be careful,' I warned. 'We don't want citizens turning this into another fight. Show strength, but only use force if there's no other option.'

He gave a short nod before disappearing with a few of our men.

Cooper cracked his back with a groan, rolling his shoulders like he'd just shed a heavy load from his frame. 'I'll check for medical buildings. If Aspen's still in the city, that's where he'll be.'

Before I could respond, a shout called out – it was my name. My head snapped around, my heart leaping into my throat. I ran, my feet barely skimming the ground, and collided straight into his arms. Spindle caught me effortlessly, pulling me close. His breath was warm against my hair, his arms wrapped around me like a lifeline.

'You're safe. You made it,' I murmured.

Behind him, Ash ambled up, his trademark smirk tugging at the edge of his mouth. He threw his arms around both of us. 'Come on, Jasmine - did you really think we'd miss the action?'

30

The dust had finally settled, blanketing the city in a muted shroud that dulled the edges of its destruction. The once-mighty capital, proud and impenetrable, now lay gutted and broken. Streets were strewn with the wreckage of a battle hard-fought, with bodies left where they had fallen.

Guards, soldiers, our own freedom fighters - all tangled together in a grotesque tapestry of death. Blood pooled in gutters and soaked the cracked pavements, mixing with dirt to form a thick, rust-coloured sludge that clung to our boots like a second skin.

The silence was unnatural. No shouts, no laser fire, no cries of the wounded - just the wind, whistling through the remains of the city. It slipped through the jagged gaps in the shattered glass dome above, breaking the stillness with a lonely, ghostly moan. High above it, the sky was choked with smoke, the ash-thick air obscuring the harnessed sun. Its artificial glow, once a symbol of dominance and innovation, hid dimly behind a veil of grey.

Ash drifted through the air, coating every surface in a thin, suffocating layer of decay. It settled on broken windowsills,

helmets, and the faces of the dead. The stench of burning flesh
and melted circuitry hung in every breath - a nauseating
reminder of the cost. In the distance, government buildings -
once towers of strength and fear - had been reduced to jagged
ruins.

I couldn't help but feel a twisted sense of relief that the only
part of the city still standing was the Control rooms - now
abandoned. It was in this same block where we had uncovered
the lab holding its dark secret - *Ashes of Eden*. Nearby stood a
luxury compound, a stark contrast, where Malus and his inner
circle once resided in opulent apartments, hidden away from
the working citizens.

Tattered flags fluttered from bent poles, their colours faded
by fire and smoke. What had once been bold symbols of order
and control now hung limp and defeated, barely clinging to
their last threads. But . . . this victory felt like a lie.

We had won the ground beneath our feet, but at a stag-
gering price. Malus had escaped, slipping through the cracks.
Aspen was still missing. Felix was barely holding on. Orion and
Jaz were dead. And the bodies - so many of them - blurred the
lines between oppressed and oppressors. Death had rendered
them the same. No rank, no loyalty, no cause mattered in the
end. They were all still now - flesh and bone left to rot together
in the dust of a fallen empire.

It was too soon to call this triumph. The fight wasn't over.
Not really. The Keepers or Curators, whatever it was Aconite
had called them, still lurked in the shadows, their strings
tangled in the heart of whatever remained. If they had their
way, none of us would survive to see the world we were fighting
to build. The scars of what had come before ran deep, and the
road ahead lay steeped in uncertainty. For now, we were alive.
Just. But survival was not the same as victory. Not yet.

I walked through the wreckage with Spindle's hand clasped
tightly in mine. Neither of us spoke. The silence was heavy with

the weight of names we'd never say again - Orion - Jaz - friends, fighters, people we'd bled beside. Around us, the city moaned in its ruin, while the survivors moved like ghosts through the rubble. They gathered intel from the fractured remains of government buildings. We still had no way to stop the nightmare looming on the horizon. However, if we didn't act soon, everything we'd fought for would be undone in an instant.

Ash strolled over, dust in his hair, a tired slant to his grin. 'Zander found the citizens,' he said. 'They've been hiding in a large hall - reminds me of the Justice of Pax, only much bigger with more grandeur. I'd bet there are still some people scattered in buildings and dormitories. As the days pass and they're no longer fed Control, they might finally be willing to come out.'

'Thanks, Ash,' I said, managing a small smile. His news was a nugget of hope, and right now, that was pure gold.

'Jasmine' Minx's voice rang out across the rubble. She picked her way over with Astrid close behind. 'I think we've found Malus's private quarters. Looks like he left in a rush - papers, clothes, even food still there. Do you want to check it out before we move on?'

I glanced at Spindle, who gave a subtle nod, his grip on my hand tightening just a fraction. 'Yes,' I said, already turning towards her. 'Let's see what secrets he left behind.'

* * *

While the rest of the citizens were crammed into bare, windowless quarters, Malus had lived in opulence. His private apartment sprawled across the upper floor of a massive building, its floor-to-ceiling windows offering an unbroken view of the shattered capital below. Gold trims lined the walls, rich fabrics hung from the curtain rails, and crystal light fixtures dangled like icicles from the ceiling.

'His masters looked after him,' I muttered, lifting a bottle of scent from a polished table and holding it to my nose. The fragrance was fresh, clean. 'He lived like a king while everyone else was mere nobodies. I doubt even Aconite had a suite like this on Ruin.'

Spindle took the bottle from my hand and set it back down. 'We'll find him,' he said. 'I promise.'

A heavy thud echoed through the room as Astrid slammed her fist against a door stretching the length of one wall. 'This thing won't budge. Must be a storage unit or a secure room. Anyone see a key?'

I stepped closer, studying the sleek surface and the small panel embedded beside it. 'It won't be a key you need,' I said, pointing at the faint red glow of the keypad. 'That's a biometric lock. You'd need Malus's microchip to get in.'

Astrid swore under her breath, wiping a sleeve across her brow. 'There's got to be something important in there. He wouldn't go to all this trouble to lock up spare robes.'

'We need access,' I said, my eyes scanning the rest of the room. 'There could be files, plans, something on Ashes of Eden or the Archipelago Island. I'm guessing that's where the masters are and where Malus and the others are heading.'

'Check with Cooper,' Spindle said. 'He's still trying to get through to Spruce from one of the ops rooms. Most of their tech was fried or wiped clean before they fled, but he's working to salvage a signal. If he can reach the outpost, maybe Cedar can replicate a microchip for it.'

'Or,' Ash said, stepping forward, 'We can blow the damn thing open.'

'No,' I said, stepping between him and the door. 'If there's anything useful behind there, we need it intact.' I glanced back at the locked panel, a chill creeping down my spine.

An hour passed, until Cooper finally emerged, clutching a battered handheld monitor. The screen flickered to life as he handed it to me, revealing Spruce's face. His features looked strained.

'I've filled him in on everything we saw and heard,' Cooper said. He knows our situation.

'Our people are combing through old nautical charts, trying to pinpoint your island,' Spruce said.

I stared into his eyes through the monitor. They looked tired - older somehow.

'We've lost too many good women and men today,' I said, feeling a stab in my heart. 'We can't let their sacrifice be for nothing.'

'I agree,' Spruce replied, though his gaze faltered, dropping from mine.

Was that guilt I saw flash across his face - brief, but intense? I knew that look. Spruce had betrayed me before. 'We'll talk when I get back,' I said, trying to keep the coldness from my tone. 'Right now, I need Cedar. There's a door we need opened.'

A shuffle, a moment of static - and then Cedar's face appeared, his expression already calculating. 'Show me the lock.'

I tilted the monitor, angling it towards the control panel embedded in the steel door. 'Can you see it?'

He studied it, his eyes narrowing. 'It's sealed. Someone will need to strip back the casing so I can look at the wiring.'

Minx stepped forward. She snapped open her penknife and knelt beside the panel, her fingers moving quickly, the tiny screws hitting the floor. The cover dropped away, revealing the tangle of wires beneath.

Cedar let out a low whistle. 'This isn't just any lock. It's a custom insignia interface. Anyone can spoof a microchip, but this . . . this is bespoke. Designed to keep everyone out.'

Of course it was. Nothing about Malus was ever simple. 'Any suggestions,' I asked. 'I want to get in there before we head off.'

Cedar's brow furrowed. 'It's a biometric failsafe with an encrypted back-loop,' he muttered. 'That insignia's more than branding - it's a data signature embedded in a private circuit.'

I frowned. 'So, it's impossible?'

He didn't answer straight away. I could almost see his mind racing. Then his eyes lit with a spark of reckless brilliance.

'Alright,' he said. 'Here's what you need to do. You've got one shot, so listen closely. Find a heat source - something that can melt through the outer circuit board without frying the wiring beneath. A micro-flame, maybe a soldering arc. You're going to short the feedback loop manually and sever the ID reader.'

'That'll open it?' Zander asked.

'Not exactly,' Cedar replied. 'It'll confuse the system - make it think the door's under maintenance override. While it's blinking out, someone has to hold a copper surface -anything conductive - against the insignia itself. That should trick the relay into opening, just for a second.'

'A second?' I said.

Cedar looked directly into the camera. 'That's all you'll get. Get the timing wrong and you'll fry the lock and possibly the person holding the metal.'

'Brilliant,' Minx muttered, under her breath. 'Who's volunteering to maybe get electrocuted?'

I stepped forward. 'I'll do it.'

Because if anyone was going to take that risk, it had to be me.

31

Z ander crouched beside the wiring, eyes darting over the knot of cables and plastic. Then he straightened. 'There were Bunsen burners in the Ashes of Eden lab,' he said. 'Back down the corridor, two turns left. We can use one for the heat source - should be enough to breach the panel without setting the whole thing alight.'

Without waiting for a reply, he turned and sprinted out of the room. 'I'll be right back,' he called, after himself.

Spindle placed a hand on my shoulder. 'You can't be serious,' he said, his tone sharp enough to cut. 'Let me do it. I'll hold the damn plate - Ive go steadier hands.'

I shook my head. 'No. It has to be me.'

His hand dropped to my arm, he squeezed it hard. 'You're not invincible.'

'I never said I was,' I replied, my voice unwavering. 'But my job - my duty - is to keep the rest of you alive. And that means taking the risk when it counts.'

I didn't say the other truth - the one lodged like glass in my throat. That whatever was happening inside me, whatever damage had already begun . . . this might just be speeding things up. I couldn't be sure I had much time left anyway. At least this way, if I died, it would mean something.

Spindle stared at me, his jaw clenched, but he said nothing more. He just stepped back, his silence louder than any protest.

'I'm with Spindle on this,' Minx said, her voice filled with defiance. 'This isn't your decision to make alone, Jasmine. I'd rather be the one to do this.' She wiped her brow, as her gaze fixed on mine.

As I secured the makeshift copper plate in my palm - a battered strip Astrid had scavenged from the debris below - I said, 'I'll hear no more on it. My decision's made. If any of you can't stomach it, then go. Now.'

Then the monitor buzzed, loud and sudden, making me jolt. I turned, pulse racing, just as the screen shimmered to life. Spruce's face snapped into view, a little blurred, the signal glitching with static.

His eyes were wide, and when he spoke, his voice trembled with a strange fusion of excitement and dread. 'We've found something,' he said. 'An old maritime chart - pre-End of Days. Hand-drawn. It's faded, but intact. It shows a series of land-masses. What we thought was a single island might actually be a cluster of smaller islands, tight together beyond the Pewter Sea.' He paused, as if contemplating the risk of giving false hope. 'You can thank Robinia, as it was she who remembered something of it - down in our basement, hidden among archives.'

'That's good news,' I said, feeling a little warmth in my reply. 'Something positive at least.'

'There's no record of anyone ever sailing that far,' Spruce continued. 'Not that we know of anyway. It could be a myth. But it's the first lead we've had that wasn't steeped in mere specula-tion. Juniper's monitoring the sea from Ruin. He's got drones sweeping the waters, scanning for movement - anything that breaks the monotony out there. If they start to manoeuvre, he'll be watching for them.'

A cluster of islands lost to time. A dying planet. A locked door between us and the next move. And to top it all, I was about to burn my way through it. No wonder the pounding at my temple began.

I closed my eyes for a moment, trying to choke back the wave of nausea twisting in my gut. The world tilted slightly, the floor no longer solid beneath me. When I opened them again, the face on the screen looked like that of a stranger. My grip on the monitor tightened, my breath caught. I must've looked shaken.

'Are you okay?' the man asked, his voice coming through the static.

I glanced up, my eyes scanning the room. It felt unfamiliar - alien, almost. The walls blurred, the faces around me faded in and out like half-remembered dreams. *Where was I? Who were these people?*

Her voice cut through the haze - soft, steady. It belonged to a woman with skin as dark as the night sky and eyes that sparkled like black pearls. She rested a hand lightly on my elbow. 'Jasmine . . . what's wrong?'

Jasmine. The name stirred something deep. I blinked, planting my feet hard against the floor, as if sheer will could anchor me. I looked up again - into a pair of blue eyes that sliced through the fog. Eyes that knew me. Spindle.

'Spindle,' I said, the tension slipping from my shoulders. 'Sorry.'

I rubbed my forehead, memories slipping back into place like a puzzle piece nudged home. 'I was . . . I was lost in thought. Trying to make sense of something that doesn't quite fit.'

I turned back to the screen. 'Sorry, Spruce - what were you saying?'

'That Juniper has eyes on the sea,' he said. 'If anything moves out there - anything at all - we'll know.'

I leaned toward the monitor. 'Did Robinia come across anything . . . anything about a tower? One that nearly reaches the sky?'

Spruce's brow furrowed. He glanced sideways, speaking to someone offscreen, then turned back. 'She did mention something,' he said, as he contemplated her findings. 'An old reference buried in one of the texts. A structure - massive, and unnatural. She's questioning Aconite at the minute. I'll have her look into it further when she's finished with him.'

Zander returned at a run, the Bunsen burner clutched in one hand, a battered gas canister in the other. He skidded to a stop beside me, breathless, and dropped to his knees. 'This was the only one left intact. Let's pray it holds.'

Minx crouched by the panel, her hands trembling ever so slightly as she wired the burner into place. A metallic snap rang out, then the burner hissed, the flame sparking to life -blue, volatile, and crackling with menace.

Spindle stood back, his jaw clenched tight. 'Careful,' he muttered, his voice rough, barely hiding the fear gnawing at all of us. His eyes met mine, holding a silent warning.

Minx hunched closer to the exposed wiring, the heat from the flame painting sweat across her brow. 'Cedar reckons we've got five millimetres before the core fries and everything goes up,' she said grimly. 'No pressure, then.'

None of us breathed. One slip, one flick of the wrist too far, and the whole plan - including me - could burn.

The burner flared as it kissed the metal, the casing beginning to blister and curl back like old skin. A sharp chemical stink hit my nose - burning insulation, scorched alloy - a foul mix that clawed at the back of my throat. I gritted my teeth and held the copper plate tighter, the serrated edge cutting into my palm. Spindle hovered close, tense, ready to haul me back if something went wrong - though we both knew he'd never reach me in time. If this blew, there'd be nothing left of me to save.

'Almost through,' Minx said, as her eyes narrowed. 'When I say go, press the plate flat to the insignia and don't flinch.'

The moment came fast. 'Now.'

I slammed the copper down. Sparks leapt from the contact point, a shrill whine rose from the circuitry, and the door vibrated violently. My muscles locked against the current jolting through the plate - my teeth clenched, vision tunnelling, pain threading through every nerve like fire. Then - clunk.

The door gave a mechanical groan, and with a final jolt, it lurched open an inch. Minx lunged forward, jamming her shoulder into the gap. 'It's open. Help me before it shuts tight again.'

Spindle held me while Zander and Ash jumped in, forcing the steel slab aside as smoke hissed from the edges. The corridor beyond yawned into blackness - uncharted, foreboding. We'd made it through.

Astrid reached into the darkness, her fingers brushing along the wall until they found a switch. With a soft click, a single bulb sputtered to life overhead - then another, and another, until a cascade of lights burst down the length of a long corridor like falling dominoes, bathing everything in a cold, bare glow.

The hallway stretched ahead, unnaturally long, lined with tall, ornate wooden stands - rich mahogany polished to a mirror sheen. Each pedestal was crowned with a glass casing that warped the shapes within - shapes I prayed, for one breathless second, weren't real. But they were. Inside each case, grotesquely preserved, sat a human head.

Some rested in unnatural stillness, eyes closed as if sleeping. Others stared wide-eyed locked forever in the last moment they'd known. And some . . . some wore expressions twisted by agony, mouths frozen mid-scream, skin drawn tight over bone. The horror of their final seconds captured like a monstrous work of art, their pain preserved. They were displayed as if it meant something - a warning, or maybe just madness given form.

We moved quietly through them, each footstep a whisper over the floor, our breathing shallow, our hearts thundering. The dead watched us as we passed - dozens of them, maybe hundreds. They watched without seeing. And still . . . it felt like they saw.

I stopped walking. The ground shifting under my feet. My lungs refused to draw in air. There, in the third row from the left, was Aspen. His lips were parted slightly, as if he'd been about to speak. His eyes - those familiar, laughing eyes - were open, glassy, and devoid of life. They stared straight ahead, straight through me, and I felt something in my chest splinter. I staggered.

Spindle caught me before I hit the ground. I didn't fight him. I just stared - hollow, weightless. Aspen. Gone. Not hidden, not buried, but displayed like some twisted trophy. My mind recoiled, but my body stayed still, frozen by the brutal clarity of it. Malus hadn't just killed him. He'd made sure we would carry the sight forever, a scar burned into the part of us that still believed in hope.

32

The road back was longer than I remembered. Every bump in the cracked earth jarred through the vehicle, but none of us flinched. We sat, sinking in a tide of grief. Dust seeped through a damaged vent, turning the air thick and grainy, coating our tongues and lungs. Whether it was the dust or the sorrow that made it so hard to breathe, I couldn't tell.

Felix lay across the long plastic seat, his head cradled in my lap. I stroked his brow with trembling fingers, each touch a silent plea. *Stay with me . . . please.* His skin burned, shiny with fever, his breathing thinning to rattling gasps. I'd heard that sound before, when Saxon slipped away, and it haunted me still. That uneven, brittle breath that told you the body was already letting go.

Something had gone terribly wrong. Aspen hadn't just vanished - he'd been taken. Malus must've discovered the truth, uncovered the fine web Aspen had spun within the system. But how? What slip, what glance, what word had betrayed him? I gritted my teeth, willing myself to hold on, to not break. My heart was cracking beneath the thought of it, but I couldn't cry.

I wouldn't. Because if I let even a single tear fall, the dam would shatter - and I feared the flood might drown me.

How was I supposed to face Robinia? She never said it outright, but I'd seen it - that hint of something meaningful when she looked at Aspen. Back on Ruin, when Coral and I were made to stand trial in the Justice of Pax, Robinia's mask had slipped for just a second. The way her gaze lingered on him - and the way he returned it.

Now, he was another name on the ever-growing list of those we couldn't save. We'd lost so much - too much - and for what? The antidote was now out of reach. Control still gripped the masses like a noose for now, and Aspen, who might've cured it completely, was dead. Not that any of it would matter, if Ashes of Eden were to be released.

The thought sent a shiver racing through me. I glanced around at the others - Larch, Zander, Minx - all locked in their own thoughts. We were returning . . . but not victorious. Not whole.

The capital had fallen, yes. Malus's regime had been fractured - but not broken. Because behind him, above him, the true masters of this rotted world were preparing to strike back. Their power lay not in public speeches or armed patrols, but in silence. In secret. How much time did we have left?

* * *

I stormed into Aconite's cell the moment I returned. Rage soared through me, wild and unrelenting, hotter than it had ever burned before. Aconite sat in the corner, calm, almost expectant - like he'd been waiting for the storm.

I didn't hold back. My voice thundered through the room. 'I hate all of you. You and your masters.' I pointed a shaking finger at him, close enough to strike, close enough to feel the heat of my own fury rising between us. 'All of you . . . sick twisted monsters.'

He didn't flinch. That only made it worse. Fury boiled over. Nails dug deep into my palms, fists trembling with the need to strike. Instead, I turned and drove my knuckles into the wall, the crack of bone on stone was savage. The pain came fast - real, but not enough.

It took everything I had not to cross the line. Not to wrap my hands around his throat and squeeze until every lie, every sin he'd ever committed was choked out of him. But I didn't. I wouldn't. Because that's what *they* wanted. That's what they were - monsters who tortured and destroyed and justified it all in the name of power. If I gave in, even for a second, then they'd win. They'd make me one of them. And I refused to let that happen.

'Jasmine.' Spindle's voice was grounding as he stepped into the room, gathering me gently into his arms. His embrace strengthened my quivering frame, his tone calm, coaxing. 'This isn't helping. Come on, let's get you some rest.'

I let him lead me out, anger still burning low beneath the surface. But before the door closed behind us, Aconite's voice cut through - mocking.

'I warned you - I told you - you'd never win.'

* * *

Outside, Cooper stood waiting, his face pale and drawn. 'I've given Robinia the bag we took from the lab.'

'Thank you,' I said, a sigh escaping me. 'I don't know if we'll have the time to study it in any depth.'

'Time is running out,' Cooper said, his voice faint, 'I want your permission to return to the caves. Freya and Nova are buried there, and I think Orion should rest with them too.

They're my family, Jasmine. When the end comes, I want to be with them. It's where I belong.'

Hearing him say this made my heart sink. I had already surrendered to the idea of losing, but I never imagined Cooper would too. His quiet resignation struck something deep inside me. I reached up and touched his cheek. 'You have my blessing,' I said, feeling I owed him more than words. 'And when you see them in the afterlife . . . give them my love.'

Cooper's gaze locked with mine. 'We'll all meet again in the afterlife. We'll all be together.'

I shook my head, unable to speak.

Robinia's voice broke through the moment, as she stepped into view. 'I've found information on your tower.' Her expression was unreadable. 'But I'm only going to tell you once you've rested.'

Not waiting for my reply, she turned to Spindle. 'Make sure she sleeps for a few hours. Then I'll meet with her. No sooner. It will give me time to sift through what was brought back.'

I leaned against Spindle as we made our way towards my suite. 'She must hate me . . . because of what happened to.' I couldn't finish - couldn't say his name without it splintering inside me. 'I can't imagine how I'd feel if I lost you.'

Spindle pressed a kiss to the top of my head, his arm firm around my shoulders. 'Aspen wasn't your fault - and I promise, you'll never lose me.'

'I need to go to the medical bay . . . I need to check on Felix.'

He stopped, turning me gently towards him. 'The medics are with him. They know what they're doing. You need to rest. Felix would want you strong - ready to fight when he's well enough to join you.'

I nodded, though my heart dragged me in the opposite direction. It would be a miracle if Felix lived . . . I wasn't foolish enough to think otherwise.

* * *

Spindle lay beside me, his body curled protectively around mine, the warmth of his breath brushing against the nape of my neck. His arms, strong and sure, wrapped me in a cocoon of love that held the world at bay. I let myself give in, surrendering to the pull of sleep.

Nightmares loomed in the sidelines, waiting to drive me insane - but I refused to let them play. I willed my mind into a void, a place of utter blackness where nothing could reach me. Not fear. Not grief. Not even memory. Just stillness.

* * *

Spindle woke me gently, pulling me up and placing a cup of herbal tea in my hands. The steam curled up in faint wisps. 'I wish we had more time,' I said.

'I wish for that too,' he replied, sitting beside me. 'Time for just the two of us'

I looked down at the tea, cradling the warmth, then let out a long, slow sigh. 'Empty. That's how I feel . . . a vast emptiness.'

He reached for my chin, tilting it up until our eyes met. His gaze held that same fierce tenderness I'd come to know. 'This isn't the Jasmine I know and love,' he said, a half-smile teasing his lips. 'The wild rebel of a girl from Ruin who never backed down, no matter what. Come on - drink up. We've got a world to save.'

The world, with all its demands and urgencies, seemed so far away, insignificant against the crushing pain behind my eyes. I couldn't bring myself to care. 'Give me a minute,' I said, feeling my head spin.' More than anything I wanted to creep back under the covers on my bed.

'Don't take too long. We need you.'

Every muscle in my body ached. It was as if it were

preparing for its inevitable collapse. Each breath felt like a battle, the rising panic tearing at my chest. I squeezed my eyes shut, forcing myself to inhale deeply, to push back against the tide of fear and exhaustion.

I made myself a promise in the silence. My voice a whisper in the back of my mind - even if my body shattered, even if my mind splintered beyond repair, I would drag myself through the ruins of this broken world. I would find Malus and his masters, no matter the cost, and I would bring them down. I had to. There was nothing else left.

33

I'd help myself together through sheer force of will, barely managing to stay upright. The suite pressed in from all sides, every corner heavy with Aspen's absence. His presence haunted the room - not in sound our sight, but in the silence he left behind. Grief tore through my heart spurring me to keep going - I had to - anything to keep me from drowning in it.

Spindle left to fetch Robinia, pausing only to squeeze my hand. His eyes lingered - tender, anxious - knowing I was on the edge. I felt it too. But this wasn't the moment to fall apart. Not yet.

I stood by the table, fists clenched at my sides, trying to steady my breath. The guilt consumed me, carrying the knowledge of everything I hadn't said, and everything I hadn't done. What kind of leader was I? When Robinia finally opened the door, her presence spoke volumes.

'Thanks for coming to me,' I said, feeling like a coward - hiding while the others carried on. 'I can't face them in the Operations Room. Not yet. I just need . . . I need some time.'

'I understand,' Robinia murmured, clutching a bound file. 'It's been a tragic loss for all of us.'

I caught the glisten in her eyes before she blinked it away, but the sadness clung to her face. In that unguarded moment, her grief mirrored my own. 'I can't imagine how you feel right now.'

'Don't,' she said, a little too sharply, the crack in her voice revealing the effort it took for her to stay composed. 'We can't afford to waste time grieving. There's too much at stake. We'll deal with our broken hearts later.'

I gave myself a mental shake. 'You said you had information.'

A shadow crossed over her features. 'I've been digging into the Archipelago islands. I found reference to a large tower which could be the one Aconite mentioned. It's said to reach the sky, piercing through the clouds like some forgotten relic. I think it's where those before us studied the sun - where the scientists from the old world charted its movements and sought for ways to harness its power. There could be data there. If we can find these islands, we might uncover something vital. Maybe . . . just maybe, there's a way to unharness the sun without ever stepping foot near the reactors sealed chamber.'

'Where do we even start to look for these islands?' I asked, desperate for answers. 'We're running out of time.' I gulped hard, forcing down a sob. 'I'm at a loss as to what to do next.' The words barely scraped out. I didn't dare admit what truly terrified me - that seeing Aspen's head trapped in that glass cage had shaken something loose inside me. I would never be cured of my condition.

'Juniper's scanning the waters with drones from Ruin,' Robinia said, doing her best to muster some hope. 'If anything stirs - large vessels, sailing craft - we'll catch it. With luck, we can track their course long enough to get a reading. Once we have a trail, we'll send our own ships after them, follow them on radar to where they go. It's a long shot,' she added, her jaw tightening, 'But it's better than standing still and waiting for the world to burn.'

Still, I couldn't summon even a spark of hope. I just wanted it all to end. 'Don't any of you get it?' I said, the words tasting bitter in my mouth. 'Ashes of Eden will be released any day now - and when it is, that'll be it.'

'While you were gone,' Robinia said, looking at the file on the desk, 'I spoke with Hemlock a few times. He told me he was relieved we didn't send him back under Malus's charge. He's consumed by guilt at what went on at Omen's Keep. He's more or less free of Control now - thinking for himself again.' She hesitated, as if weighing the risk. 'Why don't we speak to him? See if he knows anything about the islands, the tower . . . even this chemical weapon. It might be a dead end, but right now we can't afford to overlook anything.'

'It might be worth a shot,' I said, unwilling to let hope creep in too easily. We had been burned too many times before, chasing scraps that crumbled in our hands. Disappointment had settled over me so many times and I wasn't sure if I could survive it peeling away again.

Robinia smiled, a flash of relief crossing her face. 'Good. If you head for the Operations Room and see what's happening, I'll sort out a calm space for us to speak with him. Somewhere away from the tension of his cell.' She touched my arm lightly. 'If Hemlock's willing to help, we need to give him every reason to trust us.'

* * *

The room Robinia had chosen was small but welcoming, a stark contrast to the sterile cell Hemlock had been trapped in for so long. A small sofa sat in the centre, its cushions plump but sagging slightly, looked as if it had known better days. Two armchairs bordered it, their fabric worn but clean, angled inwards to make the space feel homely.

Robinia placed a glass of water in Hemlock's hands. 'Are you sure I can't fetch some herbal tea?'

He took a sip. 'No, water is fine, thank you.'

Hemlock looked shattered. The glass shook in his hands. 'Please, don't send me back,' he blurted, his voice hoarse. 'I'd rather stay and fight here with you lot ... than keep doing what they forced me to do.' His words spilled out in a rush, too fast, as if he feared he wouldn't be given the chance to finish them.

'It's okay,' I said, dropping into the armchair opposite him. 'You're not going anywhere. But we don't have much time. I need you to be honest with me, Hemlock. No messing around.' I leant forward slightly, trying to meet his darting gaze. 'If you can help us, it'll go a long way towards making up for some of the wrongs you committed.'

As soon as the words left me, regret prickled in my chest. It wasn't fair to lay blame at his feet. Not really. Hemlock had been drugged, his mind and emotions stripped away by Control until he was nothing more than an empty vessel, carrying out orders without choice. Like so many others, he hadn't truly lived the wrongs he'd been forced to commit.

He nodded quickly, almost frantically, the glass sloshing water onto his hand. 'What do you need from me?' he asked, ready to grasp whatever thread of purpose we could offer him.

'What do you know about a biological weapon called Ashes of Eden?' I asked, hoping knew something, desperate he could help.

Hemlock stiffened, his gaze darting between Robinia and me, a burst of uncertainty crossing his face. 'I've never heard of it ... honestly.'

'Do you know anything about a project called Star in a Jar?' I asked, hoping to pull something, anything from him.

Robinia, pulled out the familiar file from her bag - the same one she'd brought to my suite earlier. 'That was the name the ordinary people gave it,' she said, cutting in. 'The scientific name is Solar Ignition Amplification Junction.' She handed the file to Hemlock. 'Here, have a look.'

He took the binder from her, flipping it open, his eyes scanning the first page. His brow furrowed, his lips pressing into a thin line as he absorbed the information. Minutes passed.

Finally, I broke the quiet, my patience waining. 'Have you ever heard of a group of islands called the Archipelago?' I asked, watching him closely.

'No. This is all new to me.' Hemlock's voice was laced with confusion, his features contorting as he tried to process the information. 'The schematics of this machine . . . they're ancient. Is this what you're calling Ashes of Eden?'

Robinia clasped her hands on her lap, as her gaze fell to the file. 'What you're looking at,' she said, 'Is a reactor that was used to try and harness the sun. There was a nuclear explosion which brought about the End of Days.'

Hemlock shook his head. 'No . . . that's not true . . . it was the Goddess Pax. She was angry and took revenge on mankind. '

'Think logically.' I argued. 'We were all fed the same lie, generation after generation, to justify their war and to keep us all in line. We believe that Ashes of Eden is a biological weapon or something that will bring about the end of humanity once again. They'll rebuild - and perhaps use the same lie, that it was an angry Goddess. Perhaps they may even invent a different one.' My words hung heavy between us all.

Hemlock blinked, his eyes wide, his mouth opening and closing as though searching for the right thing to say. 'You found this in a lab in the capital?'

'Ashes of Eden . . . yes. But not the reactor you're looking at. That's hidden in an underground labyrinth, buried beneath what used to be the great Salt Flats. I had hoped to access it, to see if there's any way to reverse the damage to the Sun. But the radiation levels down there remain extremely toxic.'

'What has this to do with the islands you asked about?' Hemlock asked. 'I'm guessing you think there is a connection between all three.'

'There might be,' Robinia said. 'The notes mention a colossal tower, thousands of miles from the reactor site. But much o our history has been rewritten. We were taught there was only one mainland and a few scattered islands. That, too, was a lie.' She let the words hang before continuing. 'There are other islands - hidden from us. And on them lives an elite class, above even Malus. The true masters. Their ancestors built the reactor and the tower - one to harness the sun's energy, the other to control it. But it's only a theory. We need an expert to be sure.'

Hemlock's attention drifted back to the file. He flicked through the pages, scanning the information. 'I would need more time to study this properly.'

'We have brought some computerised files back from the capital too, relating to the Ashes of Eden,' I said. 'Robinia has them, but I'm happy for her to share everything she has with you.'

His gaze snapped to mine. 'If you'll allow it, I'd also like to examine the laboratory in the capital. Perhaps I can be of use there too.'

His words were like magic, lifting the veil of darkness that had smothered the hope inside me. I allowed myself to smile. To breathe. 'Hemlock, I thought you'd never ask.'

34

I leaned against Spruce's desk, keeping my voice casual. 'Bracken's finally making headway,' I said, letting the lie slip out.

Spruce blinked, caught off guard. 'Who?'

'Bracken. One of the scientists from Omen's Keep.'

'I've not heard you mention him. Why? What's he working on?'

'He's cracked part of the Ashes of Eden project - something that could tear Malus's operations apart. Sorry, I thought Robinia would have told you. I guess we've all been so busy and lost in what's been happening.' I watched him closely, waiting for his reaction.

Did I catch a flicker of something behind his eyes? Something calculating? Or was I just seeing what I wanted to see?

Ash entered, his face lighting up with relief when he saw me. 'Good to see you on your feet,' he said. 'You had us all worried. Spindle's busy organising the transport you asked for. He should be along any minute.'

'Where are you going?' Spruce asked, before I could reply to Ash.

I could sense his unease, the frustration simmering beneath his calm. 'I'm heading back to the capital and will visit some of the other settlements too. I need to check on the citizens - see how they're coping. We left some of our fighters behind to help organise, to bury the dead, and to help rebuild. I'd like to check on their progress.'

'Cooper's gone,' Spruce said. 'I'm not sure if he told you, but he's gone back to the caves to bury Orion next to Freya and Nova. I don't think he'll be back. But . . . we can't just disappear when we all feel like it.'

'I gave Cooper my blessing,' I said, trying not to snap. 'Do you really think he'd have left without telling me?'

Spruce hesitated. 'Do you think it's wise for you to leave now, with Malus out there? We don't know where he's gone. Like we were to him, he's a ghost now. Vanished into the shadows.'

'I know where he's headed. Just keep Juniper's drones locked on the Pewter Sea. He'll surface eventually.'

'But by then it'll be too late. Ashes of Eden will be released while he flees to safety.'

'Do we know that for sure, Spruce?' I shot back. 'Since when did you become an expert on Malus's tactics?'

'What's going on with you?' His eyes narrowed. 'You seem a bit . . . off.'

I placed a hand on his shoulder, my voice softening. 'After everything we've been through - the losses, Jaz, Orion, Aspen, and many good young men and women. I guess it's catching up with me. But I'll be fine. Don't you worry.'

Spindle entered the Operations Room, his gaze landing on Spruce. 'It's okay,' he said, clearly having caught the tail end of our conversation. 'I'll stay with her. Ash, Zander, Minx and Astrid will too. A true leader should check on her people.'

'I'll be right there,' I said, grateful for his support. 'I just need to head to the medical bay, to see Felix. Coral's taking it in turns with Robinia to sit with him. I need to confirm with them that they know to contact me the minute he wakes.'

* * *

Once again, we hurtled towards the capital, confined in yet another speeding vehicle. Hemlock barely looked up, absorbed in the tablet Robinia had handed him. He muttered the entire way - focused on copper wires coiled around the reactor.

He marvelled at the placement of each screw anchoring the framework, at the basic switches feeding into a hidden lattice of control. His gaze lingered on the power relays, the coolant pipes, and unique circuits. To Hemlock, every component stitched itself into a machine that was ancient . . . yet fascinating.

* * *

We left him to it, granting full access to the lab and the captive scientists now at our disposal. Spindle, Ash, and I wove our way through the gutted remains of the city, its bones laid bare.

'What's really going on, Jasmine?' Spindle asked. 'You're up to something - I can see it. But you're keeping it to yourself.'

For a heartbeat, I nearly confessed. But the truth snagged in my throat. 'Everything's fine,' I said, hating the fact it was a lie. 'Let's just get through today. We'll deal with the rest later.'

He let it go, but mistrust etched itself across his face.

* * *

We spent the day tending to he wreckage of lives, handing out supplies to dazed citizens who wandered the ruins in silence. Their faces blurred into one - empty, stunned, hollowed by a grief they hadn't yet named. The world had collapsed beneath them, and even with Control still clouding their minds, some part of them seemed to know - nothing would ever be the same.

The city lay scoured for any trace of Malus - any shadow, any whisper of where he might've slipped through. Our efforts yielded nothing. The sun bled into the shattered skyline as the radio screamed to life.

'It's just as you feared, Jasmine,' Coral's voice crackled through. 'Robinia and I have contained a situation for now. I don't want to say too much – but you'll be able to deal with it the moment you're back.' Then silence.

We returned to the lab. Hemlock was hunched over a desk, lit by the stark glare of a lamp. His eyes, locked to the microscope, didn't shift when we entered. He adjusted the lens and sighed.

'What did you find?' I asked, trying - and failing - to keep the desperation from my tone.

He didn't answer straight away. Then, at last, he leaned back on his stool, his expression grim. 'You were right,' he said, his tone professional, masking any fear he might hold. 'It's lethal. If this is unleashed it won't just kill - it'll decimate. The Earth itself - what little we've managed to salvage - won't survive another strike like this.' His voice cracked. 'This isn't just about wiping out a species. It's about pushing the planet past its breaking point. Generations will suffer. And they might never come back from it. Perhaps the true masters have other islands where they believe they will be immune to the fallout. But this bioweapon won't stop at borders or bunkers. It could reach them - even where they think they're safe. They haven't truly understood what they wish to unleash.'

I'd known devastating news was coming, had braced for it. But his words still hit me hard. We weren't just trying to stop a disaster. We were fighting to keep humanity from becoming its own executioner. My consolation was that when the elite decided to bring about our end, at least they'd be dragged into the abyss with the rest of us. That was the only justice left.

I stepped back, my thoughts spiralling with the weight of it all. 'And Malus?' I asked, shuddering at the sound of his name. 'Where's he hiding? We need him in custody. If there's even a chance he knows how to stop this, we have to track him down. Fast. Maybe if he realises he's going down with the rest of us, he won't be so eager to let it happen.'

* * *

We made our way back to the outpost, the high wind kicking up a storm of dust.

'I need more time with the reactor schematics,' Hemlock said, still focusing on the files. 'The fragments of intel - we're only seeing part of the picture. But I'm with Robinia on this - there has to be a link between the reactor and the tower.'

I glanced at Spindle. Then the others. My friends. My circle. 'No one speaks of this,' I said. My voice came out harder than I meant it to. 'Not to Spruce. Not to Cedar. Not even Larch. Hemlock's work stays between us. No leaks. No questions.'

Zander tilted his head, eyes narrowing. 'You really think there's a traitor among us?'

'I know there is,' I replied, without hesitation.

Ash's jaw clenched. 'You're not accusing my father.' It wasn't a question. It was a warning.

'No,' I said, too fast. 'I don't suspect Larch. He's one of the few I'd bet my life on.'

I didn't say what I was thinking - that these days, even trust felt like a trap. What was happening to me? Was paranoia part of the condition that was killing me? 'I just need Larch and Cedar focused,' I added, forcing the doubt down, shoving it deep. 'If they catch wind of Hemlock's work, they might focus too much on what he's doing and not what I ask of them.'

'Why? What is it you're asking of Hemlock that's so secretive,' Ash asked.

'I can't say right now, but I have a hunch about something. If I'm right,' I looked at all of them in turn. 'You'll all be the first to know.'

Spindle frowned, returning the subject back to my accusations of a traitor. 'You think it's Spruce, then?'

Silence fell among us.

'But if it is,' Spindle said at last. 'Why haven't they moved against us? If Malus has someone inside . . . why are we still breathing? Think about what you're saying, because it doesn't make any sense.'

'Because the most dangerous enemies don't strike head-on,' I said, meeting his gaze. 'They smile. They wait. They let you believe you've won - until it's too late to fight back.'

I rubbed a hand over my face, the tears I held back stinging my eyes. And for one awful moment, a colder thought took hold . . . was it Spruce? Or was it me - so hollowed out by fear, I was seeing knives in every hand?

* * *

I headed to my suite when we returned, needing a moment to freshen up after our intense journey.

Spindle fell into step beside me. 'Why all the secrecy, Jasmine?' he asked

I hesitated, the words pressing heavy against my ribs. 'Do you trust me?'

'What kind of question is that? Of course I do,' he said, but there was a tension in his voice - a slight note that told me he sensed the gap between us. He knew I was holding something back.

I slowed, pulling in a breath. 'It's just . . . every time I speak my fears aloud, they're waved away. Brushed off as paranoia. As if questioning Spruce somehow makes me disloyal. I can't risk that. Not this time.' I paused, searching for the right words to have him on my side. 'I need proof. Real proof. Something no one can deny or twist.'

I looked over at him, met his eyes. 'And I think . . . I think I might have it now. Just give me a little more time. Enough time to speak with Coral and Robinia.'

He looked at me, and I could see it on his face - it was trust.

35

The corridor outside the cell block was brightly lit. Beyond the reinforced doors, our hostages stirred restlessly - some muttering, others staring blankly at the walls, as if waiting for fate to remember them.

I paused at the junction where a small, secure side room branched off from the corridor. Robinia and Coral were already inside.

Robinia glanced up from the tablet she held, her expression composed, though I could see the strain carved into the corners of her eye.

'How's Felix?' I asked. It was the first thing I needed to know - the rest could wait.

Coral shook her head gently. 'Still hasn't woken since the surgery. The medic says he's stable, and every precaution's being taken, but . . . he's not out of the woods yet.'

Pressing my palms against the wall, I shook off a slight dizziness and drew in a deep breath. 'Alright. Now tell me - what happened after I fed Bracken's name to Spruce?'

'Are you okay?' Coral asked, concern flitting across her face.

'I'm fine.'

Robinia's eyes darted from Coral to me. 'Spruce acted quickly. He made enquiries about which cell Bracken was held in. Claimed it was routine - and wanted to personally oversee his interrogation.'

'Did anyone challenge him . . . or wonder why this hostage was to be questioned?' I asked.

'Not outwardly,' she replied. 'But I asked Cedar to log the time-stamps.' She held up the monitor. 'There all here. Later that evening, one of Spruce's low-level operatives, Fern, entered Bracken's cell. However, we had already moved Bracken to a different room.'

Coral picked up the story. 'Fern had something in her hand - a syringe. Our medics ran tests on it. It contained a serum with a very specific compound - designed to mimic a heart attack. It's quick, clean, and nearly undetectable unless you're looking for it.'

'So, we would have had a silent execution had she gotten away with it,' I said, more to myself than them. My voice hardened. 'And where is Fern now?'

'We isolated her straight away,' Coral said. 'She's in a holding cell, with a guard posted outside.'

'Alright then . . . let's pay her a visit. See what she's got to say for herself.'

The three of us made our way out into the corridor, heading for Fern's cell. The guard standing watch gave a brief nod and stepped aside without a word. Robinia held up the key card to the lock. With a slow creak, the heavy door swung open, and I slipped inside.

Fern sat slumped against the far wall, her knees drawn to her chest, one trembling hand hovering at her mouth. She looked up, her terror filled eyes locking with mine. Raw, unmistakable terror. Then, without any warning, she popped something into her mouth and bit down hard.

I lunged forward - but it was too late. Her body jerked

violently, before she collapsed sideways onto the floor. A thin trail of foam bubbled at the corner of her mouth.

Coral and Robinia darted across the threshold. They dropped to their knees beside the body, Robinia pressing her fingers to Fern's neck, and then to her wrist. Nothing.

'Cyanide,' Robinia muttered. 'She's gone. Sorry - I never even thought to check. I know we all carry it when we're out, in the event the enemy catches us. But I never for a moment thought any of the operatives would have it here, in the outpost.'

My stomach turned. Resistance soldiers were issued a pill - one final escape if capture seemed inevitable. But she wasn't captured. She was one of ours. Questioned, and contained. Protected. And still - she'd rather die than talk to me.

I clenched my fists, taking one last look at Fern's body. Her features were twisted. Lips tinged blue, eyes wide in frozen horror. There was no calm, no pace. Only the grim finality of pain and panic. Another name to add to the list of the dead.

* * *

I slid the door open with all the force I could muster, storming into the Operations Room. 'You murdered Fern. Your own operative. How could you?' I said, my voice trembling with a fury I could barely contain. The words felt like they'd been building up inside me for days, but now they were out and there was no taking them back.

I balled my hands, knuckles white, and held them firm against my thighs, forcing myself to stay grounded. If I let the anger take over now, I wouldn't be able to stop. The room fell silent Everyone froze - as if time itself had been suspended – all eyes fixed on me and Spruce.

His brow furrowed, a flicker of uncertainty crossing his face.

'What are you going on about?' he asked, his voice laced with confusion. It wasn't performative - not entirely. There was a crack in his composure now, a tremor beneath the usual veneer of control. He genuinely didn't know which thread I was about to pull - or how much of the truth I'd already unravelled.

My chest tightened, each breath shallow and strained. A sudden throb flared at my temple, sharp enough to make me flinch.

Spruce stared at me like I'd lost my mind, his eyes narrowing, disbelief and irritation flitting over his face as his mouth twitched. It was as if he was forming words he couldn't quite bring himself to say.

'You ordered Fern to take her own life if she was caught doing your dirty work,' I said, each word cutting sharper than the last. 'She was caught in Bracken's cell, with the clear intention of ending his life. That wasn't a coincidence. You must have ordered the hit.'

A trickle of blood slid from my nose. I wiped it away with the back of my hand, barely noticing. 'I fed you Bracken's name,' I said, my voice dipping. 'It was a lie - a trap. You're the only person I ever spoke it to. So, tell me, Spruce . . . why are you working against us?' I swayed a little, catching myself just in time.

Zander took a step towards me, his hand half-raised. I couldn't tell if he meant to steady me or hold me back. But before he could make contact, Robinia grabbed his arm.

'Let Jasmine be,' she said, her tone firm, her angry stare enough to have him back away. 'She's got this.'

Spruce looked genuinely shocked, his eyes flicking from me to Robinia. 'Robinia,' he said, a note of disbelief colouring his voice. 'Surely you don't believe this . . . fabrication. Can't you see? Jasmine's unwell. Look at the state of her. If she wasn't at the counter here, she'd be falling over.'

He turned to the others in the room as if seeking validation, as though the performance of his concern might be enough to sway them. 'Aspen warned me this could happen. Paranoia. Forgetfulness. We've been through this before, haven't we? How many times must we watch her unravel before someone does something?'

I forced a breath through the tightness in my lungs. Shaking my head, I pushed back the fog threatening to scatter my thoughts and steal my memory. Not now. I couldn't let it take over. Not when I was this close. 'It was strange,' I said, clearing my throat, 'That Jaz's detonators didn't work on the water vessel. She lost her life making sure it blew. Then there was the pier - the detonators there sprang to life far too soon. Premature. Sloppy. You oversaw their packaging into the vehicles for delivery. Did you tamper with them?'

Spruce let out a short, incredulous laugh, shaking his head. 'Don't be so stupid,' he scoffed. 'Jaz should never have been allowed near the munitions room. She clearly didn't have a clue what she was doing.'

'Then there was confusion . . . you wanting us to pull back, retreat, claiming we had lost control of the settlements.'

'We were in the middle of a battle. It was chaos. I struggled to know what was happening with all the firepower and noise.'

I stepped forward, fury rising, and stabbed a finger at his face. 'Then explain the uniforms - the ones meant to help us blend in. Malus's soldiers didn't hesitate. They fired on us instantly, like they knew exactly who we were. What did you do to them? What did you change to have us marked so clearly?'

'I didn't do anything' he snapped, his voice rising. 'Your paranoia has you grasping at straws.'

Before I could answer, Spindle appeared in the doorway, taking in the scene with narrowed eyes. 'What's going on?'

I didn't hold back. 'I want you to arrest Spruce - right now.

Get him out of my sight and prepare him for an interrogation. I don't care what methods are used . . . I want the truth out of him.'

Spruce shrugged casually, raising both hands in the air as though he were shrugging off the accusation itself. 'Your girl-friend has clearly gone mad, Spindle,' he said, his voice oozing with contempt. 'She dares to barge in here and accuse me of all sorts.' He threw a glance my way, a smirk curling on his lips. 'I think you should take her to the medical bay. Have her checked over.'

His words were designed to undermine me, to shift the focus away from his own guilt and onto my mental state. The way he spoke, as if the truth had no bearing and my accusa-tions were the ramblings of someone unhinged, made my blood boil. He was trying to play the concerned ally, but I could see through it - the thinly veiled manipulation, the desperate need to deflect.

Spindle pulled an ink marker from his pocket, the sleek black pen catching Spruce's eye.

Holding it up, Spindle asked. 'How do you explain having one of these? It's standard government issue. It should have been declared when you brought it back from your last appointment.'

Spruce's expression shifted to one of unease. 'I've never seen it.'

'What is it?' I asked.

'It's a thermo-reactive marker,' Spruce said, handing me the pen. 'It coats any surface with an invisible dye that reacts when hit by a laser beam. When Malus's soldiers fired on us, they must have seen it on our uniforms. That's how they knew where to target. How else could they have been so precise?'

Spruce's face drained of colour, his lips pressing into a thin line. 'You've got this all wrong. That's not mine.'

Spindle didn't back down. 'When Jasmine intimated she had concerns, I searched your apartment. I have Cedar looking into some high-tech apparatus I found there, too,' he added.

'I think you should come with me,' Ash said, gesturing towards the door. 'We'll get you settled in a cell first - then the questioning can begin properly.'

36

The door slid shut behind me, sealing the lab. Hemlock didn't speak. He sat stiffly, his hands clasped on the table as if holding back something dangerous. A thin vein pulsed in his temple.

'I trust you have everything you need?' I asked, breaking the quiet.

'Yes, more than I expected,' he replied, not looking up. 'The files Robinia gave me are packed with data. It's old technology, but easy enough for me to understand.'

'Good. I'm glad. Is there anything you've found out that you'd like to share with me just now.'

'The tower isn't just symbolic, Jasmine . . . it was the breakthrough. At the time, it was science pushed to the very edge of reason. A solar conduit, designed to harness and direct the Sun's energy to the reactor. It used a lattice of ionised prisms to capture the radiation, funnelling it through a cryogenic relay buried beneath the structure. From there, the energy was pulsed - not scattered, but focused - through deep-under water channels that threaded across the Archipelago. The tower

234

MARTI M MCNAIR

didn't just store the power it gave it direction. That's why the alignment matters. Without it, the energy has nowhere to go.'

I stared at him, trying to keep up, but it felt like the words were skidding past me without any understanding. 'Right ... so it's like . . . a funnel for the Sun's energy?' I asked, my brow furrowed. 'You're saying if the alignment's off - even slightly - that power could just . . . scatter? Or worse, hit the wrong place?'

He nodded, his face solemn. 'Exactly. That's why we need to know which islands the tower is on. Old maps Robinia found show many clusters of islands before the End of Days. Everything depends on that connection being perfect. Otherwise, we won't be saving the planet. We'll be wiping it clean.'

'And what about the elite - if we turn the reactor back on . . . and channel the energy to where they are . . . what happens to them.'

'If they're still hiding out where the tower is, then they're doomed. However, if you look at maps of the old world . . . there were many such clusters of islands. Which set still remain? With our limited knowledge of what lies beyond the Pewter Sea - how do we find them?' Hemlock asked.

'Larch and Cedar are searching through some of the data we backed up before Malus fried their systems.' I got up and paced the room. 'And you really think that this will reset the imbalance.'

'The Sun would be free,' he said, with a wistful smile. 'Its natural balance restored. The Earth would begin to heal - no more droughts or violent sandstorms, no more black rain. It would take a scientist willing to make the ultimate sacrifice, stepping into the heart of the reactor, knowing it's a one-way journey. A painful, agonising death, yes - but one that might just save the world.'

I thought for a moment. 'Does it have to be a scientist?'

'Someone with some knowledge, at the very least,' he

replied. 'They'd need to be briefed - primed on exactly what to do once they're inside'

'And there's definitely no other way?'

He shook his head. 'We could try to mimic the reactor, but without the tower's infrastructure, it's guesswork. The original design was lost. We're working with fragments. And we don't have time - with the oncoming Ashes of Eden to contend with - accessing the reactor is the only way.'

I stopped pacing and turned to face him. 'No one hears about this conversation,' I said, my voice tight. 'Not yet. Do you understand?'

Hemlock met my gaze. 'You have my word.'

A knock at the door broke the moment. I opened it to find Spindle standing on the threshold, his brow drawn and arms folded tight across his chest. 'Why all the secrecy again. You don't usually go around locking doors behind you.'

'I must have done it by mistake. What's up?'

'Spruce is ready,' he said. 'We've got him hooked up to an old lie detector – I dug it out of the basement. It's a relic, but it works, as we've tried it out a few times when larking around. At least it's better than jumping straight to more aggressive methods. I think it's best to try this way first.'

Hemlock inclined his head slightly. 'I'm happy to help if the machine fails to do its job. I can prepare a cocktail that'll loosen his tongue. One dose and he'll be spilling truths he didn't even know he'd buried. I'm sure you'll have the ingredients I need in the medical bay.'

'Good. Start mixing it now,' I replied. 'If it comes to that, I want it ready.'

We left him to it and strode down the narrow corridors. When we reached the interrogation room, Spindle pushed the door open, and I was greeted by the low, steady thrum of the bulky lie detector.

Spruce sat slumped in a battered metal chair, his wrists

strapped to the arms. A series of thick, coiled wires snaked from his forearms and chest into a clunky console beside him. The machine itself looked like something from centuries ago - chipped steel, with gauges waiting to twitch. A paper spool was held in place ready for the ink needle to scratch its surface in jagged little lines. A cracked monitor flickered above, pulsing faintly with each beat of Spruce's heart.

'Are you sure you know what you're doing with this?' I asked.

'Sure. We've had fun messing around with all the old tech and equipment we found. When I first brought Ash here, I hooked him up to it. That's how I know he's still in love with you.'

I opened my mouth to speak, but he cut in.

'I asked him outright - and the readings confirmed it. But, let's not dig up the past. We need to focus,' he said, pointing at the machine. 'Ask spruce a question that we know the answer to. That will give us a baseline.'

I stepped closer to Spruce, hands resting on my hips. 'What's your name?

He rolled his eyes. 'Spruce.'

'Did you grow up on Ruin?'

His lips curled into a grin. There was a darkness behind it - a sort of mockery that said he wasn't afraid, not of me, and not of the machine. As if this was all theatre, and he'd already read the final act.

'Have you ever lied to me?'

A pause. 'No.'

The needle on the spool stuttered - just enough to make Spindle raise an eyebrow. I stepped closer, watching the machine carefully. 'Why did you betray us?'

'I didn't.' His voice was calm . . . almost mechanical. 'I've always had your back. I'm being framed.'

'Did you make contact with Malus while working with the Resistance?' I asked, clenching my jaw.

'I didn't. You've got it wrong.'

Frustration coiled in my gut. I turned to Spindle. 'This is a waste of time. He's lying - I know he is. Either the machine's goosed, or he knows how to cheat it. Fetch Hemlock's serum. Now.'

Spindle hesitated, eyes flicking to the machine, then back to me. 'You're sure about this?' he asked. 'It could be dangerous.'

'I don't care,' I replied. 'And if the serum doesn't work . . . we'll move on to other methods.'

Spindle left, and I turned back to Spruce, my gaze cold and full of contempt. I let the silence stretch, letting my stare unsettle him.

Eventually, I said, 'I never trusted you. Not truly. Not after you tried to have me killed.'

He didn't flinch. 'I feel sorry for you. That your paranoia has come to this. It's actually sad. You're dying . . . your brain is rotting . . . and this is where these ideas are springing from.'

I sighed. 'Everyone told me to let it go - that you'd changed, and you were loyal. And I tried. I really did. But here we are.' I leaned closer to him. 'What I don't understand is why? Why did you sell yourself out to Malus? What was worth trading us for?'

Spruce let out a slow, exaggerated sigh, as if he were the one growing tired of the game. He leaned back in the chair, the old metal frame creaking beneath him, and cast his eyes to the ceiling - as though my accusations were nothing more than background noise to him.

'Let's see how truthful you feel with a little help,' I said, part of me hoping he wouldn't cave - just so I'd have an excuse to beat the answers out of him.

Spruce didn't respond - just smirked again, tapping his fingers idly against the chair as if counting down to the end of a bad joke.

The door creaked open moments later, and Spindle stepped in. In his hand, he carried a slim vial of murky liquid and a syringe. As he moved closer, Spruce's smug expression faltered for the first time, the arrogant veneer slipping from his face. His eyes flitted between the two of us as Spindle prepared the syringe. The liquid swirled menacingly within. I held my breath. Whatever mask Spruce had been wearing - it was about to crack.

Spindle slipped the needle beneath Spruce's skin. For a moment, nothing happened - Spruce merely blinked, his jaw clasped, his eyes darting back and forth. Then, a fine sheen of sweat broke across his forehead, beading along his temples despite the coolness of the room. His breathing quickened, as though the air had thickened around him. Words tumbled from his lips, incoherent at first - then half-formed thoughts laced with confusion.

'No . . . not them . . . we were just following . . . she can't,' he murmured, his voice slurred, the syllables dragging like a slow bleed. His pupils dilated, darting erratically as if his mind fought to stay in charge. Then his head lolled slightly to one side, and the dam broke.

'I didn't want to die, Jasmine. They made me do it. They said it was the only way for humanity to survive.' His body trembled, caught between defiance and surrender

His voice grew slacker, his defences crumbling under the serum's grip. 'I didn't trust where you were taking us,' he said, sweat soaking through the collar of his shirt. 'Too much of a hot head without thinking about the risks. You would drag us all to ruin just to spite Malus.' His gaze twitched to Spindle, a flicker of shame crossing his loosened features. 'You can see that, can't you. Look at the amount of times she set off on her own course regardless of those around her.'

'How long have you been deceiving us?' I asked.

'Not long. On my last appointment to the capital, I stole a

patching device. It's new - high tech, long range. It allowed me to make contact - and scramble the trace. Malus took my call happily. You have to believe me . . . I never gave the outpost location away. Malus still doesn't know where we are.'

'So, what did you give away, Spruce?' I asked. 'What was your bargaining chip?'

His voice dropped to a hoarse whisper. 'Malus asked how he could trust me.' The next words spilled with dreadful clarity. 'I told him . . . I'd give him one of our own. I advised he was already in the capital. That he was a medic. Aspen.'

The words struck like a whip. I shot to my feet, my chair clattering backwards as rage surged through me. Before Spindle could stop me, my fist smacked against Spruce's jaw, flinging his bead back – blood spraying form his mouth. 'You betrayed Aspen,' I screamed. 'You handed him over like scraps - and for what?'

Before I could lunge again, Spindles arm wrapped around my waist, pulling me back. His voice murmured against my ear, his other hand pressing gently on my shoulder. 'He's not worth breaking yourself over. Breathe. You need your head clear for what comes next. You're stronger than this.'

Spruce groaned, dazed but still under the serum's thrall. 'I didn't give them our location . . . never that. I tampered, yes – enough to give Malus signs that I was helping. I marked the sleeves with the ink pen he gave me, made sure the sensors on Jaz's detonator delayed . . . just enough. I never thought for one minute that it would all blow up so violently. But I never sold you out completely. I never gave away our plans – not fully. I needed leverage.' He blinked slowly, his eyes rimmed red, broken and drifting. 'I only wanted a place inside the inner circle. A real life. A family. Peace. Let's face it, Jasmine - we were never going to win this war.'

37

B ack in the lab, Hemlock stood beside a large screen, tapping its surface with a metal pointer. He gestured to a cluster of coloured modules. 'This quadrant regulates the containment field - each dial controls magnetic stabilisation. These here manage thermal output, and the flux converter . . .'

I raised a hand, cutting him off. 'Hemlock. In layman's terms. Please.'

He paused, the pointer mid-air. A flicker of embarrassment crossed his face as he nodded. 'Right. Sorry.' He lowered the stick and took a breath. 'The suit you'll wear is biochemical - it'll protect you from the radiation and heat for a short window. You'll have ten minutes, give or take, before the chamber becomes uninhabitable.'

I stepped closer, breath shallow, eyes fixed on the reactor's image. The schematic looked ominous on the screen - no longer a drawing, but something aware, something waiting. It pulsed . . . not with power, but with deadly intent. The enormity of what needed to be done pressed in around me.

'And how will I know it's worked?' I asked, my voice barely a whisper. I knew the minute I stepped into the chamber there would be no return.

Hemlock's answer came slowly, each word weighted with the burden of inevitability. 'You'll know - a split second before it happens. You want just feel it, you'll see it. The chamber, your body, the walls around you - will be torn apart in an instant - in a blinding light - the minute the Sun's energy breaks free.'

'And what about the islands and the elite?'

'Like I said before, the tower is the conduit. When you start the reactor and release the energy - if the alignment is exact, the solar force won't just surge. It will erupt. It will tear through the tower and lance skyward, a pillar of fire and energy reaching beyond the clouds. It will be a cosmic explosion - similar to what happened at the End of Days. Only this time its blasting outwards into the universe and not inward. The Archipelago won't even have time to burn. They'll be gone. Erased - Just like *you* - in that same heartbeat.' He looked at me, before adding, 'But only if we are aligned with the correct cluster of islands. If not, we can kiss this world goodbye.'

I could accept sacrificing myself - knowing I was taking the elite with me. But I couldn't face risking humanity with a miscalculation. 'Larch and Cedar are working on it,' I said, rubbing a hand through my hair.

'Let's hope they are successful,' Hemlock said, 'And that they find them quickly.'

'Thank you, for everything.' I replied, though my voice faltered. 'But are we sure? No stray fallout, no shockwave? The mainland. The other islands. They'll be safe? They won't feel it?'

'As I have already stated, as long as we set the right alignment, all will be well. The Earth will shudder as it tips back to its correct axis. Now, regarding radiation - we'll need to construct a sealed vacuum tunnel for you to enter. Think of it like a pressurised plastic corridor, reinforced and sterilised.

And once you're inside the chamber, you'll need to seal the entry behind you immediately.' He tapped the corner of the schematic on the screen. 'I'm happy to speak with whoever you need me to, so we can design a secure and stable gateway.'

'Yes, that would be useful. But remember - I don't want anyone knowing what we're planning. Not until I'm satisfied we have everything in place.' I glanced at the clock on the wall. 'I need to go. We're questioning Spruce again, see if he lets anything else slip about Malus. How the hell does a man like that just vanish? We thought he'd show up somewhere along the Pewter Sea, but there's been nothing. Maybe if we knew where he was, we'd have a better sense of how much time we've got left before Ashes of Eden is released.'

* * *

The storage room was cold and stank of old metal and mould. A single bulb swung overhead, casting fractured shadows across the walls. Spruce sat shackled to a chair in the middle of the room, his face gaunt, the bruises on his jaw still fresh, and his mouth swollen. He didn't look at me right away - his gaze fixed on the floor. Spindle stood at my side, silent and still. We weren't here to play games. Not this time.

Spruce finally looked up, and something passed over his face - a flicker of defiance, then resignation. 'No serum today?' he rasped, the corner of his mouth twitching. 'Guess it's just the two of you and a lot of awkward silence.'

'Watch your tone, or Jasmine might loosen another tooth,' Spindle said.

I kicked at a roll of thick polythene sitting on the ground next to his chair. It unravelled with a soft flap across the concrete. 'We don't want to make a mess of the cell,' I said, my voice flat.

Spindle stepped towards Spruce. 'You said Malus wanted to

trust you, so you gave him Aspen. But trust goes both ways. Did he ever tell you where he was heading? Where the Archipelago islands and the tower are?'

'Why should I help you,' Spruce asked, glancing at the polythene. 'You're going to kill me anyway.'

I knelt down in front of him, placing my hands on his knees - leaning in until our faces were inches apart. 'Here's the thing, Spruce,' I said. 'The elite are going to unleash their bioweapon, and when they do, we're all going to die. That's the part you've always failed to grasp. But you?' I let the corner of my mouth twitch. 'You just might go sooner. And I can promise you this – you'll go with a hell of a lot more pain. Ashes of Eden will be bad, but not as bad as what I can inflict on you in the time we have left.'

He flinched, just slightly, and that was enough to make my blood boil with justification. 'What was it Malus offered you? A first-class seat on his watercraft? Passage to some untouched cluster of islands while the rest of us choked on ash?'

Spindle picked up a small, sharp knife from a nearby table, turning the blade over in his hand. 'I've wanted to do this since the time you thought you were transporting Jasmine to her death. Back then . . . I only let you live because Robinia spoke up for you. She regrets that now. No one here will save you now.'

His shoulders sagged. 'He did promise me a ticket out of here . . . but only if I gave him the outpost.' His voice was hoarse, brittle with defeat. 'I refused. So, he offered me another way in. He said if I helped in other matters, he'd still see me right. But if I don't make contact soon . . .' He paused, a shadow falling over his expression. 'He'll know you've caught on. And then I'm nothing to him.'

'Were you going to meet him somewhere?' Spindle asked.

Spruce hesitated. I felt his knees tense beneath my hands.

'Spruce,' I warned, my grip tightening. 'I know you want to make this right. Tell us all you know.'

His eyes darted back and forth. He leaned back, the chair creaking beneath him. For a long moment, he said nothing. Then he exhaled. His words came in a quiet manner. 'Malus always watched from above,' he murmured. 'Liked the high ground. Said it gave him clarity.' His gaze lifted to mine. 'Before the End of Days, man managed to create a flying vessel that streaked through the sky. They could travel all around the world in a matter of days.'

I reeled back a step, my stomach twisting. 'Are you telling me Malus has a vessel that can fly?' I gasped, the words catching in my throat.

Spruce leaned forward slightly. 'Well . . . Malus couldn't perfect it - not that form of transport. But what he did manage wasn't flying at all - but sailing on the wind.'

I frowned. 'What does that even mean?'

Spruce leaned back, a glint of amusement in his eyes. 'You see, it's all about the air. You start by heating it up - blast enough warmth into the fabric above, and it begins to rise, light as a feather.'

I turned to Spindle. 'Have you any idea what he's talking about?'

Spindle raised an eyebrow, giving me a side glance. 'Not a clue,' he muttered, his voice dry. 'Something about fire and air.'

Spruce smiled at my puzzled look, his tone shifting a bit. 'As long as its fed heat, it stays afloat. Too little, and the vessel starts to sink. Too much . . . well, let's just say we don't want to find out what happens then. I believe Malus calls them hot air balloons. While you'll be looking for him to cross the Pewter Sea, he'll be flying high above it. Higher than our drones.'

A faint memory stirred - something from early childhood. I remembered the images from a lesson on Ruin - baskets drifting through the sky, carried by nothing but shifting wind and the careful release of heat. A great flame would roar beneath a silk canopy, warming the air until it lifted. 'We were told in class that such a thing would be impossible - that the oxygen levels would be too dangerous to attempt such a feat.'

Spruce''s reply was simple. 'We were told may things.'

It made finding Malus harder. No warning. No engine noise. No heat signature. Just shadows, soundless in the clouds above.

'If Malus didn't want our location, then what did he want?' I asked.

Spruce shook his head. 'They said the outpost didn't matter. My task was to get them back in to our systems - they'd handle the rest. I never gave up our plans. I swear. I was only meant to flag any signs of attack - nothing more. That's what the pen markings were for. The detonators at the pier. I thought it would cause a small explosion. A warning, not devastation. It wasn't supposed to go down like that.'

'I still don't get it,' Spindle said, frowning. 'How were you going to escape? I don't believe you'd go to all that trouble just for him to leave you behind.'

Spruce looked at me as he spoke. 'He demanded small pieces of intel in exchange for safe passage. If Ashes of Eden were to be release, I had one task - kill you and display your body in a gruesome spectacle, something to fill every heart with horror. He wanted the Resistance to witness the humiliating fate of their leader while toxins tore through them. Once he received proof, he'd send coordinates to a watercraft - something fast, built to slip past the Pewter Sea unnoticed.'

My eyes widened. 'Do you know where the Archipelago Islands are?' I asked, hope rising in my chest.

'No,' he said, shaking his head. 'I don't. But the computerised engine on the watercraft does.'

38

Solemn quiet descended, the kind that highlights grave decisions. Spruce sat at the head of the table, shoulders square, the bruise on his face still prominent, but the swelling on his lips had died.

Ash sat beside Coral, the two of them deep in conversation, light laughter bubbling between sentences. Zander and Larch worked nearby, checking weapons spread across the floor. Minx paced at the edge of the table, her eyes fixed on the high-tech comm device Spindle had jut finished setting up.

I looked around, missing Cooper. Orion. And Felix. My heart ached at their absence. They should've been here, shoulder to shoulder with us, part of this reckoning.

'It's ready,' Spindle said, turning to Larch. 'Do you want to put a tracer on it?'

Larch hobbled forward pulling a small drive from his pocket. He slotted it into the side port of the comm device and keyed in a rapid sequence of symbols. The machine responded with a short chirp. 'Running trace diagnostics now.' He straightened after a few seconds, his eyes never leaving the screen. 'It's ready. If they answer, we'll get a bounce point and backtrack their signal. Even if it's masked, we'll get close.'

'Close is enough,' Ash said. 'We'll take it from there.'

Spindle tapped the comm casing once, as if setting a trap and hoping the prey would take the bait. 'Okay, Spruce, you know what to do. If you deviate in any way . . .'

Spruce rolled his shoulders back, though the motion did little to disguise his tension. 'I told you - I don't want to die. I'll play my part.' His eyes moved over every face. 'Remember your promise. You're all witnesses - I get to live. I walk free.'

'Spruce,' Spindle said, motioning to the comms station. 'Sit. It's time.'

I stepped out from the shadows near the archway, fury burning through every word. 'Oh, I'll keep my word. But don't think for a second it's mercy. Now do what you were brought here to do - before I change my mind.'

Robinia leaned into him, fingers laced together, her voice firm. 'Malus will test you. He doesn't believe in loyalty - only leverage. Be ready for him to ask more than you've prepared for.'

Spruce gave a tight nod. 'I know what's expected of me.'

Spindle hit the sequence. The comm crackled and static weaved through. The screen blinked twice, then Malus appeared. Spruce was the only one visible; the rest of us remained just out of frame.

A beat of silence - then Malus's voice. 'What happened to your face?'

Spruce lifted a hand to the bruise. 'Jasmine is dead,' he said, flatly. 'I made it look like her illness took her. That she eventually lost her mind.'

Across the table, Coral's brow furrowed. She turned to me, eyes narrowing, and silently mouthed, *'What illness?'*

I met her gaze. *'Not now.'* I mouthed back, and watched her confusion deepen.

'Her death wasn't supposed to happen yet. Explain the deviation.'

'She found the marker pen in my quarters. Put two and two together. I had no choice but to take her out.' A humourless chuckle escaped Spruce. 'She didn't go easy - put up a fight. Not that I would expect anything less.'

'Do the others suspect you?'

'I told them I got hurt trying to save her, that she snapped and came at me. Said she fell and cracked her skull. Honestly, I think they expected it. She'd been unravelling ever since she came back from the capital.' He paused, his eyes locking with mine. 'Seeing Aspen's head in your trophy case . . . it broke something in her.'

A low, guttural breath rasped through the speaker. 'If only I'd known how much Aspen meant to her. I'd have killed him rather than Salix during her trial.' He paused, as if contemplating what to say next. 'I want to believe you, Spruce. But I'll need proof of her death.'

'I can't risk staying here any longer,' Spruce replied. 'They're mourning. Distracted. But not for long. I've got to slip away before the window closes. I'll bring what I can - hair, blood, clothing. Whatever satisfies your masters. But if I wait, I'm done.'

'I'm not sure they'll accept your word alone. Proof is everything.'

'This is my only chance. I'm begging you. I won't have another opportunity to disappear.'

Another long pause stretched out, the screen flickering in the silence. Then his voice returned. 'Very well. I'll send the coordinates - a secluded port with access to the Pewter Sea. It was built to receive our masters in secret when they visited the mainland. Few know it exists. The watercraft should carry you safely.'

Spruce nodded. 'Understood.'

But then Astrid's voice rang out from the sidelines. 'Why aren't you travelling by sea then? Why the balloons?'

The question escaped her before she could stop it, hanging in the air as all of us froze in stunned horror.

Malus voice lifted, taut with suspicion. 'Who's that?'

Spruce didn't flinch. 'One of the medics tending to my burst lip. She's a friend and has offered to help cover my exit. But she makes a good point about the balloons.'

His tone changed from one of confidence to one of suspicion. 'The sea's not safe anymore. You've seen the sabotage. We've lost two vessels in the last cycle. The upper jet stream is untraceable, and the balloons use organic propulsion - no digital signature, no thermal trail, no engine noise. The last thing we need is to be found before we release Ashes of Eden.'

'That's understandable.'

'With your training, you should be able to manoeuvre the watercraft at great speed. Once you leave the Pewter Sea, it will be plain sailing. Feel free to bring your medic friend. It's a good skill to have and we can never have enough.'

With that, the screen turned black and Spindle shut off the comms. A breath released from every chest in the room.

Astrid lowered her gaze. 'I'm so sorry. It just slipped out without me thinking.'

Spruce was quick to reassure her. 'I think his suspicion only lasted a moment. Saying you were a medic seemed to settle it. They'll need skilled people if their so-called next generation is going to survive.'

'I think he bought it,' Ash said, almost to himself. 'Or, he wants us to think he did.'

Robinia sighed. 'Either way, we should receive coordinates that lead us to the watercraft. And onboard, there's a nautical map that shows exactly where the Archipelago islands are. No more guessing.'

Larch smiled faintly. 'And with the tracker now embedded

in his comms frequency, we'll know if he so much as twitches. Hopefully, it will kick in soon. I'm going to run it through a few programmes - see if I can pinpoint his exact location.'

Coral stood, her gaze finding mine. 'Jasmine, I know you're busy, but can we talk? I need to know about your illness.'

'Sure,' I said, guilt creeping in. This wasn't how I'd wanted her to find out. 'I need to check in on Hemlock, but we could grab something to eat and talk then?'

Spindle, who'd been leaning casually against the wall, gave me a look of mock suspicion. 'You've been spending a lot of time in the lab with your new scientist friend. Should I be jealous?' he asked, pulling me into a quick hug and planting a kiss on my forehead.

The gesture lingered a second too long. His body stiffened - realising too late he'd broken his own rule. No affection. Not while Ash was in the room.

'Let's just say I'm becoming a science geek,' I replied, forcing a smile, trying to ease the guilt I knew Spindle felt.

To be fair, I think Ash was over me - or at least doing a good job of hiding it. He didn't look back as he escorted Spruce out of the suite. Maybe he'd finally learned how to let go.

* * *

It was easier now - moving between the settlements without the constant fear of being tracked by government guards. Our fighters had began to rebuild, and though the citizens still looked dazed, they were coping. There'd been no reports of mass hysteria as minds adjusted to life free from Control. I would leave that part of the recovery to Spindle - once I was gone.

The hidden pier sat like a fortress carved into the cliffside - dark, grey stone walls rising in notched layers, weathered and battle-worn. It looked as though it had been carved straight from the mountain itself. Moss clung to the cracks between the bricks, and rusted chains hung from ancient mooring hooks embedded in the wall. A narrow cobblestoned path led to a flight of crumbling steps, descending toward a small watercraft that bobbed gently in the shadowed inlet below. It was exactly where Malus's coordinates had stated it would be.

We watched from a concealed ridge above, shielded by dense rock. The sea churned with a strange stillness, the sky above a low ceiling of bruised clouds. No movement. No guards. Just silence and grey.

'I'll go,' Spindle said, tightening the strap of his laser. 'In the event it's a trap.'

Astrid cut in quickly. 'No, let me. I think we're just being paranoid.'

Before any of us could protest, she stepped from the cover, following the winding path to the edge. We watched her descend, her figure shrinking with every step until she vanished from view. A second passed. Then another. And then - Boom.

The blast didn't hit - it rolled, a heavy, thundering wave that bent the air. Heat came next - violent and searing, rushing up from below in a sudden wave. A column of flame and black smoke swallowed the pier, casting a blinding light across the waves. I dropped without thinking, driven by instinct.

Time fractured around me. Everything moved with surreal slowness. Stone and salt exploded upwards in a violent spray. For what seemed like eternity, there was only the sharp, metallic ring screaming through my ears, drowning out everything else.

And then - voices, distant at first, rising like echoes from under water.

'Astrid,' Minx roared.

Zander caught her as she darted forward, his arms locking around her in a firm hold. Minx thrashed against him, her fists pounding against his chest, her cries raw with anguish. 'Let me go,' she sobbed, her voice ragged and broken. But he held her tighter.

His chin rested against the top of her head. 'Breathe, Minx. I've got you. You're not alone. I promise, you're not alone.' She sagged against him, her strength spent, her grief spilling out in silent, shaking sobs.

A fine ash began to fall, drifting like grey snow. Smoke curled up from the shattered remains of the pier, cloaking the water below in a swirling veil of soot and flame. The heat licked at our skin, even from our vantage point, and the scent of scorched stone and burning saltwater clawed at the back of my throat.

'I can't see her,' Spindle muttered, scanning the wreckage through a handheld scope. 'The craft is gone. The lower steps - gone. Just debris and fire.'

Zander turned to me, his face contorted with anger. 'It was a trap. Malus either knew we'd come, or he double crossed Spruce. We need to get back to the outpost.' Without waiting for a response, he gently gathered Minx in his arms and helped her back to the vehicle.

I stood - frozen in shock. My mind reeled, refusing to accept what my eyes had seen. Astrid. Gone. Another name on my list. Another life lost because they followed me.

The world around me seemed to blur, the smoke, the voices, even the heat - all of it dulled beneath the sharp, cold clarity of guilt. How many more? How many before Malus took everyone I cared about?

My legs felt heavy, rooted to the stone. I wanted to scream, to run down the slope and tear through the wreckage with my bare hands. But I didn't move. Because I knew. This was the cost. Again and again. And still, we kept paying it.

39

I sat beside Felix's bed, my fingers wrapped loosely around his clammy hand. The machine beside his bed beeped softly, its rhythm far too calm for what I felt inside. Not only had we lost Astrid - we'd also lost our chance to pinpoint the Archipelago islands.

The sobs tore through me, raw and unstoppable. I could barely form the words through the tears, but I told him about Astrid.

'I'm sorry,' I whispered to him, my voice shaking. 'None of you deserved any of this. But I'm going to make it right.' I squeezed his hand tighter. 'You have to hang on, Felix. You hear me? I'm counting on you to make it through - to be part of the new world we're fighting for. A world that needs people like you.'

Eventually, I forced the grief down. Locked it away. Rage replaced it.

* * *

I stormed into Spruce's cell, the door slamming back against the wall. Spindle and Ash were already there.

Spruce looked up, his hands slightly raised. 'I promise, Jasmine . . . this wasn't on me. Malus must have wanted me dead too. I'm just another loose end that needed cutting.'

I turned on him, my anger deadly. 'You better pray Larch finds a fix on Malus's signal, or I swear on my life - your last breath is coming a lot sooner than you think.'

Hammering my fist against the wall, the fury burned through me. I spun on my heels and stalked away.

'Wait,' he called out. 'You still have Aconite.'

I stiffened, eyes narrowing. 'This had better be good, Spruce. I don't have time to waste.'

He looked at the three of us in turn. 'Aconite. You do still have him . . . don't you. Or did you kill him off without telling me.'

'Go on,' I said.

'Aconite and Malus are joined at the hip,' he replied. 'If Malus finds out he's alive, you could use him - force a trade, anything.'

'No,' I replied, 'Malus won't risk exposure, not with the Ashes of Eden project so close to release.'

A small smile flickered across Ash's face. 'Actually, you might be onto something,' he said, rubbing his chin. 'What if Malus is tying up loose ends? He'll believe Spruce blew himself up. We could have Aconite contact Malus on the comms, claiming Spruce managed to break him free. Poor Aconite finds himself stranded on the mainland, with nowhere left to run.'

The idea took root - but was it viable? 'Do you think Aconite will cooperate?' I asked.

Nobody answered.

* * *

Larch's voice burst through the monotony of the Operations Room, his face alight with something I hadn't seen in days - hope. 'We've got it,' he announced, barely pausing to catch his breath. 'The tracker worked. We've pinpointed the location of Malus and his inner circle.'

'Where?' I asked.

'I'll transmit it to the plasma,' he said, keying commands into his keyboard.

A large map of the mainland appeared on the screen, and in its most southern part near the coastline, a red dot flashed.

'We don't have any eyes out there,' Robinia muttered, frowning. 'That's way beyond our drone range.'

'It's way beyond any travel that I've ever seen too,' Ash added.

Larch's fingers flew over the keyboard again. 'I'm going to try sending one of our drones anyway. Let's see how far we get.'

We all watched, captivated, as Larch launched the scout. It darted from the safety of he outpost, a sleek speck disappearing into the distance. We followed its progress in stunned silence - until the screen flickered, stalled, then went dead.

'Damn it' Larch said, slamming his palm on the console. 'The distance is too far. We lost the feed the second it reached the outer boundary. I should've known.'

Cedar lifted his head. 'What if we don't rely on just one drone?' he said. 'What if we send a chain? Juniper's team still has drones operating on Ruin, right? They could fly theirs part-way, and we fly ours from this side. If we coordinate the flight paths, each drone could boost the signal, relaying it from one to the next.' His gaze fell on me. 'We've piggybacked before. This time, it's just a little further ... but definitely worth trying.'

Minutes later, we had Juniper on screen, explaining what needed to be done.

'Okay,' he said, without preamble. 'Give me fifteen minutes to recalibrate our airborne units. I'll have them flying in formation and ready to link with yours by the time you hit launch altitude.'

We moved fast. Juniper and Cedar plotted the overlapping flight paths. Larch recalibrated every frequency. The Operations Room vibrated with the energy of renewed purpose. When the time came, Larch advised they were ready.

'Send them,' I said.

The drones lifted into the sky, one after another, buzzing like mechanical insects. We tracked their progress on the plasma, the signal feeding through stronger with each link - Juniper's machines bridging the vastness. The image came slowly - pixelated at first, then clearer.

I gasped. Ten enormous balloons floated in a still pocket of air above a wide clearing, their surfaces ghostly grey and mottled with stitched seams. Suspended from each was a broad basket - too large for simple transport, and anchored to the ground with thick rope. The clearing also homed a temporary camp, the tents in all shapes and sizes.

We zoomed in on Malus's inner circle. No longer cloaked in government robes but dressed in combat uniforms, their weapons slung casually over their shoulders. They circled fires and tables, deep in conversations, unaware we were watching. Among them, Malus's silhouette stood tall - unmistakable.

'This isn't just a camp,' Cedar said, coming to stand beside me. 'This is a staging ground.'

'It looks as if they're preparing to move,' Zander added.

'Look at the baskets again,' Minx said, narrowing her eyes. 'Those aren't just transport carriers. They're equipped - solar cells, weapon racks, comms panels. They're airborne command units. Do you think he's going to release Ashes of Eden when he reaches the sky.'

My mind raced. We had found them. But the window to act was small - mere hours, maybe less. And if they lifted off - if they scattered across the clouded skies . . . we'd never get another chance.

I stepped back from the screen, the blood humming in my ears. 'We need to speak with Aconite.'

* * *

Aconite's pain was undeniable. He'd eventually succumbed to the torture. I couldn't deny the dark satisfaction that I had savoured every second. After all he'd done, all he'd stolen from us, he deserved every cut and bruise.

We drove to the pier. To where we had lost Astrid - but I couldn't afford to think of her now. I needed to stay focused.

I leaned in, pressing my laser into Aconites ribs. 'Speak into the comms. Just like we agreed,' I said.

He jerked, yelping as the charge danced beneath his skin. 'I'll do it,' he said, his chest hitching as the pain rattled through him.

'And remember,' I added, watching his pupils dilate. 'I'm doing you a favour. In the new world, you'll live. Locked in a cell. Forgotten. But breathing. Betray us - give anything away - and you'll die with us slowly, when your masters release their final weapon.' His eyes widened, and I felt a surge of joy seeing his fear.

Spindle crouched beside the comms, making the connection. A beat later, the line sprung to life - and Malus answered.

Aconite almost choked as he rasped out his name. 'Malus - help me. Please. You have to come. Get me out of here.'

There was a pause, then Malus's voice, edged with surprise. 'What happened? Where are you?'

'I'm at the pier,' Aconite said, his voice strained, desperate. 'Spruce broke me free - but he got on the watercraft with his medic friend. It exploded. I was behind, carrying the comms. The blast knocked me out cold.' He coughed. Shivered.

It was Perfect.

'I didn't think Spruce had it in him,' Malus muttered. 'If I had, I might've spared him. But it doesn't matter now.'

'Please come for me. I need medical attention. I'm bleeding. My head's not right. You have to come yourself.'

Malus was quiet. Calculating. 'Stay where you are,' he said, finally. 'I'll send someone to fetch you right away.'

Aconite's eyes flitted to me. He was playing the part well. Desperation clung to his every word. 'No. I don't trust your group anymore. Someone's been feeding information back - you've got a traitor, Malus. Inside your inner circle.'

That landed. I could hear it in the stillness, in the sharp inhale that followed. 'I don't believe you,' Malus said, slowly. But there was a crack in the conviction.

Aconite begged. 'Please, believe me. You have to - for the sake of us all. One of your own contacted Jasmine before she died. She boasted of it. Said she was close to finding your camp.'

Even Spindle stiffened at how convincingly Aconite played his part. The bait was set, suspicion sown. Now, all that remained was to wait.

40

We heard them coming before we saw them. A dark shape rumbling over the cobbled roads, its black paint dulled by dust and war.

I turned to Aconite, dragging him roughly from the shadows. Blood still streaked his face, and one eye swollen - nearly shut. I drove him forward with a hard thump on his back.

'Remember what I said. Lure him out of the vehicle. Zander's above us - he's got a clear shot. So don't even think about deceiving me. You'll be dead before your feet hit the road.'

The vehicle drew closer, tyres crunching over the uneven stone. A ripple of tension spread through the comms.

'Only Malus and a driver.' Ash said, his voice clear through my earpiece. 'No sign of any additional bodies and no other vehicles in the horizon.'

'Visual's clean,' Zander added from his perch. 'They're in my line of vision.'

'Spindle?' I asked.

'It's a standard government vehicle with no rear windows, no armaments on the roof. I don't see any incoming backup,' he replied. 'He'd have brought a larger vehicle if he was bringing a group. So, I agree, two at the most - but be vigilant.'

The vehicle rolled to a halt ten paces from where Aconite swayed weakly in the road.

Then - the faint hiss of the doors sliding open. The driver emerged first, cautious. His eyes darted over the terrain. He slowly moved toward Aconite, his hand hovering near his belt.

Aconite dropped to his knees, again, playing the part better than I'd expected. The driver reached him, knelt down, and tried to hoist him to his feet - but Aconite slumped like a dead weight. The driver grunted, struggling to lift him.

It wasn't until Malus stepped out of the vehicle and strode towards Aconite that I spoke through the comms. 'Okay. That's our cue.' Raising my weapon and levelling it at the centre of Malus's forehead, I stepped out from behind the rusted barricade. 'Welcome to the party, Malus.'

The driver turned, instinct moving his hand towards his weapon.

'Don't,' I warned, flicking my aim in his direction. 'Put your weapon down. Now. Kick it over here.'

He hesitated - then slowly laid it on the ground, sliding it across the road.

'Good,' I said. 'Nice to see someone with self-preservation instincts.'

Then, in perfect timing, my team stepped from the shadows. Spindle from the rear, Ash and Minx from the slope behind the vehicle, Zander descending the crumbling scaffolding overhead. In seconds, Malus and his driver were completely surrounded.

Malus offered no resistance. But a flicker of something darker passed over his face - rage. His eyes locked onto Aconite with a venomous glare, sharp enough to draw blood.

'Put them in the vehicle,' I ordered.

Ash took Malus by the shoulder, twisting him forward while Spindle bound the driver's wrists with rough cable.

For the first time in what felt like weeks, I let out a long, quiet breath. The kind that settles in your ribs and reminds you what peace might feel like - even if it's fleeting.

* * *

Malus didn't take kindly to his interrogation. He howled, raged, thrashed against the inevitable - as if fury alone might undo the noose tightening around him. I didn't stay. Whatever he had left to scream wasn't meant for my ears. Others handled it. It was only a matter of time before he'd crack, and when he did, the Archipelago Islands would no longer be a secret location.

But I could feel it - that low sensation in my blood, the hollowness creeping behind my eyes. The constant headaches and nosebleeds. My time was drawing to a close. So, I chose not to spend it in the Operations Room. I chose to live what little life I had left.

We gathered in the canteen, feasting on homegrown root vegetables and greens. They weren't as sharp as the veg grown in the caves but still tasted good. There was laughter - the kind that felt foreign on our tongues but warm in our bones. Zander passed around a bottle of moonshine, and we drank like we had something to celebrate. And we certainly did.

Coral asked about my condition again, trying to mask her worry, but her eyes always gave her away. I told her not to let it linger - that these things had a way of deciding for us, that the future made its own choices whether we liked them or not.

She confided something unexpected - a quiet, blushing admission about Ash. A crush, she said, too softly, but with enough joy in her eyes to make it real. It explained more than I wanted to admit. His glances no longer lingered on me. And oddly, it brought me peace. Whatever they'd found in each other, it was untouched by bloodshed or obligation. For that, I was glad.

News came that Felix had woken. His voice still faint, his movements slow and uncertain - but awake. It was more than we'd dared hope. I sat with Zander and Minx that evening, and we raised our glasses. To Cooper. To our fallen. To everything we'd had to lose in order to get this far. And maybe - just maybe - to the hope that Cooper would return, and I could say good-bye. A proper goodbye.

Later, Robinia and I walked the perimeter of the outpost, the dust settling behind our boots as we traced our journey from beginning to end. We spoke of Rowan, and her bravery. Robinia tried to convince me to let the medics take over where Aspen had left off. She still believed in a cure, somewhere buried in blood and science. But I only smiled and humoured her.

I celebrated with Larch and Cedar - the drone work, the restored comms, the tactical clarity they'd brought to our chaos. Quiet victories, but they mattered. I visited Hemlock too. Not to plead for a different path, but to learn more of the one I would walk. The reactor systems, the final fail-safes. Everything I would need to know to keep all of them safe. I memorised every last diagram, every line of code etched into memory. A memory I hoped would not fail me - hence my fate had to be sooner rather than later.

And then - when the outpost surrendered to sleep - Spindle came to my door. He didn't speak, and neither did I. We let our silence communicate - in every glance, every touch, every breath. We undressed slowly, like we had all the time in the world, and made love as if it might be the last time either of us remembered how. In those hours, I wasn't a soldier, or a symbol, or a dying girl. I was just Jasmine. Someone I had longed to be.

I woke early, the outpost still hushed in silence. Spindle

stirred beside me, his breath soft against the pillow. I kissed his cheek, slow and gentle. His eyes blinked open, heavy with dreams, and he smiled a sleepy smile. Reaching out, he pulled me into the space between his arms, where the world always seemed safe.

I traced slow circles on his chest, losing myself in the rhythm of his heartbeat. 'There's something I need you to do for me,' I whispered.

He didn't hesitate. 'For you - anything.'

He propped himself up on one elbow, the sheet slipping slightly across his waist. His other hand reached for me, his fingers brushing the edge of my jaw. His touch was featherlight and I savoured the feel of it.

'I've been working on something,' I said. 'Something secret. With Hemlock. It's important. I'll need your help after its done.'

His gaze didn't falter. Not once. 'You can always count on me.'

I searched his face, memorising every line, every scar, every bit of love it carried. 'Is that a promise?'

He smiled. Not the casual smile he gave to the others, but the one he saved for me. The one that made the world tilt back into place. 'I promise.'

I kissed his lips gently, lingering for just a moment. 'Good,' I whispered. 'Now go back to sleep. It's still early.'

41

The salt flats stretched endlessly before me, a cracked and colourless expanse where nothing dared to grow. I could only imagine its once glistening plain of mirrored beauty. It now lay in ruins, its surface warped into ridges and fissures.

Winds scoured the land, whipping up fine white dust that stung my eyes. Salt crusted the broken ground in slated patterns, glinting dully under the waning sun. I stood, eyes scanning the wasteland. In my mind's eye, I saw the flats restored - shimmering with life and light, not ruin. What I was about to do might be madness, but I carried that one belief - that from ruin, something pure and beautiful would rise. A new world.

'It's not too late,' Hemlock said, helping me into the hazmat suit. 'I can radio for Spindle to come . . . even Zander. I feel someone should be here for you, before you head down.'

His eyes drifted to the four feet concrete hatch at our feet, sealed tight with a rusted wheel-lock.

'It's all good,' I said, not wishing to dwell on it. 'I've said all my goodbyes . . . and I left Spindle a letter.' I forced a weak smile. 'Took a while. I wanted to write it in ink - not punch it into some soulless tablet. Anyway. He'll know what to do. He knows the kind of world he needs to build. And he has wonderful people working with him.'

Hemlock nodded, but his face twisted. 'Still, someone who loves you should be here. I'm just a scientist with a view this job needs doing. Even free of Control - which I thank you for - I'm still a little detached.'

I stepped forward and pulled him into a quick embrace. 'And that detachment is exactly what I need to help me open that door,' I said, nodding toward the hatch. It loomed like a tombstone, silent and final, the edges smeared with soot and the faint stain of salt. The air around it felt wrong - too still. 'The others,' I said, 'Especially Spindle, Coral and Zander . . . they'd never let me do this. Not if they knew. Even though it makes the most sense.' I looked back at Hemlock, my voice more stable than I felt. 'I'm dying anyway. It has to be me.'

Hemlock double checked all the seals on the suit I wore. The fabric hissed faintly as it locked into place around my wrists and collar, the weight heavy on my shoulders. I adjusted the respirator, then glanced at him through the transparent shield. 'You're sure we'll be able to hear each other?'

He gave a firm nod. 'Loud and clear. And I'll be able to see what you see - the chest cam is active.'

I exhaled slowly, the breath fogging against the inside of my visor. 'I'm ready.'

Hemlock crouched beside the hatch, unfolding a compact popup tent the engineer had designed. It was a dull grey shroud of reinforced polymer and carbon mesh, able to seal tight against any surface. He clipped it into place around the hatch perimeter. 'This will definitely hold the breach,' he said. 'No radiation, no airborne toxins - nothing gets out unless we let it.'

I placed my hand on Hemlock's shoulder, my fingers trembling slightly as my eyes began to mist. 'Tell them how much I love them . . . and don't you dare let any of them know I was afraid.'

Hemlock's gaze faltered, his own eyes glistening. 'I don't think you've ever been afraid, Jasmine. You've followed your calling - to free humanity, and to heal what was broken. That takes more courage than most could ever summon.'

I stepped into the tent, the material whispering faintly as it settled behind me, sealing the world out. I turned toward the hatch. 'Let this be enough,' I whispered.

The wheel groaned as I turned it, the metal stiff with years of disuse. It took all my strength - arms shaking, shoulders burning - to wrench the heavy trapdoor open. A gust of stale air rushed up to greet me, thick with dust and the ghost of rot. I slipped through the gap and hauled the hatch shut behind me, sealing me in. Darkness swallowed the chamber. I unhooked the torch from my belt and its narrow beam cut a trembling path through the gloom, swaying left and right as I moved forward. Reinforced walls emerged on either side, thick with rivets and cold, vault steel.

My footsteps echoed until they met the edge of a stairwell. I descended carefully, each step creaking underfoot, until the light caught on the rusted grate of a lift - old, caged, its iron bones groaning with time. I slipped inside, but the buttons stared back . . . lifeless. No glow. No response.

'Hemlock,' I said, my voice shaking.

His reply hit my ear, calm and focused. 'Check just beneath the main panel - there should be a manual override, probably tucked behind a rusted latch or sliding cover. It won't look like much. Just a small lever or a reset switch.'

I ran my gloved fingers along the metal, searching blindly until I felt the edge of a corroded flap. I tugged it open. 'There's a red toggle.'

'That's it,' Hemlock said. 'Old emergency systems like these were built to run independently of the main grid - powered by a separate capacitor. Flip it, and give it a second.'

I did as instructed. After a few seconds vibration stirred beneath my boots. The caged walls shuddered, and a low mechanical groan echoed up the shaft. The buttons blinked to life, flickering like tired eyes slowly waking.

'You're good to go,' Hemlock said. 'But be careful - there's no telling what condition the lower levels are in.'

It seemed to take forever. The lift groaned and juddered as it descended, each passing second stretching into eternity. In the silence, my thoughts turned to Spindle - to the moment he'd wake and find the letter. He'd be angry at first. Hurt. But he'd understand, in time. He'd have to. He made that promise without knowing what I would ask of him. But with it, he gave me his blessing. I'd clung to that, knowing it would hold him in good stead in the years to come.

Inside the envelope, I'd tucked a drawing of a jasmine flower for him - sketched from memory, from a picture I had as a child on Ruin. I'd lost that precious flower along with Mary's small wooden cross when I was first dragged to the mines. If only I still had the cross, I would have passed it on to Coral, a piece of faith and comfort she could carry - with her memories of Mary and me.

Instead, I left the necklace Larch had given me when I went to visit him in the caves - the one that belonged to Laura. It felt only right that Coral should wear it now. Spindle had instructions to place it in her hands, with all my love. I could see it clearly - Larch sitting with Coral and Ash, telling them the story of Laura - and the strong, enduring love they had shared.

I thought of Cooper, and a deep ache settled in my chest. I never truly said goodbye -not properly. When he left, I was too tangled in grief and fury over Aspen to see what he needed from me. I wanted to tell him I was on my way to meet Orion, Freya, and Nova - and I would be their family in the afterlife, until he came. He'd realise, in time, that we'd won. That no biological weapon had been unleashed. He'd make it back to the outpost and find Zander, Minx, and Felix.

Astrid would be waiting for me on the other side, I was sure - with Rowan, Lucy, and Willow. And Salix too, my beautiful friend, kind and loyal. And then there was Saxon . . . who had believed in me. Finally, Mary - the old woman who had made me who I am. The one who had clung to hope when everything else had failed, who refused to let her grandson be taken, and who had looked on both Coral and me as her family, blood or not.

I didn't spare a thought for Malus or Aconite and their cruelty - they meant nothing to me now. I hadn't even asked Spindle to show them mercy. Their fate was no longer mine to shape. I'd left that choice in his hands, and he'd made no promises to them. Whatever came next, they were his responsibility now.

* * *

The machine's Core towered before me, a hulking beast of steel. It wasn't just a machine - it felt alive, almost breathing, its low, guttural drone vibrating through the soles of my feet. Generations ago, it was built to steal and shackle the Sun's energy, chaining it to the Earth. What began as the dream of limitless power had curdled into a nightmare - one that birthed the End of Days, ushering in the One World Order.

Now, that nightmare pulsed in front of me, its rhythm heavy and merciless - the heartbeat of a monster that had long forgotten compassion. The air was electric, bitter with ozone. Each breath scalded my lungs even through the hazmat protection. My boots felt fused to the metal grate, as though the machine itself was claiming me, making me part of its vast, devouring body.

Its black cables shimmered with seething plasma, veins surging with molten light. I was small, so painfully small - nothing but a speck before this monster. But I was also the only one who would end it. The levers had to be pulled. The final switch had to be flipped. And I would be its last offering.

My hands trembled as they hovered over the console. Above me, the warning light blinked red and relentless, flashing in time with the Core's hunger. My memory did not fail me. I could see all the schematics and drawing Hemlock had drummed in to me. I could do this. I pulled the first lever. The machine groaned, a grinding, monstrous sound - like it was waking from centuries of rage.

The second switch released a hiss that ricocheted around the chamber. The heat surged higher, pressing against my suit as I turned to the navigation panel. My fingers danced awkwardly across the controls, aligning the core's release with the path to the correct cluster of islands - a final act of intention. Perhaps, when the world began to heal, Spindle would journey far beyond the Pewter Sea, to lands no longer shrouded in ash and sorrow.

Magnets screamed as plasma spiralled faster, hotter. Soon, it would all be cinders including me. There was no turning back. The Earth needed this. For too long, the elite had poisoned her because of their greed, had burned her breath and buried her beauty. Only fire could free her now. Only ruin could bring rebirth. The oceans would live again. Perhaps forests would stretch like prayers into the sky, and birdsong would return to the morning.

Tears blurred my vision as Spindle returned to my thoughts. My heart ached for the life we'd never share, but I knew he - and all of them - would do just fine. They would carry my hope forward. They would remember me. Perhaps Spindle would plant a garden full of jasmine flowers, each one a quiet echo of what we lost, and what we dared to hope for. I smiled at the thought - soft, bittersweet, and full of light.

I reached for the final switch. My fingers quivered, hovering over the activation pad. And then, through the static in my comms, Hemlock's voice came - quiet, comforting.

'You've done enough, Jasmine. Go with peace.'

I smiled, just a little. I wasn't truly alone. I pressed the button.

The core howled - a sound too loud, too ancient for human ears. The floor buckled. Fire surged. The metal around me melted, screeched, folded in on itself. Heat consumed me, blistering through flesh and bone. The pain was immense. Infinite. And then . . . Light.

And in that final, blinding moment, as I surrendered to the flames, I heard it - The Earth, exhaling.

ACKNOWLEDGMENTS

Where to begin? Thank you to my wonderful husband, Martin, and my two beautiful grown-up children, Rebekah and Sam. For all you do for me, and for your love and encouragement.

Family and friends are everything, and for that, I am truly blessed. You all know who you are - too many to list.

Special thanks to my editor, Wendy H. Jones, who has supported me from the very beginning, encouraging me every step of the way.

A special shout out to all the writing organisations who have been a huge part of my writing journey. To name but a few - Ayr Writers' Club and History Writers. Not to forget my friends and colleagues on the Council of the Scottish Association of Writers. I must also mention Wendy again, and Shoma, my partners in Auscot Publishing and Retreats.

To Linda Brown and Kirsty Hammond for always being there, and bouncing ideas around.

Finally - all those who have played a part in my writing journey - I extend my heartfelt thanks.

ABOUT THE AUTHOR

Having had a passion for reading and writing since an early age, this passion has only grown over the years. Marti M. McNair has been writing since she could pick up a pen, and after her children flew the nest she turned to writing seriously. Her main focus is writing for a YA audience, and her books feature dystopian settings, dark political undercurrents and places her characters in precarious situations which tests them to the limit. She was the winner of the prestigious Scottish Association of Writers, Barbara Hammond Prize. She is also a partner in Auscot Publishing and Retreats and a graphic designer for Writers' Narrative Magazine. In addition she is the Vice-President of the Scottish Association of Writers.

ALSO BY MARTI M MCNAIR

Island of Ruin

Rebels of Ruin

A Right Cozy Christmas Crime

Coming Soon

Resurrection

A Right Cozy Culinary Crime

A Right Cozy Historical Crime

Cozy Christmas Crimes

Printed in Dunstable, United Kingdom